I Only Want to Be with You

I Only Want to Be with You

Lisa Norato

FIVE STAR
An imprint of Thomson Gale, a part of The Thomson Corporation

Detroit • New York • San Francisco • New Haven, Conn. • Waterville, Maine • London

Five Star Publishing, an imprint of The Gale Group.

Set in 11 pt. Plantin.

LIBRARY OF CONGRESS CATALOGING-IN-PUBLICATION DATA

Norato, Lisa.
I only want to be with you / Lisa Norato. — 1st ed.
p. cm.
ISBN-13: 978-1-59414-611-4 (alk. paper)
ISBN-10: 1-59414-611-X (alk. paper)
1. Young women—Fiction. 2. Americans—England—Fiction. 3. Manhattan (New York, NY)—Fiction. 4. England—Fiction. 5. Chick lit. I. Title.
PS3614.O7I3 2007
813′.6—dc22 2007031722

First Edition. First Printing: December 2007.

Published in 2007 in conjunction with Tekno Books.

Printed in the United States of America on permanent paper
10 9 8 7 6 5 4 3 2 1

To my mother, Caroline Norato, with love.
The first person to teach me to read and inspire me with a love for books.

Chapter 1

Would an urban professional woman leave an exciting career with a major New York magazine publisher to settle in the English countryside as the wife of a vicar?

Yep, you bet she would.

Crazy, huh? Marcella Tartaglia didn't comprehend such a match, having left her own small Italian neighborhood on Providence's Federal Hill for the great adventure of working in New York. But hey, that didn't mean she wasn't all for the union.

In fact, she saluted the cupid who'd shot his arrow in this bizarre twist of kismet. She lifted her cocktail glass in his honor.

Tomorrow, when Senior Editor Lynne Graham married the Reverend Henry Swann, the position of Senior Decorating and Entertainment Editor at *Gracious Living* magazine would be up for grabs.

There was only one obvious choice for a replacement. Only one woman at the magazine possessed the creative genius, innovative thinking, and leadership skills needed to fill Lynne Graham's sophisticated designer pumps. One woman, with her obsessive-compulsive work ethic and tireless dedication to organization and design, embodied the editorial integrity of *Gracious Living* magazine.

Me! Marcella thought with glee.

Modesty was not a virtue in the media, and Marcella expected to be offered the title as soon as she returned to Manhattan.

"Salute," she toasted with a nudge to her traveling companion, a.k.a. best girlfriend, Sallie, who, lost in the groove of her MP3 player, was paying absolutely no attention.

In private celebration, Marcella brought the martini glass to her lips and sampled her Potion for Passion. A blend of lemon vodka, Grand Marnier, and passion fruit juice, the cocktail had become her favorite since she and Sallie visited a certain midtown Manhattan lounge last spring.

But what happened here? *Blah.* This cocktail tasted more like a potion for nausea with a bitter citrus kick, and Marcella narrowed her gaze at the responsible party. The male flight attendant Brad had substituted pink grapefruit juice for the passion fruit.

Well, so much for the luxury of first class. Accommodations on board this British Airways Flight 0178 en route to Heathrow were courtesy of the magazine, because not only was Marcella flying across the pond to attend Lynne's wedding, she was also on assignment.

Marcella had six pages to capture all those wedding details readers craved. Details to illustrate how a simple garden party could be turned into a romantic fantasy, in what would ultimately become a feature article in next June's issue.

With the reception to be held in the gardens of a private Oxfordshire estate dating from 1635 and a theme to reflect the essence of a summer's day, she didn't find the task much of a challenge. But for obvious reasons, she wanted everything to be perfect.

Nothing was going to screw up this promotion.

She opened the organizer in her lap to review her notes for the zillionth time.

In addition to the usual photographs of the church, gardens, and traditional English fruitcake, she'd need Sallie to capture the finer details. Details like the feathery and lifelike paper butterflies that would serve as napkin rings on the reception tables and ornaments in the junior bridesmaids' hair. Then there were the hand-stitched, lavender-filled pillows Lynne had commissioned as favors. Each pillow had been tied with a silk ribbon, hand-painted by special order with the couple's name and wedding date.

Ah, and of course, the vintage tent for the children filled with parasols, pop guns, and crayons.

Lynne had certainly done a thorough job with the arrangements. More correctly, she'd assigned Marcella to do a thorough job, seeing as Marcella had been the one to track down and order most of this stuff. Further indication she deserved the promotion.

She was grateful for the opportunity. Still, she couldn't help wonder aloud. "Is Lynne making the right decision in dropping everything to follow this man into a new life?"

Marcella waited for an answer. When silence continued to fill the air-conditioned cabin, she leaned back against the headrest and turned towards Sallie.

Sallie was bopping her head to music only she could hear.

Marcella gave her another nudge. "Hey, you've been ignoring me this whole flight. Pull that thing out of your ear and talk to me."

Sallie rolled her eyes, then, with a patronizing sigh, turned off her music. "I always try to ignore you when you've got your head buried in that organizer."

"I want to go over some stuff."

Sallie finger-combed the straight, honey-brown hair that flowed down her back. "Tell me tomorrow at the wedding."

"I feel we should review a few things so we'll both be clear about which images we're trying to capture."

"Look, you don't interfere with my creative process, I won't interfere with yours. I'm a spontaneous photographer. I see; I create. And right now, I don't see anything artworthy but a flight attendant with a cute ass."

Marcella sipped from her drink, frustrated by this lack of co-operation. Her taste buds cringed in horror, reminding her of her botched Potion for Passion.

"Yuck." She swept the cocktail away from her, extending her arm into the aisle lest she make the mistake of sipping from it again. "Cute? Maybe, but he can't mix a drink to save his life." She pushed the overhead call button, then as the attendant emerged from the galley, said, "Excuse me, Brad, but could you please take this drink away?"

Brad hustled over to reclaim the glass and asked if there was anything else they needed before he brought the hot towels. Behind the polite smile and gracious manner, Marcella noted the interest in his eyes as he glanced back and forth between Sallie and herself.

But for their Amazonian stature, she and Sallie made for a sharp contrast. Brad had to be wondering how two such opposites had come to be traveling companions.

Marcella, with her short black curls and exotic look, wore a conservative, black linen suit over a chocolate brown shell and her tiger's eye choker beads. Her figure, though still slim, was no longer the gangly thing it had been in childhood when she'd been tagged with a nickname of *"Ragno"*—the skinny, long-legged spider.

Sallie Madigan, photographer extraordinaire, on the other hand, was the all-American athletic type, fair and solidly built, never to be caught without her beloved Birkenstocks. Sallie had just made muster into first class with her low-rise capris, which she'd had to hike up over her backside to hide the butterfly tattoo on her left hip.

Years at the magazine, with Marcella styling countless photo shoots and Sallie photographing them, had brought them together. Now they were the best of friends, which was why they shared a comfortable, say-what's-on-your-mind rapport.

Sallie reminded Brad about her vegetarian meal, thanking him with a smile that revealed none of the attraction she expressed earlier for his physical attributes. Flirting had always come easily to the confident Sallie, but not so these days. Her heart was reserved for the jazz musician she was dating back in Manhattan.

At Brad's departure, Marcella leaned across the armrest. "Sallie, I've been wondering. Do you think Lynne's making a mistake? You know, giving up her career in New York to marry a . . . um, vicar?"

Sallie snickered. In her sassy tone, she said, "For cryin' out loud, Marcella. In England, a vicar is just like any other working Joe. But you feel this guy might be too tame for Lynne, huh? And this is an issue with you, why?"

Marcella drummed her fingers distractedly over the open pages of her organizer. She was stunned the day Lynne returned from visiting her family in England to announce she was engaged to her widowed college sweetheart.

With a shrug, she said, "Lynne's a very independent woman, and this marriage . . . well, it just isn't something I would have expected of her. Granted, Henry Swann may seem like the perfect man at the moment, but why wasn't he the perfect man thirty years ago? Do you think, perhaps, as a fifty-something, Lynne feels her chance for a great love has passed? I mean, should we women settle for a man we believe might be good for us or hold out for that one true soul mate? Is it ever too late for fireworks?"

"Whoa . . . the age-old question springs eternal."

"Any thoughts?"

"Well, this is all a little too deep to assimilate after an hour of zoning out on jazz, but here goes. The optimistic view is—no, it's never too late. And if Lynne Graham wants to marry a vicar, who are we to question? Love very often comes as a surprise. It hits like a brick. It just happens, like shit. And when it does, it turns your whole world upside down. Like in the movie *Moonstruck,* when Ronny tells Loretta how love ruins everything, breaks your heart, makes things a mess, yada-yada. I forget the rest, but you get the gist. Oh yeah, and he tells her the storybooks are bullshit."

"Wait." Marcella whipped out her pen. "Let me get this straight. Okay, now—the storybooks are bullshit, but movies tell it like real life. Uh-huh, right." She shook her head, pressing her fingertips to her temple. "That's what I get for asking the opinion of an L.A. native. I do so need a real Passion."

"Maybe you'll meet someone at the wedding."

"I meant the drink, Sallie. I need a real Potion for Passion cocktail. Not that nasty brew Brad served."

Sallie laughed. "Relax Marcella. You should be in celebration mode. With Lynne out of the picture, you now have the opportunity for that big break you've always dreamed of."

She paused in consideration when suddenly her eyes narrowed into an intense and serious stare. "Marcella, is this about Lynne or you? As long as I've known you, it's been career first, whether or not it's allowed you time for a relationship. You do want this promotion, right? Or are you rethinking the whole single woman, professional lifestyle thing?" Her voice lowered to a whisper. "Are you worried about finding someone special?"

"Who me?" Marcella burst, loud enough to attract Brad's attention. "I hadn't given it a thought. No, this is just me overanalyzing again, that's all. Celebration mode, here I come." Marcella settled back in her roomy seat. She pushed the inside button to eject the footrest, then shut her organizer with a snap, zipping it closed. "After all, what do I care whether a magazine editor and an English vicar can make it work? It's not like it's my life."

The following morning, over two hundred guests gathered at St. Cross Church, Oxfordshire, to witness the union of Lynne Graham to the Reverend Henry Swann. Already, the organist had played "O Perfect Love" three times. The ceremony was running late and a collective murmur drifted up from the filled pews.

Out in the foyer Sallie focused her Leica for one more shot of a hand-scribed brown envelope, opened and spilling over with dried delphinium petals. An envelope like this would be handed to each of the guests as they left the church, for confetti tossing at the bride and groom.

"Minor adjustment!" Marcella stepped into the shot. She scattered a few more dark purple petals across the opened envelope flap.

"Thank you, Editor of Anal." Sallie shooed her out of the way, then zoomed in and took the photo. Behind her camera, her glossed lips curled in a satisfied smile. "Got it."

They'd arrived an hour early. Sallie had already shot two rolls of film. Only a small percentage of those photographs would make it to the finished article, but Marcella was leaving nothing to chance on this assignment. "Guess we'd better get seated. I wonder what the delay is? Hey, Sallie, you don't suppose Lynne's having second—"

A thundering blast of motorcycle exhaust drowned out her voice. Insult seethed in Marcella. This lovely wedding morning, assaulted by motorcycle noise pollution. How dare anyone. She stormed out to the front steps of the ancient stone church, Sallie following behind, and watched as a large black and smoke motorcycle roared into the church lot.

The bike was ridden by a man in mirrored sunglasses,

rolled-up shirt sleeves, and black dress trousers. He wove between the parked cars and stopped in the shade of a towering oak several feet away, where he hit the kickstand before turning off the ignition. Silence. *Thank you.*

Sallie let out a low whistle. "Whoa, a three-cylinder Triumph Thunderbird."

Marcella lost interest in the motorcycle. Its well-dressed biker raked a hand through his windblown chestnut hair as he climbed off the seat. Sunshine dappled his head through the foliage, creating a prism of sienna, gold, and auburn light in the thick waves.

He stood facing the bike, his back to Marcella, and as he removed the sunglasses, she took this opportunity to check him out. His white wing-collar shirt stretched across broad, square shoulders and tapered to lean hips. She figured him for no less than six-three, if not taller.

At once, her opinion of him soared. She adored tall men. As the long-legged *Ragno,* who had towered over her peers in her small Italian neighborhood, she had developed quite an appreciation for men of generous stature.

Marcella moaned the same sensual moan that escaped her whenever she bit into a dark chocolate raspberry truffle. *Deelish!*

She moistened her lips. To Sallie, she said, "I never realized you were into bikes."

"I've done some riding," Sallie admitted with a shrug. "I agree. That biker's a bit of a triumph himself."

Marcella smiled. "I wondered when you'd notice."

He turned, and just as they prepared for their first glimpse of his face, he slipped a handkerchief from his back pocket and bent down to polish his shoes.

Marcella and Sallie exchanged expertly tweezed raised brows.

They continued to observe. The instant he straightened and

began to roll down the cuffs of his sleeves, Sallie raised her camera.

"What are you doing?" Marcella demanded although she already had a pretty good idea once she saw Sallie adjust the zoom on her Leica.

"Having a closer look. This is a ninety-millimeter lense." Sallie's smile grew as she brought her subject into focus. "Whoa." She pressed the automatic shutter and clicked off a series of shots.

"Whoa? Again whoa? Whoa, what? Why'd you take his picture? Is he gorgeous? Let me see." Marcella reached for the camera but Sallie waved her off.

Too late, anyway. The guy was now walking to the back of his bike where he unzipped a tote attached to a small luggage rack.

Sallie lowered her Leica, and the excitement on her face boosted Marcella's anticipation to a frantic level.

"Well?"

Sallie let out a breath, then, "Awesome face. He has, like, a totally awesome face."

"Shut up!"

"No kidding. I'm talking movie-star handsome. Classic features, an unassuming expression, intense eyes. Lots of character."

"Shut up, shut up!" Sallie's articulate description excited Marcella, so much so she did a happy dance in her Sergio Rossi black stiletto mules. She turned for another eyeful, only to discover he was now shrugging into a knee-length suit jacket. She could see from his bearing, he had a confident, aristocratic air about him.

And was she hallucinating or was that a frock coat? On the seat of the motorcycle sat a black top hat. Huh? "Hey, what'd we miss?"

"It appears he's getting dressed for a wedding."

They watched him tie a perfect white cravat, then slip a pair of white gloves from out of the pocket of his morning coat. He pulled them on.

"Maybe we'll meet at the reception." Marcella sighed wistfully. "Maybe I'll make a point of meeting him. Who is he, I wonder?" She wondered a little too long because suddenly a disturbing thought occurred. "Oh-no, Sallie. You don't suppose?"

"Nah. Much too young. Even for Lynne."

Marcella couldn't believe the relief that washed over her. Already, she was beginning to fall for this guy. She'd be heartbroken if he were about to be married. Or worse, married to her boss.

He set the top hat upon his glorious head at a rakish angle.

"Do you believe this? This tall, sexy stranger appears from nowhere, and in minutes transforms from biker to aristocrat right before our unsuspecting eyes."

"It's a turn-on, isn't it?" Sallie gave a seductive growl. "A new age Mr. Darcy."

Yes, Marcella was turned on, she had to admit. She lingered over her last glimpse of him as he headed for a side entrance with long, quickened strides, looking for all the world like some nineteenth-century Regency lord. His royal hotness.

"He never even noticed us," Sallie said.

"He's in a hurry. And good thing, too, or he'd have cause to suspect he was being stalked by a couple of pervs. As it is, I feel like a peeping tom. Speaking of which, I want those photos when we get back to New York."

"Oh yeah? And what do you intend to do with them?"

"Sleep with them under my pillow and hopefully improve the quality of my dream life."

Sallie linked her arm with Marcella's. "You know, it is a truth universally acknowledged, that a single man in possession of a good motorcycle must be in want of a sexy American fox. As opposed to an English bird, that is."

Marcella fanned herself with her hand. "Do we know he's single?"

"Okay, let's review the facts. He arrives late for a wedding, on a motorcycle, half-dressed, and with no date. What do you think?" Sallie spun her towards the door. "Let's grab a seat, shall we? Before you combust and Jane Austen rolls over in her grave."

Inside, Sallie scooted into an empty pew, dragging Marcella in behind her. A fresh herb scent filled the air. The church had been decorated with garlands of greenery and herbs—mint, purple sage, thyme, and rosemary. Henry had taken his place at the altar by the vicar. He was a distinguished, white-haired gentleman with half-moon-shaped glasses. A white rose filled the buttonhole of his frock coat.

The vicar and the vicar, Marcella thought, *hee-hee.* "Geez, I think I'm getting giddy."

"What?"

"I think we're sitting on the wrong side," she whispered to Sallie as the organist began to play the processional music. "Family and friends of the bride are supposed to sit on the left."

Sallie rolled her eyes.

The congregation rose to its feet, and Marcella rose with them. She turned to face the back of the church. There, at the door, stood Lynne in a white silk column dress with a bouquet of white roses, her newest shade of ash blonde hair swept up in an elegant, classic, Grace Kelly style.

She took the right arm of the gentleman beside her and together they entered the church. *Whoa.* It was the guy from the parking lot. Adrenaline shot through Marcella in a rush, setting her libido on fire.

Then it hit her. Lynne's nephew. The guy from the parking lot was Lynne's nephew. Yes, she remembered now. With her father deceased, Lynne had mentioned she'd asked her nephew to give her away.

Lynne and her nephew proceeded down the aisle together.

Sallie's description fit. He was gorgeous, intense and elegant all at the same time, and he was about to pass right by her.

Keep your focus on Lynne, she reminded herself. *Happy, gracious smile for the bride. This is her moment. This is not a damned nightclub. Do not give her nephew the eye.*

As they approached her pew, Marcella smiled at Lynne, then stole a quick glance at the nephew. His aquamarine blue eyes had already found her and held a meaningful glint that was more than casual. Marcella exchanged smiles with him. His gaze lowered to the cleavage peeking from between the lapels of her tailored black pantsuit, then returned to her face, where he cocked a brow, gave her an approving nod, and continued down the aisle.

Marcella stared after him, speechless for once in her life. The tables had been turned. He'd just checked *her* out.

Sallie nudged her in the ribs and sing-songed, "I saw that."

As a trail of six little bridesmaids, ranging in ages from four to twelve, followed them down the aisle, Marcella tried to recall anything and everything Lynne had told her about this hottie nephew of hers.

His name? What was his name? She didn't know, but Marcella did recall Lynne mentioning he was an Oxford grad. He was acquainted with Henry because Henry taught at Oxford. In his day, her nephew had been a popular oarsman on the University's rowing club.

Must be where those shoulders came from.

Bugger him, she nearly took his eye out, she was so beautiful.

Henry stepped forward as they approached the altar, and William handed him his bride, then moved to the left.

His gloved hands folded before him, William stared up into the stained glass and wondered, who is she? One of Aunt Lynne's friends from the States? Yes, of course. Who but a cheeky American would wear her bosom to church as a fashion accessory? He'd always found them a big distraction during service. Breasts, that was. Nearly as tall as he, she was obviously of Italian descent with her short black waves, dark deep-set eyes, and full, expressive mouth that reminded him of a young Sophia Loren.

Aunt Lynne waved her bouquet, jostling William from his musings. First, late for the wedding, now slacking in his duties. He wasn't used to being on this side of the altar.

He took Aunt Lynne's roses and turned around to set them on the front pew. As he did, he glanced down the row of pews and across the aisle, looking for the exotic giantess. Her dark head appeared above the crowd because she was straining her neck to watch him. Their eyes met across the congregation.

"The grace of our Lord Jesus Christ, the love of God, and the fellowship of the Holy Spirit be with you," the vicar greeted everyone.

William quickly turned back round and joined with the others in answering, "And also with you."

He had committed his life to taking the tedium out of the Church of England and replacing it with fun, but a posh, impertinent American with a career in New York was a little too much fun for even this bloke. As the bishop and his mother had lately reminded him, it was time he got married.

William agreed, but a long-distance relationship and separate careers . . . not bloody likely he'd be going that route again.

The dark-eyed beauty in the back was no choice for a vicar.

Chapter 2

After the ceremony, the Reverend and Mrs. Henry Swann marched out the doors of St. Cross through an arch of oars hoisted by Oxford University oarsmen wearing striped suit jackets of Oxford blue.

Marcella exited her pew and melded into the throng of guests following the wedding procession outside. When she reached the foyer, she was handed a little brown envelope. Tucking her organizer under one arm, she broke the embossed seal and emptied a handful of petal confetti into her palm.

Cheers went up along with a shower of dark purple petals. Well-wishers gathered around the couple to offer congratulations. Marcella searched the crowd, waving when she spotted Sallie, who had slipped out early for photographs.

Farther away, among a group of college students gathered on the courtyard lawn, stood Lynne's nephew. The Duke of Sexual Fantasies himself was speaking with a petite brunette in a silky bob. The girl reached up to snatch the top hat from his head and placed it on her own, while a few of the oarsmen made obscene gestures with their oars, everyone laughing and generally having a good time.

Immature, Marcella thought, though she was still very much intrigued. She unzipped her organizer.

Sallie joined her at the bottom of the church steps and held up her Leica. "I got the most fantastic shot of the bride and groom under the oars. What's next on your list?"

Marcella flipped through the pages, distracted. "That's all for now, Sallie. Great job. Thank you. We'll get Lynne to pose with her bridesmaids in the gardens once we get to Rousham House. Damn, I don't believe this. I'm chronically thorough. I jot down everything. How could I have nothing in my notes about the man who gave away the bride?"

"Ah, Mr. Darcy on a motorcycle. The obsession continues." Sallie slipped an arm around Marcella's shoulders and gave her a squeeze. "Brace up, old girl. Cheerio." She gestured to the surrounding crowd. "If Lynne's nephew gave her away, he's likely one of her dearest and most popular relatives. Who needs notes when any one of these two hundred guests could give you the scoop? No problem, right? Part of what makes you such a good editor is your ability to talk to strangers, to meet people up and down the social scale."

Marcella beamed.

"Look, that woman seems pleasant enough." Sallie pointed, directing Marcella's attention to a statuesque older woman in knee-length chiffon and matching hat, the dark purple of the delphinium petals. Definitely upper-class. She was helping one of the little bridesmaids into a lilac cardigan.

Marcella gave Sallie the thumbs up, then casually strolled towards the pair. She gazed overhead at the day—the green English countryside, the church steeple against a clear blue sky—and sighed. "Beautiful wedding," she offered to no one in particular, but the woman glanced up and agreed. "Yes, lovely."

She gave Marcella a slow, elegant smile.

Marcella needed no further invitation. "Hi. My name's Marcella and this is Sallie. We're friends of the bride. We work with Lynne at *Gracious Living* in New York. I've seen family photos in her office, but I'm not familiar with the gentleman who gave her away. Do you know who he is?"

"William? Yes. Of course, I know him."

William. Marcella replayed the name in her head. Not casual-guy Bill or Billy, but *William.* Sophisticated, charming William. Handsome, refined William. William, as in Prince William. As in Will, for short. Or long Willy. *Oh, don't get me started.*

"Handsome, isn't he?" The woman straightened to assess Marcella from beneath the wide brim of her hat, jostling Marcella away from her naughty imagination.

Marcella tittered in feigned innocence. "Oh-no, don't misunderstand me. It's nothing like that. I'm producing an article for the magazine featuring Lynne's wedding, and I've just been trying to orient myself with who's who before Sallie starts clicking away."

"I'm the photographer," Sallie explained, holding up her Leica.

"Fabulous photographer," Marcella confirmed. "Speaking of which, don't you just love those frock coats? They're going to make for some great photos."

The woman smiled down at the child by her side. "Yes, I suspect they'll be quite smart."

These Brits. So tight-lipped. "William, you said?" Marcella repeated, writing the name in her notes even though it was already implanted in her consciousness. "Such a dignified, noble name. William. Makes one think of royalty."

"Indeed, William is, in fact, descended from the peerage. The Honorable William John Anthony Grafton Stafford, third son of Lord Wiltshire, the Eighteenth Viscount of Wiltshire. Not only is he Lynne's favorite nephew and godson, he is a man of extraordinary principle and wit, an accomplished sportsman and gardener, educated at Eton and Oxford." As she sang William's praises, her voice rose with authority. Then much quieter, on a more wistful note, she added, "He lives in the village of Bramble Moor in a beautiful stone cottage with no wife."

Marcella scribbled furiously, trying to contain her glee.

Sallie stepped closer to the woman. "You seem to know a lot about him."

"I should, dear. I'm his mother."

Marcella dropped her pen.

"Oh . . . ah . . . his mother," Sallie twittered. "How cool."

Marcella chuckled. "I'm hardly surprised, Lady Wiltshire. I could hear the pride in your voice." She affected a composed smile before Will's mum caught on that the heightened glow to her cheeks was not the result of a heavy-handed application of shimmery cream blush, but mortification.

The little bridesmaid picked up the pen. "Here you go, miss."

"Thank you, sweetie."

"This is my granddaughter, Mae."

"It's a pleasure, Mae." Marcella gave the child a wink. "You look very pretty in your linen dress with paper butterflies in your hair. Sallie take her picture. That face belongs in a magazine if ever I saw one."

Sallie crouched down for the shot, then thanked Mae for being such a good model.

The girl blushed, then tugged on Lady Wiltshire's skirt. "Gran?"

"Yes, sweetheart, let's go find Mummy, shall we?" Lady Wiltshire took the child's hand. As she turned to go, she smiled into Marcella's eyes with an amused expression. "Lovely to meet you." She moved past. "You also, Sallie."

"Hope to see you at the reception," Marcella called. She turned to Sallie and mouthed, "His mother!"

Sallie shrugged. "Sorry. But look at it this way. You've survived the scariest part of the relationship. You've already met his mother."

"Mother, aunt. It's a nightmare. This party is going to be crawling with relatives."

"Less competition for you."

"I wonder what he does. He does work, I assume. She didn't say."

"Ah, but she did say he was honorable," Sallie quipped.

"Technically, the third son of a viscount is a commoner just like you and me." Marcella raised a brow and whispered in a seductive voice. "But we'll see just how 'honorable' once we're better acquainted."

Sallie laughed. "Look, the crowd is thinning. Let's go congratulate the bride and groom."

They maneuvered over to the newlyweds, where they were immediately introduced to the soft-spoken, even-tempered Henry. *Quite a contrast from Lynne,* Marcella thought, *but then opposites attract . . . or so they say.*

Marcella ooh-ed and aah-ed over Lynne's dress, her radiant glow, her handsome new husband. She squealed and kissed and congratulated, never once mentioning Lynne's fake tan or new hair color, and generally sucked up in all the ways expected at such a momentous occasion. So Lynne's curt dismissal came as a shock, especially when compared to the attention she seemed to be lavishing on Sallie.

"My nephew William has insisted on traveling by motorbike, so we now have an empty seat in the wedding car. We've a lovely old Bentley. You're welcome to join us, Sallie, if you need a lift to the reception."

"Me? Ah . . . well," Sallie glanced helplessly at Marcella. "That's generous of you, Lynne, but I don't think—"

"Oh, forgive my rudeness." Lynne turned to Marcella, and with a haughty expression, explained, "We only have room for one, I'm afraid."

Ouch, Marcella thought. Lynne knew she and Sallie traveled as a pair. What was up? Why the slight? She tried to recall if she had unknowingly done something to piss Lynne off. Nothing came to mind. In fact, she'd gone out of her way to help with preparations for the wedding. This just better not have anything to do with her promotion.

"Go with the Bentley, Sallie," Marcella encouraged, hiding her hurt feelings behind a smile. "You need to be at the reception early to take pictures."

"That's exactly what I thought," Lynne agreed.

Sallie wasn't buying it. "Thanks just the same, Lynne, but Marcella and I will find a ride together."

"Oh, don't be silly, love," Lynne argued, "Marcella's quite capable of finding her own transport."

"Sure, I can bum a ride. Don't worry about me."

"Excuse me, Aunt Lynne, but aren't you going to introduce me to your American friends?"

That proper, British-accented baritone came from directly behind Marcella and sent a warm, fuzzy shiver down her spine. She turned and found herself staring into the dazzling aquamarine eyes of the Honorable William.

They twinkled with that unassuming expression Sallie had spoken of earlier. He touched the brim of his top hat to her and grinned before returning his attention once again to Lynne. "Not still cross with me, are you, Auntie?" His voice was rich with warmth and laughter.

Lynne pouted at him. She set her blonde head at a tilt while she regarded him, then threw up her hands and sighed. "William, darling, where were you? You had us all worried, wondering why you were so late. Whatever made you take that awful motorbike when you drive such a smart little Fiat?"

"Terribly sorry 'bout that, Aunt Lynne. Babette refused to get out of bed this morning. You know how I depend on her to wake me. Wasn't pleased with the fact I was going to leave her behind, I suspect. I'd arranged to borrow Angus Harsley's Land Rover for the drive, but it lost an axle on the A-Four-Twenty-Nine. Too late by then to ring up one of the family. I had no choice but to go back for my bike."

"But your Fiat, William! Where is your Fiat?"

"The Fiat. Right. Babette was quite disappointed, actually. She loved our long drives. I traded it in only last month, you see, to help purchase a minibus for Bramble Moor's seniors. Bit difficult to get around once you reach a certain age, and you know how cranky seniors get come Sunday morning when they've missed their Saturday evening of bingo and tea. Or you will know soon enough, won't she, Henry?"

Henry and William enjoyed a private chuckle.

Lynne scoffed. "Stop it, both of you. Trading decent transport for a minibus. Absolutely ridiculous. I don't want to hear another word." She drew herself up and assumed a happy wedding face. "William Stafford, my godson, please meet Sallie Madigan, a photographer friend of mine from *Gracious Living* magazine."

William offered his hand and exchanged greetings with Sallie.

"And this is my assistant, Marcella Tartaglia."

"Associate Editor," Marcella corrected, extending her hand while her poor confused brain was still trying to process Babette and the senior bingo players.

"Honored to make your acquaintance, Miss Tartaglia."

William's firm grasp enveloped Marcella's hand, but instead of shaking it, he gave it a gentle squeeze while he leaned forward to kiss her on the cheek.

Sexy, elegant man. It was all Marcella could do not to turn her face into his lips.

He drew back slowly, his gaze locking into hers where Marcella caught a glimpse of longing, similar to what she was experiencing herself.

"Umm . . . Marcella," she corrected, remembering to breathe. "Call me Marcella."

He smiled. "Beautiful name, Marcella. Italian?"

She nodded.

"Some of us call her Tart," Lynne interjected.

"Short for Tartaglia," Sallie amended. "No other reference implied, of course," she added, laughing off the jibe, thank God, because suddenly Marcella felt uncharacteristically like a shy schoolgirl.

"Of course." William joined in Sallie's laughter.

My kinda guy, Marcella thought.

Lynne's nostrils flared.

"Right. I'd best dash, then, if I'm to be in the receiving line. Mustn't risk another late arrival, eh, Auntie?" He chuckled at the jibe, which Lynne pretended not to appreciate. Still, she smiled fondly at him as she offered her cheek for a kiss.

William kissed his aunt, then waved goodbye to Sallie. "I hope to speak with you again at the reception."

"Oh, don't worry. You'll be seeing me. I'll be the one following you around like the paparazzi. I have a feeling you're scheduled to be in lots of photos."

Marcella's silent plea to shut up was lost on Sallie, who seemed to be purposely avoiding her gaze. Marcella resumed her smile when William paused before her.

"I couldn't help overhearing you were in need of a lift," he said. "I'd love to run you over to Rousham House, Marcella, if you don't mind my motorbike. In all good conscience as a gentleman, I simply cannot stand by and allow a beautiful woman to . . . er, 'bum a ride' from strangers. So, what d'you say?"

Lynne twittered. "Surely not, William, you silly-willy. Marcella can't ride with you. Her clothes, her hair—they'll be a gastly mess in all that wind. She has a wedding reception to attend."

William cocked a brow. "So do I, as I recall."

Marcella scrambled to take this all in. William thought she was beautiful? He wanted her to ride with him to the reception. Wonder of wonders, it was a fantasy come true, but she couldn't. Lynne was right. She'd spent all morning styling her hair, perfecting her makeup. Vanity ruled. She was not going to make an appearance looking like the Bride of Frankenstein for any man, no matter what color his eyes were.

Besides, William was already taken, apparently. What about Babette, huh? Babette, whom he'd been sleeping with earlier this morning.

Marcella opened her mouth to politely refuse when Sallie shouted, "Great! It's settled. I'll ride with the wedding party; Marcella will ride with you. Thank you, William, for solving our problem."

William turned to Marcella with a smile she could see was meant for her alone. "Pleasure."

Before Marcella could respond, Sallie grabbed her by the arm and dragged her away, calling, "Excuse us a moment, please. I need to discuss some photo shots with Marcella before we go."

Once out of earshot, Sallie spat, "I saw your face. You were going to refuse him, weren't you? Have you lost your mind? You've been hot for him from the moment he roared into the parking lot."

"Sallie, I can't get on that bike. Do you realize the state I'll be in by the time I reach the reception?"

"You'll be fine. You're wearing a pantsuit. So what if you get a little windblown? The helmet will cover your hair."

"Oh great. Severe hat hair."

"A little fluffing, a shot of hair spray and you'll be good to go. Don't screw this up. The guy is obviously interested. And it's really pissing Lynne off."

"Yeah, what's her problem? You'd think she'd be in more

generous spirits on her wedding day."

"Strange, I know. But enough of her. Look at him, Marcella." Sallie turned back for a peek at William who was speaking with Henry.

Marcella watched. William Stafford was incredibly handsome to begin with, but dressed in a frock coat, top hat and white cravat . . . well, he simply took her breath away.

"Looks like he's just stepped out of a Jane Austen novel," Sallie commented, reading her mind. "Hell, I'd hop on that Triumph myself if I didn't have my camera to protect. How can you just let a guy like that slip by? C'mon, did Elizabeth refuse Mr. Darcy?"

"Yeah, as a matter of fact, she did."

"I never read the book myself. But that's beside the point. You're not some freakin' two-hundred-year-old debutante. You don't have time to waste being coy."

"Oh. Was I being coy?" Marcella begged to differ.

"Where's that adventurous spirit we all know and love? Deep inside I know you want to do this, Marcella. Now, march back there and accept his offer. You swing your legs up behind that son of an English viscount and wrap your thighs around his bike like you mean business. You little Tart, you."

Marcella laughed. "Okay, I'll do it. Elizabeth did change her mind eventually, but unlike her, I don't have the luxury of time. Might as well go for it now. Come Monday morning I'll be boarding a plane to New York, and then it's back to my dateless, workaholic life."

CHAPTER 3

William drove into the busy roundabout, following the flow of traffic round the loop. As he leaned his Triumph into the circular turn, it tilted at a sharp angle.

Marcella shrieked. She resisted, shifting her weight in the opposite direction so that William had to fight against her for balance. Wrapped in his frock coat and wearing a cycle helmet with its goggles pulled down over her eyes, she squeezed him in a bear hug that forced the breath from his body. Her nails clawed his midsection as she clutched a handful of his billowing shirt.

"All right back there?" he shouted over the rush of traffic. "Not scared?"

She leaned close to his ear. Her breathy gasps drowned out the sonorous rasp of the Triumph's twin exhausts and caused his heart to pound like waves of torque through his gears.

It was all he could do to concentrate on driving. Those fantastic breasts were pressed to his back. Right, there they were again, as distracting on the road as they were in church, as distracting when he couldn't see them as when he could. He'd bloody well dream of them tonight.

She caught her breath and yelled, "No-o-o-o, not scared at all. I love zipping through traffic at high speeds in an open vehicle with nothing but gravity keeping me in my seat. Do all the intersections in England converge in a circle? No stop signs?

No traffic lights? Geez, and I thought New York City traffic was hectic."

William grinned. He adored her sarcastic humor. "What d'you mean? We have signs. How about that sign at the entry point that read 'Give Way'?"

"I don't know about you, but I don't see anyone giving way."

"Right. Bloody nuisance, signs. But seriously, it'll make things much easier on both of us, if next time we make a turn, you lean with me in the same direction as the bike. Anyway, try to relax. It's only a twenty-minute ride to Bicester. I know it can seem a bit scary if you're not familiar with riding motorbikes, but you're safe with me."

"Safe? Bummer. And here I thought hog riding with Will Stafford was going to be a walk on the wild side."

If the wind wasn't whipping his face, William thought he might have blushed. He was feeling a bit awkward. For a man in a profession which exposed him to all sorts of men and women in all walks of life, a man who daily shared their greatest joys and sorrows, where an instant rapport and ease of conversation were essential skills, this sudden shyness was uncharacteristic.

Nevertheless, there it was.

Maybe he was smitten. She was quite dishy.

In the six years he'd been a vicar, he'd found it difficult to meet eligible young women outside his parish. The moment they spotted his dog collar an awkwardness took over.

They'd adopt a saintly air. They'd endeavor to shield him from reality by discussing noncontroversial subjects, like the weather. They'd feign wholesomeness and become cautious of their language. Meetings were always the same. Always unstimulating.

'Course, on the opposite side of the coin were those encounters which were too stimulating for comfort. Some women spotted his dog collar and immediately thought what great sport it would be to shag a vicar.

Either way, a woman who could not be genuine with him was hardly worth his time. William was looking for someone he could truly get to know and enjoy, someone he could, in turn, share himself with, someone who liked to joke and laugh.

Someone like Marcella. Marcella flirted. Marcella was amusing. Marcella made him feel as though she was attracted to him for no other reason than liking him for himself.

Something was happening here. Relationship-wise, where could he possibly be headed with this cheeky American? One would think a man would learn from his past. One would think a broken heart would be lesson enough. But when he spotted Marcella chatting with Aunt Lynne, a blood-rushing excitement he hadn't experienced in years took hold of him, and in a moment of daring, William seized the opportunity for an introduction.

And now, here she was, on his bike.

"I hope you'll allow me to buy you a drink at the reception," he called to her. "I'd love to get to know you better."

"I'd like that, too! Hey, did you really trade in your Fiat for a minibus?"

"Yes. Actually, I did."

"Why?"

William laughed. "I'm perfectly content getting round on my motorbike. Most times, in fact, when I don't have far to travel, I just peddle a bicycle about. Exercise, you know. Anyway, I thought it rather a good deed to put the money for the Fiat towards service for those who need it more. But in so doing, I seemed to have inconvenienced a lot of people today. I'm sorry I don't have a more comfortable ride to offer."

"Nah, don't worry about me. I thrive on being taken out of my comfort zone. You sound like a very generous man, Will. But don't you find it difficult getting back and forth to work without a car? What is it you do? Does your family own a business? Who do you work for?"

A black Saab convertible blew past, cutting rather close.

"Jesus!" she screamed.

"Right, that's him."

"Huh? Who?"

Rather than explain, William gestured up ahead. "Ah, we've arrived, Marcella. There it is. Rousham Park."

He'd have to show his hand soon, though. William hesitated, not because he was ashamed of his vocation. No, he worried Marcella would hide herself from him once she found out he was a priest. That would be a bloody tragedy, because William had a feeling Marcella Tartaglia, beyond her obvious beauty, which would attract any man, was a refreshingly genuine person he very much wanted to spend time with.

Marcella pushed open the ladies' room door with the flat of her hand and ducked inside. She made a dash for the mirror, and noticing she was alone, dropped her organizer on the vanity for a critical inspection.

She cringed at her reflection. Her thick black waves were packed around her ears in a smooth cap. Those funky biker goggles had smudged her mascara. The wind had swept the blusher from her cheeks. Her lipstick . . . well, she'd probably chewed it off herself. So now, in addition to black circles under her eyes, she was ghastly pale. And this was the image she'd left with William before he drove off to park his bike? Hello, Halloween was over four months away. *Nice, real nice.*

A long wig and she could make an appearance as Elvira, Mistress of the Dark.

Speaking of whom, Marcella's cleavage seemed to have disappeared. She straightened the double-breasted jacket of her pantsuit until it once again sat square on her shoulders, its deep neckline centered over her bosom.

Ah, much better. And while she was at it, she might as well lift and adjust. Reaching between the wide lapels, she slid a hand into one cup of her black satin demi-bra and repositioned her breast over the push-up pad.

She switched hands and had just scooped up her right breast when the door burst open and in walked that little brunette she'd seen flirting with William on the church grounds.

Marcella immediately jerked her hand out of her underwear, then leaned over the sink to fluff her hair, hoping the girl would disappear into one of the stalls, but she marched up to the vanity beside her.

Marcella tried to ignore her, rejecting any possibility she could be competing for William's attention with this pixie of a woman-child who barely looked old enough to drink. She straightened and ran the faucet to wash the smudged mascara from beneath her eyes, until finally the staring became so palpable it was ridiculous to go on pretending she didn't notice. She glanced down to meet the girl's gaze in the mirror.

"Hi! I'm Darcey." She waved excitedly at Marcella's reflection. "Darcey Little, actually. Darcey with an E-Y. Mum's a big Jane Austen fan."

Marcella smiled curiously into Darcey Little's heavily, although expertly, made-up eyes. "Funny, I was thinking of *Pride and Prejudice* earlier this morning. Hi, I'm Marcella Tartaglia."

Who could have imagined a pierced eyebrow would complement a classic silky bob, but Darcey pulled off the look.

A sequined fabric tote featuring a Parisian café scene hung from her shoulder. She slipped it off, opened it, then shook it upside down. Compact cases, lipstick tubes and glosses, moisturizer jars, liner pencils, mascara wands, eyelash curlers, eyeshadow discs, perfume sprays, and makeup brushes of every shape and size scattered over the vanity.

"Help yourself," Darcey offered.

Marcella eyed the spill suspiciously.

"It's all right," Darcey assured. "William sent me."

"William?"

"William, yes. I mean, he told me to be discreet. Didn't want you to know he'd noticed your makeup running all down your face, but I thought, sod it. Any girl'd be keen to know what a thoughtful fella she had in William. Perfect gentleman, isn't he? Not a bit like Bertie. His younger brother, you see." She leaned closer and whispered, "My boyfriend. Yes, complete prat, Bertie. A sex god, but still a prat, unfortunately. Especially on days like today when he's got all his mates round. You must've seen him. He's one of the Oxford rowers in the striped jackets."

Whoa, too much info, too fast. If she gave it some thought, Marcella might be mortified, but she was busy enjoying this newfound discovery that the relationship between Darcey and William was not a romantic one.

Which made her think. Darcey was the person to ask for the scoop on William, but as she obviously couldn't be discreet, Marcella dismissed the idea. Interrogating William's mother had been embarrassing enough. She wouldn't want William thinking she was pumping his entire circle of acquaintances for information.

No, anything she wanted to know about William Stafford, Marcella would learn by herself, thank you very much, including his rating as a sex god.

So, William wanted to buy her a drink. A drink meant conversation, an opportunity to get to know one another. *Whoopie!*

Marcella nosed through the makeup. "Yes, I believe I did

notice Bertie," she admitted. He must've been the one humping his oar.

"Do you fancy him?" Darcey asked. With a shake of her head, she snorted a laugh. "Not Bertie, obviously. William."

"What's not to fancy?" Marcella countered.

William's refined British elegance in combo with that laid-back, biker-dude attitude and dry sense of humor was the sexiest. With the wind blowing through his thick chestnut hair, it had been all Marcella could do not to bury her face in the back of his neck as she inhaled his clean scent. And what about those abs, huh? She'd admittedly capitalized on being frightened by the ride in order to snuggle up to his buff bod.

"You're a lucky girl," Darcey said. "William's not the type to chat up a woman unless he's pretty certain he's interested. 'Course Bertie says how could William not be interested with bosoms like yours? They are real, aren't they?"

Marcella was rather taken aback. Not by the question, but by these small, shiny purple packets she kept noticing mixed in with Darcey's makeup stash. At first, she assumed they were perfume samples. Then it dawned on her. Condoms.

"Not that it matters," Darcey was saying. "I hear it's done all the time in the States. Having one's breasts enlarged."

So, William was a boob man, was he? Something to keep in mind. Marcella threw back her shoulders and noted the effect in the mirror. "Oh, they're real, all right," she boasted. "I inherited them from my Italian nana."

She didn't mention she was, in fact, a modest B-cup. Her slim frame and the push-up pads did wonders for creating a fuller bustline.

Darcey chose a lipstick and a powder compact from amongst her things and offered them up like pocket change to a beggar. "Go on then," she encouraged. "Wouldn't you like to use something?"

"Well . . . maybe just some blusher." A person could pick up some serious germs using another's makeup, but all Marcella had for repairs of her own was a thin lipstick tucked into one of the pencil slots of her organizer.

"Blusher . . . right . . . very good." Darcey rooted around before producing a gel stick of cheek stain.

She unscrewed the cap. "This is all the rave of the fashion magazines. Very natural. Leaves a dewy hint of color. This one's mauve with blue undertones. Perfect for a light olive complexion like yours. It'll look fabulous, trust me. Would you like me to apply it for you? I'm really quite good."

"Sure, why not?" Marcella turned on her mules and strutted over to a nearby chair where she took a seat, then crossed her legs. *What the hell, right?* She couldn't look any worse than she did right now, and if Darcey could repair Marcella's makeup with half the skill she'd used to apply her own, then great.

"I'm all yours, Darcey."

Darcey beamed. "Fabulous!"

Church bells rang through Rousham Park as guests of the Swann wedding arrived in carloads to mix, mingle, and celebrate.

The extensive gardens, designed by William Kent in the early eighteenth century, remained unspoiled by time. "One of the few gardens of this date to have escaped alteration," Marcella read off the brochure she'd snatched from the manor house upon exiting the ladies' room.

The setting included a walled garden with herbaceous borders to wander through; Venus, cupids and various other statues to lend ambiance; shade trees to relax beneath; and cozy gathering spots on terraces or by fountains.

Just outside the marquee—a reception tent large enough to accommodate table seating for over two hundred and draped in herbs and greenery—the wedding party lined up to receive their guests.

William, ever so tall and resplendent in frock coat and top hat, winked at her from the end of the line, his smile as intoxicating as that first sip of a full-bodied, but slightly sweet cabernet sauvignon on a Friday night after an alcohol-free workweek. A tingle of warmth seeped through her veins.

Marcella smiled giddily and wiggled her fingers back at him. She folded the brochure and tucked it inside her organizer, excited and full of anticipation at the knowledge William was waiting for her.

She extended her hand to the first in line, an elderly woman in salmon pink and a coordinating shade of lipstick. Beside her, the woman's husband introduced them both as Henry's parents. They accepted Marcella's congratulations, and when Marcella explained her relationship to Lynne, the senior Mr. Swann joked about how Marcella's losing a boss now meant Henry was gaining one. His wife swatted his arm.

Marcella was still grinning when she moved on to kiss the thin, fragile cheek of Lynne's mother and compliment her embroidered silver suit.

Feeling Lynne's watchful gaze hurrying her along, Marcella turned to offer her best wishes. Lynne gave a curt smile and offered up her cheek. Marcella leaned forward to bestow the expected peck.

"I saw you flirting with William as I walked down the aisle," Lynne muttered. "Could anything be more inappropriate? Really, Marcella, only someone like you would make advances to a man like William, in church, no less."

Huh? . . . *oh, geez.* Marcella rolled her eyes. You'd think William was a freakin' saint or something, the way his family went on. Well, there wasn't anything saintly about the way his eyes were all down the front of her suit. In church, no less. Not that

Marcella was complaining. *Au, contraire.* But how convenient of Lynne to pretend not to have noticed.

Marcella got in her former boss's face and whispered, "I returned his smile, Lynne. No biggie. I have nothing to apologize for, but if somehow I unconsciously offended you, I'm sorry. Now, what do you mean, 'only someone like me'?"

Lynne's stern expression mellowed to a mere disapproving pout. "You're quite talented and dedicated, Marcella, but outside of work, you and Sallie are always looking to have a bit of fun. Not at all serious. And if we must be honest, William does come from a royal family, while you've been raised in your little ethnic neighborhood. Quite very different backgrounds. Actually, you've nothing in common. I hope you're not considering pursuing him."

Marcella seethed. For anyone's information, William was the one doing the pursuing. When Marcella spoke, her voice was almost a hiss. "You think I'm not good enough for William? Is that why you kept him such a secret all those months I was helping you plan this wedding? Well, what about Babette, huh? I suppose, then, Babette is from a royal family?"

Lynne arched her practically bleached-to-nothing brows. "In a manner of speaking, yes, she is . . . quite. She's a top pedigree dog."

While Marcella blushed at the mistake, Lynne touched a hand to her forearm and spoke in a low, more sympathetic tone. "You must understand William's exemplary character. It's complicated, but trust me, he's not the man for you. He's not some disposable date to entertain yourself with while you concentrate on your career, then later chuck because you don't have time for a relationship. William deserves more than just your passing fancy. We've discussed your career objectives, Marcella. It's no secret you're after my job. I don't know what the executive board will ultimately decide, but I want you to know

I've given you a favorable recommendation as my replacement. Senior Editor is a demanding job, and as I recall, you did tell me your career takes priority over a relationship."

Marcella remembered that conversation. "Don't put words in my mouth, Lynne. What I said was, I'm not a woman to pass up important life experiences just to be with a guy."

"And being promoted to Senior Editor is not an important life experience? What is it you really want, Marcella? Something to think about, dear."

Lynne released her and stepped back, raising her voice as she commented. "Now, tell me what you've done to your eyes, darling. They look lovely!"

"Just a little eyeliner," Marcella mumbled and moved on to Henry. As was her intention, Lynne had given her plenty to think about. *Bitch.* Marcella offered a smile to the groom and said loud enough for Lynne to hear, "Did you know, Henry, that my family is in the iron and steel business?"

"No," Henry admitted, he didn't know.

"Yeah," Marcella confirmed. "My mother irons and my father steals."

Henry's eyes crinkled at their corners as he burst into chuckles.

Lynne sniffed.

Marcella would have congratulated Henry but felt offering her sympathies to be more appropriate. She wished him luck instead. As he turned to introduce his three grown children, one of whom was recently married, Marcella zoned out, greeting them in robotic, pasted-smile mode. Could Lynne have a point? Beyond the need to assert her controlling nature, that was. Lynne might be leaving the magazine of her own free will, but Marcella imagined she was resenting it every step of the way.

As for herself, just what exactly was her interest in William? A couple of casual dates? A fling? She had no intention of pursuing a serious relationship at this stage in her career. And not that she was speaking from experience, but a long-distance romance was sure to be an emotionally draining undertaking filled with longing and insecurity. On the other hand, was she willing to let this great guy pass her by? Did she want to pursue a relationship with William?

Questions! Decisions! This was too much soul-searching to dump on her. She'd known William for all of a half-hour. Still, how many guys lately had held her attention for even that long?

Bottom line, though, nothing or no one was going to get in the way of this promotion. It meant everything to her. She'd been working her whole life towards her own personal dream of working in the media, living in an exciting city, traveling, meeting new people. As early as age eleven, she began washing dishes in her grandfather's restaurant on Providence's Federal Hill to earn money for college.

It floored her how William could distract her from her career goals for even a moment.

Marcella hadn't realized she'd reached the end of the line until she held out her hand and it was enveloped by a firm, comforting grasp. She glanced up and fell headlong into the depths of William's smiling aquamarine eyes.

"Ah, nice." He nodded approval. "Lovely, actually. I see you've met Darcey?"

"I did, yes." Marcella batted her lashes at him. "Thanks." Darcey had encircled her eyes with a smoky shadow to give them a wide-eyed look, soft and subtle, but adding a touch more drama to her face. Her lips were painted in a nude shade to accentuate their fullness then brushed with gloss until they shone like glass.

"Not that you didn't look lovely before, mind. I rather fancied those two big black smudges beneath your eyes, but this is a smart look, too."

Marcella had to force herself not to stare. *Man, was he hot.* Maybe she hardly knew the guy, but she felt . . . sensed more like, something incredibly wonderful in him. She truly believed him to be the extraordinary person his mother, aunt, and Darcey had raved about and realized she could fall—and fall hard—for this Will Stafford. Suddenly she was terrified.

"So, what d'ya think? Shall I fetch our drinks and meet you by the goldfish pond once they release me from this queue? What d'you fancy? A cocktail? Wine?"

"Oh, William, I'm sorry, but I'm going to have to pass on the drink," she heard herself say. "You see, I've been assigned to cover the wedding in an article for *Gracious Living.* There are still several shots I need from Sallie, and I want to take care of business before the party gets under way and things get crazy around here. You understand."

"Oh, right." He was obviously disappointed. His smile wilted. In an unconscious gesture, his hand rose to the cravat tied at his throat. "Aunt Lynne explained about the dog collar, did she?"

Marcella didn't quite catch his meaning. "She enlightened me to the fact that Babette is your dog and not a girlfriend, but I don't think I've heard the story about the dog collar."

He gave her an ambiguous look. "What exactly did Aunt Lynne say to you?"

"Keep the line moving, please," Lynne shouted at them.

"I'd better go, William," Marcella said. "Thanks again for the ride."

As she hurried off to look for Sallie, Marcella thought she heard him mutter, "Bloody hell."

Chapter 4

Marcella picked her way across the grass in her stiletto mules to join Sallie by the dessert table. She hugged her organizer to her chest and assessed the spread as she went.

A crystal cake stand held the wedding cake. White garden roses and rose leaves decorated three iced tiers of traditional English fruitcake, along with an evergreen called *Alchemilla mollis,* which Marcella remembered from her notes.

Mountainous platters of strawberries had been set out alongside pitchers of fresh cream. Excellent choices for the simplistic yet elegant theme of a perfect summer's day. Marcella greeted Sallie, ready to get down to business. The table merited a thumbs up, and a photo was a must-have for her article.

Not surprisingly, Sallie was already armed with a cocktail. Her camera hung from a strap around her neck. "You've been gone awhile. You missed the fun. I love that dark smoky thing you've done to your eyes, by the way." She raised her glass and sipped slowly. "Yummy." She lifted her brows for emphasis, then made a show of running her tongue across her upper lip and sighed. "So? Tell me. How'd it go with William?"

Marcella didn't want to think about William. Thinking about William would only make her depressed. She reached for a strawberry.

"Yeah, taste those berries," Sallie encouraged. "They're incredible. Sweet, but not too 'tart' . . . like someone I know."

Marcella tried to muster some spark of amusement for the

pun, but she could only stare blankly at the strawberry. Her appetite had vanished.

Sallie sipped again from her cocktail. She frowned impatiently, then pumped. "Okay, Marcella. Tell me what happened."

Of course, there was no way to avoid telling Sallie. Actually, Marcella was grateful for the opportunity to unburden herself. "William was great. Fun, courteous." A smile touched her lips at the memory. "Even Lynne noticed how much we were hitting it off."

Sallie gawked. "And this has you in a funk, why?"

"I freaked, Sallie. William offered to buy me a drink, and I told him I was too busy with work."

"You shot him down? The Honorable William? You bitch."

Marcella nodded. "I know, I know. I should live in the moment. I could be having fun, but I don't think I can dismiss William as just someone to hang with for a while. He scares me."

"How so?"

"A girl doesn't meet a hottie like William every day. A hottie who also happens to be a genuinely nice guy. I could really fall for him. I'm afraid if we spend time together, I'll only grow to like him more. And then when this weekend ends and we go our separate ways, I am going to be so bummed."

"It doesn't necessarily have to be like that. You can keep in touch."

Marcella snorted. "I can't adopt a pet because I don't have time for a relationship with a goldfish. How would I manage to stay connected to a man who lives an ocean away? I'm on the verge of achieving everything I've worked my whole career for, and at this point in my life, I'm not willing to walk away from that for any man." Marcella managed a weak smile. "Not to mention what the phone bills would do to me."

"You are such a hopeless case."

Sallie shook her head, and this time when she raised her martini glass, Marcella recognized with astonishment its golden, yellow-orange contents topped by a twist of lime.

Sallie beamed at her shocked expression. "Duh, took you long enough to notice. I all but waved my drink under your nose. Here, have a taste."

Marcella accepted and downed a mouthful. She puckered, savoring the citrus intoxicant, and wondered aloud, "Sallie, where'd you ever get such an excellent Potion for Passion?" For the first time since leaving William behind in the receiving line, she felt happiness return in a warm glow.

"William got it for me."

The glow waned. "William?"

"Yeah. I hate to rub salt in the wound, Tart, but you're right. William is a great guy. While you were gone, we got to talking, and I asked about his Triumph. He even posed for me in his Regency duds."

Sallie positioned her Leica for a shot and mocked, "Yeah, baby! Fabio's got nothing on you." She lowered the camera with a shrug. "Anyway, he told me he used to bartend in college. When I told him about Potion for Passion being your absolute fave, he suggested we see how well the bartender could mix one. Then, if it passed my inspection, he was going to surprise you."

A cold, sickly feeling overcame Marcella. If she believed she'd done the right thing by refusing William, then why was she left with such regret?

Over two hundred guests rose to their feet in applause and cheers as the bride and groom entered the marquee to take their place of honor at the top table.

William glanced out over the rows of long dining tables and scanned the faces as he clapped along. Jolly fat lot of good it'd do to search her out, he thought, keeping his smile in place. His gaze wandered idly over the garlands of greenery that draped the interior of the tent. Marcella wasn't interested.

But why wasn't she interested? Bit odd, wasn't it, the way she'd changed her mind for apparently no reason?

Had Darcey said something in the loo to turn her off, he wondered. He couldn't imagine Darcey giving him anything less than the highest of praise.

Aunt Lynne! Right. More had been exchanged there besides kisses and congratulations. He'd seen the distress on Marcella's face. 'Course Aunt Lynne would never speak uncomplimentary of her godson, but she might get rather cheeky with a woman she believed unworthy of him. In this case, a working-class American of no particular fame or title: Marcella.

Rather dense bloke, wasn't he? Smitten with a woman so intent on pursuing her career she couldn't spare him the few minutes it took to sip a drink? Mind, how he could have grown smitten so quickly, when all he knew of the exotic giantess was her occupation and favorite cocktail, was quite the mystery.

No, Sherlock. No mystery a'tall. He was simply bowled over with attraction for her.

But enough of that. Time he focus on the festivities, being as he was about to toast Aunt Lynne and Henry before the whole assembly. It also had been assigned him to confer the blessing over the meal.

William reached into his trousers' pocket for his notes. He'd jotted down a few thoughts he didn't wish to forget, but the pocket turned up empty. Where had he lain those notes?

As he searched the inner pocket of his frock coat, he noted flutes had been filled with champagne at each table. Centerpieces held more herbs set in white bowls, and each place setting was marked by a paper butterfly napkin ring.

The applause faded, as one by one the guests resumed their seats.

William remained standing. He removed his notes from his frock coat and unfolded the sheet. He took his reading glasses out the same pocket and was just about to slip them on when a familiar voice arrested him.

"Well done, Vicar, chatting up those Americans. Fabulous. So, which do you fancy? I'd concentrate on the dark one, if I were you. She can't resist undressing you with her eyes."

William had rather gotten the same impression himself. He'd been mistaken, obviously. "Bertie," William implored, turning to his little brother, "what did Darcey and Marcella discuss in the loo?"

Bertie's eyes lit up. He drew closer. "Her breasts," he whispered into William's ear. "They're quite the real thing. A pair of jolly good handfuls, I'd say."

William's brain exploded at the thought of Marcella's breasts. He stood dazed. Signals of excitement shot through his body and his face warmed, due in part to a stab of anger that Bertie should be discussing Marcella with such intimacy.

Bertie burst into laughter. "Red in the face, are we, Vicar? Knew you'd be pleased. You can't fool me. You're a classic breast man." He slapped William on the back. "Everyone fancies you for such an icon. William, the perfect son. William, the scholar, the champion rower. Even his damn dog's a bloody champion. Who better than our own dear vicar to represent the family and give Aunt Lynne away? Bullocks! I often wonder whether you didn't join the clergy just to have a better go at the ladies. That collar attracts more birds than suet."

"Don't be an ass, Bertie," William grumbled. "Take your seat. I was just about to give the toast."

"Toast? Is that what you're doing? Bloody hell. I thought you were rummaging through your pockets."

"Go on, then. Sit down."

William scowled, but Bertie laughed once again, made a bow to Aunt Lynne, who was shooting him daggers, then dashed off to find his table.

William smiled apologetically to the crowd as he drew himself up to his full height of six-foot-three.

"Ladies and gentlemen," he greeted, "I'd like to thank you all for coming. I know some of you have traveled quite a distance farther than others, and you are all welcome on this joyous day. As Lynne's nephew and godson, it is my honor and a privilege, not only to have been chosen to give away the bride, but to toast Henry and Lynne on the happiest day of their lives."

At one of the back tables, seated between Sallie and *Gracious Living*'s art director, Nicole Sterns, Marcella hung on William's every word. She'd been jotting down a reminder to balance the vibrant garden photographs with some black and whites, when William's refined voice reached out to the crowd and all thoughts of her article disappeared.

"I've always known Aunt Lynne to be a beautiful woman," William was saying. "An independent woman who's always known her own mind and what she wants out of life, but I have never seen her look more radiant or confident than she does today. We are all very proud of her. You see, our family was a bit surprised when Aunt Lynne announced her engagement. She claimed she would never marry. None of us ever imagined she'd change her mind. It's been said—though I have no firsthand knowledge of this myself, mind you—that our dear Auntie Lynne is possessed of a rather uncompromising nature."

"A diva," Nicole summarized.

She said it; I didn't, Marcella thought as she exchanged grins with Sallie.

"But Henry wasn't intimidated," William continued. "Certainly not. Why, I heard the night before his wedding he wasn't a'tall nervous about marrying Aunt Lynne. Slept like a baby. Right, woke up every half hour crying for his mummy."

Laughter arose, especially from the front tables, which Marcella knew to be occupied by Lynne's and Henry's families.

Meanwhile, up at the top table, Henry blushed, while the diva herself pouted with faux insult. William smiled at her with a look of total adoration and Lynne melted.

William gestured to his aunt and announced, "All joking aside, my point, as you can see, is that not even our dear, headstrong Aunt Lynne could withstand the power of love."

The crowd applauded. Sallie nudged Marcella from beneath the table, which Marcella knew was meant to remind her of their conversation on the plane.

All right, she'd made a mistake. She'd overreacted. What had she accomplished by blowing William off? Nothing. She'd never be able to give full attention to her work when her libido jumped into overdrive at a mere glimpse of him.

William went on to explain that he wished to recite a short poem, which he believed expressed the nature of Lynne's and Henry's love. He slipped on a pair of round, wire-framed spectacles.

"Oh God, and just when I thought he couldn't get any hotter," Marcella groaned.

Nicole nodded. "He is a dish, as they say here in England."

Marcella listened attentively to his skillful recital, enhanced all the more by his British accent. He looked thoroughly at ease, as though it were the most natural thing in the world for William to be the center of attention. Marcella wondered whether speaking to the masses wasn't something William did on a regular basis.

She sat back and processed this new information, then flipped a page in her organizer and wrote "Natural public speaker" next to William's full titled name and the rest of his bio. As she tapped her pen on the page, she ran down the list. Born of a royal family, well-groomed, well-educated Oxford grad, team athlete, good sense of humor, strong moral character.

Marcella leaned into Sallie and whispered. "Look at him, Sallie. The glasses, his ease before a crowd. I'll bet you anything William is a professor."

Sallie considered for a moment before countering, "Lots of professions require public speaking. William used to bartend in school, remember? I bet he's real good at listening to other people's problems. Why couldn't he be an attorney? Can't you imagine him in a courtroom fighting for justice?"

"Get real, Sal. A lawyer who donates his car to senior citizens?"

"Point taken. I suppose he could very well be a professor. I'd take the bet, Marcella, but there's no chance we'll find out now, will we?"

Marcella frowned. Perhaps she could figure out some way to apologize to William and rekindle his interest.

She turned her attention back to his toast.

William was now addressing the groom. "Henry, in you, Aunt Lynne has found her perfect partner, and I know I speak for us all when I say I'm delighted to have you join our family. Your loyalty, honor and sense of humor have never failed, and I know you will make a truly loving and dedicated husband to my aunt. I wish you both every happiness."

William raised his champagne flute and told the guests, "Ladies and gentlemen, please charge your glasses, I give you the Reverend and Mrs. Henry Swann, the bride and groom."

After a traditional dinner of roast of beef with Yorkshire pudding, Dover sole for Sallie, served in an elegant presentation on white china with fine linen, the dancing began.

The bride and groom shared their first dance, then the rest of the wedding party joined them on the dance floor in an exchange of waltzes. Finally, the floor opened to guests. The music switched to the beat of Sixties British pop. As "Love Potion Number Nine" rocked out the sound system, the Oxford oarsmen shed their striped jackets in search of a partner. One in particular, tall and ruddy-cheeked with a shock of pale blonde hair, asked Sallie to dance.

Nicole wandered off to the shade trees for a cigarette. Left to her own devices, Marcella took her organizer and headed for the bar. All this crooning over potions put her in the mood for one.

As she sipped her Potion for Passion, Marcella checked out Darcey, who was on her way to the dance floor walking hand-in-hand with her so-called sex god.

Just as she'd guessed. So this was Bertie. Marcella figured him for about five-ten. Much shorter than William, but with his wavy chestnut hair and British good looks, he bore a remarkable resemblance to his older brother. Of course, Bertie's unsophisticated youth left him slightly rounder in the face, a touch gangly. He lacked William's grace, even on the dance floor.

Marcella nursed her drink as she watched William boogie with Lynne. After having debated her options all through dinner, she still hadn't come up with a workable plan for restoring herself back into his good graces.

The obvious, most direct approach would be to apologize for being a jerk and offer to buy him a drink. "Care for a taste of Passion?" she would cleverly ask. But no, apologizing would only draw attention to the fact she'd been a jerk in the first place.

She thought of asking Sallie to take photos of the entire wedding party and then use the opportunity to engage William in conversation. Unfortunately, Lynne was part of that wedding party, and her disapproving presence was bound to put a damper on Marcella's rusty pickup lines. Strike that.

Maybe she'd casually stroll over and ask William to dance. No groveling, no apology. Just, "Care to dance?" Simple, right? Problem was, William's dance card appeared to be full.

After getting down with Lynne, William danced with his mother, followed by Darcey, one of the junior bridesmaids, and a continuous stream of women of varying ages and sizes whom Marcella chose to believe were relatives. Between dances, he held court on the lawn where he inevitably picked up another partner from amongst the many guests.

The more she watched, the more vulnerable Marcella felt. Didn't it just suck, caring about someone? Someone who, by the way, she did not need, nor had she desired, to come into her life. Someone so dashing and handsome he obviously didn't need or desire her.

Defeated, she set her empty glass on the bar and opened her organizer to double check she had everything she'd need to produce a finished article.

She was scanning her list of photographs when a tiny voice interrupted her thoughts.

"Please, miss."

Marcella peered over her organizer and looked down in the direction of the voice. There in her linen bridesmaid dress, arms bare now that she had discarded the lilac cardigan, was Mae, the tiny attendant Marcella had met outside the church along with William's mother.

Mae's face was flushed from dancing. A single paper butterfly clung to a few loose strands of her baby soft, mink brown hair. She held a white rose, obviously scoffed from one of the floral arrangements inside the reception tent.

"Hi, Mae! Whatcha' got there, honey?"

Mae offered up the rose, then extended her right arm, pointing to some location yonder in the garden. "Please, miss, that man would like a dance. Shall I tell him yes?"

Chapter 5

Adorable, Marcella thought as she smiled down at Mae. Absolutely adorable. Could anyone refuse such a charming offer? Still, as a single woman, her instincts of self-preservation demanded she have a look-see before accepting the rose.

She glanced about the garden, attempting to identify the man who had sent Mae, but not one face sought her out. She noticed several guests had gathered beneath the shade trees. Nicole was still sucking poison into her lungs while she gossiped with two other *Gracious Living* staff members. A few elderly ladies admired the flower beds. A young couple locked lips beneath the rose arbor. Everyone seemed otherwise socially engaged except . . . that man . . . across the green, gazing into the goldfish pond . . . turning towards her . . . was that? . . . *yes!*

Looking her way, William stuffed his hands in the front pockets of his black tux trousers and shrugged. Slowly, one corner of his lips curled in a mischievous, sexy grin.

Her heart began to race. Gone was the frock coat. His winged-collar shirt shone stark white in the bright sunshine, its sleeves rolled past his forearms. With his excellent posture, William made for one fine, broad-shouldered, aristocratic biker dude.

Marcella waved, pointed to Mae, then mouthed, "From you?"

He nodded.

Marcella burst into a big, goofy smile she was certain broadcast her excitement and left no doubt she was up for a dance. Up for more than a dance, if everything went her way. All she could think was, *Yes! yes! yes!*

She returned her attention once again to Mae, who waited patiently with the rose. Marcella reached down to claim it. "Thank you, Mae, honey. Tell your Uncle William I said yes. Yes, I'll dance with him."

Mae beamed. "Thank you, miss, thank you."

She gave Marcella a curtsey before skipping off to deliver the news. *Enthusiastic kid,* Marcella thought. Probably just excited for her uncle. Probably just another devotee in the Honorable William fan club.

Speaking of which, Marcella fully intended to become a groupie herself. Her new strategy was to gorge herself until she regurgitated William Stafford right out of her system. Excess and enjoyment. *Yup. Uh-huh.*

As Mae approached William, Marcella watched their exchange. William offered the girl what Marcella recognized as a pound coin. Mae refused and stomped her foot. William squatted before the child and tried again with the coin. They debated for a few moments, then William straightened, and with a shake of his head, reached into his back pocket for his wallet. He slipped out a note, which he presented to Mae.

The kid snatched the money and split.

Marcella hid her laughter behind the rose. William spied her and returned the smile. His gaze never left her face as he pocketed his wallet and began to bridge the distance between them with long strides.

Her anticipation increased with his every step. The scent of rose petals stirred her senses. She couldn't be any more turned on if she were naked in bed between nine-hundred-thread-count Egyptian cotton and this royal descendant of the peerage was about to slip her the Crown Jewels.

The moment was so perfectly romantic, she could hardly

believe it. So perfect, in fact, paranoia set in. A white rose signified innocence and purity. Had William meant to deliver a message? Was he trying to explain his interest was purely innocent? Maybe he'd noticed her drinking by herself, scribbling in her organizer like some workaholic geek when she should have been socializing, and took pity. Maybe he was just being polite in asking her to dance.

Hey, if that were the case, Marcella would just have to make the most of this opportunity. Besides, William was wonderfully articulate. He didn't need the language of flowers to express himself. He'd swiped the rose off a floral arrangement, and white was, after all, the color *du jour. Nah,* she reconsidered, no hidden message. Except . . . when you got right down to it, didn't all flowers convey thoughtfulness and affection?

Cool. She was psyched. Marcella nestled the rose in the spine of her opened organizer. As William approached, she lowered them both and zeroed in on his gorgeous face.

"Hi," she welcomed.

He smiled warmly into her eyes. "Hello . . . Marcella," he greeted in a slow exhalation of British-accented breath. His damp chestnut hair curled over his forehead. His cravat hung loose around his neck, yet the top button of his shirt remained fastened.

"I hope you've managed to enjoy the reception despite your work," he said.

"Well, now that I've gotten everything I need for my article, I'm hoping to enjoy it a lot more with you here."

William's aristocratic face brightened in a bashful, totally adorable sort of way. "Yes, well, I thought I'd have another go."

"I'm glad you did. As a matter of fact, *I* was waiting for an opportunity to ask *you* to dance, but unfortunately for me you've been quite the busy socialite."

He grinned. "Lots of family I haven't seen in a bit, you

understand. So . . . you say you were thinking of asking me to dance, were you?" With a jerk of his head, he gestured in the direction Mae had disappeared. "You mean, I've just let that little kipper talk me out of a fiver for nothing?"

Marcella twittered. "Absolutely not. Loosen up that collar and I'll show you." She stepped closer, and in a bold sexual overture, breached his personal space by unclasping the top button of his dress shirt.

His aquamarine eyes widened with pleasant surprise. He breathed, then slowly his gaze narrowed to devour her with an intensity that left Marcella oblivious to everything except the fact she was here with William in the gardens of Rousham Park on this perfect summer's day.

He leaned forward and softly said, "That's much better, yes. Thank you." His gaze dropped to her lips. "I'm so used to a collar I hadn't noticed."

Marcella smiled and strained upwards. "You're welcome."

What were these references to a collar? Must be a British term for a suit and tie. So William was a businessman? Guess that ruled out professor. Right now, he could be the school janitor and she wouldn't care.

His lids grew heavy, his eyes glazing as though he'd fallen into a drugged haze.

Tilting her face up in invitation, Marcella's lips relaxed into a soft pucker, her own lids preparing to close—

At once, they simultaneously bumped into the organizer Marcella still held between them and sprang apart.

"Oops." Marcella giggled, offering William a sheepish smile by way of apology. She'd mourn that near kiss the rest of her life. Or at least until another opportunity presented itself. "What d'ya know, huh? Work gets in the way again."

"Oh, right. Work." William's smile was marked by disappointment. "Let's do something about that, shall we?" He took her organizer, saying, "Here, shall I find a safe place for this while we dance?"

Marcella agreed. "The key word there being *safe,*" she warned him. "That's my career in your hands." Career perhaps, but that organizer had been coming between her and a good time all day. Her rose lay on the ground between them, crushed. *C'est la vie.*

William didn't seem to notice. He glanced instead at the opened page, where something had caught his eye. He began to read her notes.

"John Anthony," he said, without looking up.

"Uh, excuse me?" Marcella didn't understand what in the world he was taking about, but found it an invasion of privacy, and frankly, presumptuous that he should continue to linger over her personal thoughts and writings.

"You have the names reversed." Lifting his head, he met her gaze. "My name. It's William John Anthony. Not Anthony John."

What on earth? Oh, his name. *Oh! Oh crap.* Before Mae's interruption, Marcella had been doodling hearts while pondering a few more updates to the info she'd gathered on William. That was the page he was reading. His page. She'd just handed over her own private rundown of his dating profile.

She felt like a teenager who'd just discovered her diary in the hands of the cutest guy in school. Could anything be worse?

"Please don't read that," she whined, making a desperate grab for the organizer.

William stepped back, lifting it out of reach. "Tell me, is this the 'business' you needed to take care of?"

Between his wise-guy expression and the amused glint in his eye, Marcella prepared herself to be teased for all she was worth. *Damn, damn, damn.*

He lowered the organizer to eye level for another peek at her notes. "This is what you've been slogging away at all afternoon, is it? Third son of an English viscount," he read aloud. "Rides a three-cylinder Triumph Thunderbird motorcycle. Oxford graduate. Stone cottage residence in Bramble Moor."

He queried her with a raised brow. "It's all rather impersonal now, isn't it? I mean, in Bramble Moor, even the Village surgery's a stone dwelling. But there is this bit which I find intriguing." He cracked up with laughter, and between guffaws, managed, " 'NO WIFE.' It's bloody underlined three times."

He had an infectious laugh which Marcella couldn't help but enjoy. Still, pride demanded she not encourage him further. "Don't flatter yourself."

"Oh-no, I'm quite flattered, actually." He blinked back a tear, and with another glance at her list, resumed reading. "Perfect gentleman. Natural public speaker. Compassionate eyes." His brows shot up suddenly and he sobered, then cleared his throat. "Potential sex god?"

"Hey, that's my personal and professional journal. Whatever's written there was meant for my eyes alone. You really have no business reading it. But hey, while you're at it, why don't you do me a favor by crossing out the 'perfect gentleman' part. I was mistaken, obviously. And as for your 'potential' . . . well, that was just me being optimistic."

He narrowed his gaze at her. Then slowly, one side of his mouth rose in a crooked grin. "Damn cheek." Marking the page with a finger, he snapped her organizer shut. "Is this part of your article? Judging the potential of male guests attending Aunt Lynne's wedding? If I turned the page, would I find your comments on Uncle Roy's untidy eating habits, perhaps? Have you been watching him pick his teeth? Or listening to the maiden aunts boast of Cousin Jeffrey's boyish charm?"

Holding back a chuckle of her own, Marcella considered her options. Should she continue to play the injured party or suck it up and come clean? So William had discovered she was hot for him? So what? If he was interested, and she felt confident he was, this knowledge would only encourage him. And wasn't that the whole point? After all, if William wasn't feeling attracted himself, he wouldn't be teasing her. Darcey had told her William was not the kind of guy to lead a woman on, and Marcella believed it was true.

"I haven't been observing anyone but you, Will." She enticed him with a seductive smile. "My interest is . . . personal, if you know what I mean."

His eyes sparkled. "Bugger, you could have saved us both some time if you'd have let me buy you a drink earlier."

"It isn't too late for a drink together . . . I hope."

He considered this briefly. "Where are you and Sallie staying? A hotel here in Oxford?"

"We're about eight miles away, at The Bear. Near Blenheim Palace."

"Of course, The Bear. Charming old inn. Perfect spot for a drink. After the reception, I'm going to arrange a lift for you and Sallie back to your hotel, and I could meet you at The Bear later, if that's all right. What d'you say?"

"I say great. It's perfect. I'll be looking forward to it. There'll be no work to interfere this time, I promise."

"Fantastic. Can't have you returning to the States with the impression there's nothing more to me than a few boring facts and the biased praise of my family. You've been talking to Darcey, I see. Bertie's the sex god in the family. I have to say, I do appreciate your optimism, though."

Marcella giggled. She was feeling more and more optimistic, minute by minute.

He lifted her organizer. "I'll have you know, there's quite a rather lot more to William Stafford than what's written here. For instance, nothing was mentioned about my cooking skills."

Marcella beamed. *Wow!* Great. They had something in common already, she being descended from generations of Federal Hill restauranteurs.

"Really," she asked, "you enjoy cooking?"

"Not particularly, no. I'm rather a terrible chef, unfortunately. Thank God for takeaway. My favorite nights are Tuesdays when the touring fish and chip van visits Bramble Moor."

Marcella rolled her eyes. "You're quite the kidder, William. Did I write that down? 'Cause I really think it should have been first on my list."

He reopened her organizer, slipped her pen from its holder, and pointed to the page. "May I?"

"You're, uh, going to revise my notes?"

He began to scrawl something in her journal. "I'm jotting down my numbers and address so you can get in touch with me. In case you have questions on anything we don't cover this afternoon."

Marcella restrained herself from letting loose a low whistle. What a cool cucumber. Man, did he turn her on. She was inspired.

"Excellent idea." She stepped closer to touch his bare, sinewy forearm while she peered down at the page. Mutual attraction had been established. Time to advance to an affectionate caress or two. "So that's your home phone, I suppose. And the second number? That would be your, er . . . office?"

He smiled. "Office? In a manner of speaking, yes. That's the number for Bramble Moor's village church, St. Francis of Assisi."

Huh? "Church? Your office is in a church?"

He chuckled, replacing the pen before closing her organizer. "Naturally. Look, there's my gran with her whist teammates." He motioned to the group of elderly ladies Marcella had seen earlier admiring the flower beds.

Escorting her by the arm, he began to lead Marcella towards

the group. "Can't think of anyone more reliable to guard your journal while we dance," he said.

Marcella tried to sort through her confusion. She was sure she and William had made a connection. Two single people, both with the same thing on their minds, sharing the same desire to get to know one another, flirting in sync, aroused by lust.

Pretty straightforward. So why did she suddenly feel she was talking to an alien? "I don't understand, William. Why is your office in a church? Exactly what sort of work do you do?"

Glancing askance, he noticed her blank stare and stopped, jerking Marcella to an abrupt halt.

He regarded her with a curious look. "You don't know? Aunt Lynne hasn't told you?"

"Told me what?"

"I saw you both conversing about something or other in the receiving line."

"Lynne informed me Babette was your dog and not some supermodel you bedded this morning, but I don't think that's what you're referring to, is it?"

"Supermodel?"

"What hasn't Lynne told me, William?"

"I watched you, Marcella. You looked rather upset. What did Aunt Lynne say?"

"Nothing. It was nothing, really. Lynne was just hassling me about work stuff. Apparently, she still considers herself my boss, but after today that won't be an issue," Marcella admitted, which was the complete truth, minus Lynne's bald confession that she didn't find Marcella good enough to associate with her nephew.

"Speaking of work, let me in on the big secret. What is it that you do, William?"

"No secret." He grinned proudly. "I'm a vicar. The vicar of

Bramble Moor. Did you wonder why I live in a small village?"

"You like the countryside?" Marcella heckled, with a shrug. Her brain screamed, *What!? A vicar?*

She gurgled up a hysterical giggle. You're joking, right? she wanted to ask, but his dead serious expression silenced her.

Had she heard correctly? William, a priest? William, the sexy biker dude with the cocky, confident expression? William, the ex-bartender, cool cucumber, sex god she'd nearly kissed and had made a date with, who only moments ago she'd been visualizing naked and seriously contemplated seducing, was the Reverend William Stafford?

No-o-o-o way. The two conflicting images overloaded her circuits and she slipped into brain freeze.

William shook her gently by the arm. "Marcella, are you all right?"

Her glazed eyeballs refocused. Marcella gathered herself and managed a smile. "So, that's where all those references to a collar came from, huh?"

He shrugged. "I didn't bother wearing it today, with the cravat and all, you see."

"Yes, of course." Marcella smiled into his eyes. Compassionate eyes. Natural public speaker. It was all beginning to gel. William, the man who had traded in his Fiat so the senior citizens of Bramble Moor could buy a minibus. William, who'd said grace over the wedding supper instead of the presiding vicar.

The truth hit her like a kick in the gut. But gosh, he was gorgeous. All those Sundays her Italian mama had dragged her to church and never had she seen a face like that behind the altar.

"Forgive my surprise, William. A vicar, huh? That's wonderful. I had no idea you were a vicar. No one mentioned it. I suppose it was obvious to everyone except me. Obviously, because I'd never met you until this morning. You certainly don't look like a priest, though. Henry—now there's a guy who's got a classic vicar look. Sweet-faced and mild-mannered. But you? You don't act like a vicar. You don't even talk like a vicar. Why, just a moment ago, I heard you use the word 'damn.' "

He gave a wry smile. "Right. Bit of a slip there. Not a word choice for the pulpit, is it? Pity how a vulgarity like 'damn' manages to pop into everyday conversation. Surprised I've never been struck dead."

Marcella chuckled. She deserved the sarcasm. She just hoped she hadn't insulted him. "It's just that you're such an ordinary guy," she explained. "Well, not that you're ordinary. Oh, no. Hey, you're extraordinary, really. Quite the dude. Charming, handsome, full of fun. Not the type I would have pegged for a member of the clergy. You're too . . . er, forgive me . . . normal."

He laughed. "Thank you. I'm flattered you think so."

She was babbling like a fool. Talking too fast. Digging herself deeper and deeper. What she really meant to say was, William was too hot to be a priest, but she could hardly tell him that, now could she? Did this mean they wouldn't be making out after drinks tonight?

Up till now, she'd felt confident coming on to William as the sexy male he was, but how did she handle a vicar?

She shook her head. "Sorry, I didn't mean—"

"I understand. I get this quite a lot, actually," he explained. "As a student, I had great fun bartending at a local pub during my vacations. I'd clown around with my workmates, chat with the customers. But once I let on I was intending the Church as my career . . . once they stopped laughing, that is . . . they'd react exactly the way you have."

He cleared his throat, hesitated, then gazed deep into her eyes as though he were about to make a confession. "Possibly, I've been a touch shy declaring myself. Not that I'm ashamed of what I do. It's just that once people discover I'm a vicar, they usually end up putting on a bit of an act, d'you know what I mean? They blush, stumble over their words, apologize for their language, for their jokes, their high spirits. It's rather like apologizing for being oneself, don't you agree?"

Marcella nodded. She saw his point, although to be honest, she was still having a hard time grasping the reality of William as a vicar. He spoke with levity, but had she detected a touch of loneliness in his voice? She held her tongue because she could see he had more to say.

"I don't want that to happen with you, Marcella. I've quite enjoyed your company and sense of humor. I'd be terribly disappointed if you were anything but your natural self with me."

He offered her his hand.

Marcella went all squishy inside.

"Shall we have that go at a dance?" he asked with a wink.

Marcella smiled into William's beautiful aquamarine eyes. "Let's," she said and slipped her hand in his without hesitation. "I'm really enjoying your company, too, William."

Presently, "I Only Want to Be with You" was booming out the sound system.

Call her crazy, but Dusty Springfield's crooning pretty much summed up William's effect on her. Nothing was going to stop her from enjoying his company today. Tomorrow would be too late. Tomorrow was Sunday. Tomorrow William would be back behind his pulpit, and she'd be preparing for her return flight to New York, where a busy career awaited.

They danced for nearly an hour, rocking to a few Sixties British pop songs, before the disc jockey announced, "Get ready for an eighth-some reel!"

The music started and eight couples formed two lines, men facing the women. William wanted to sit this one out, but Marcella begged him to stay. He agreed, albeit reluctantly, leaving a woman to wonder how this hottie of a vicar would pull off dancing on the balls of his feet.

As for herself, Marcella was prepared. Back in New York, she'd researched the steps for Lynne, and together they'd practiced them in Lynne's office.

The reel began. In her black pantsuit and mules, Marcella proceeded through the dance, careful to avoid Lynne's cold stares, with much less grace than she would have preferred, while William moved with the ease of an aristocrat.

As the reception wound down, the music slowed with a string of classic love songs. Marcella stepped into William's arms. She rested her hand atop his strong, broad shoulder, and as they swayed to the music, he held her close, then leaned forward to press his cheek to hers, his face moist with perspiration and slightly abrasive with the beginnings of a five o'clock shadow.

Marcella closed her eyes. Her senses whirred. She caught a whiff of his clean-scented cologne and fell into a heady rush.

In his British-accented baritone, William whispered softly, "Quite the cheeky monkey, aren't you? Jotting observations of me in your journal, when all the while I'd got the impression you weren't interested. Bit of an ego boost, that." His husky chuckle tickled her ear. "All I can say is I feel like a very lucky man, indeed, knowing I'll be seeing you again tonight."

Beneath her clothing, her body purred with desire. She longed to rise on her toes and stretch up against him like a feline in heat. Who'd have guessed a vicar could make a woman feel so sexy?

Bertie agreed to chauffeur the girls. "Brilliant. That's great," he whooped once Marcella had left to find Sallie, and William explained his plans for the evening. "I knew you two would get on," he rejoiced, his eyes alert with vicarious conquest. "Splendid, isn't it? You may well get a leg over tonight."

Leg over? William rebuked his brother with a disapproving

glare. Surely not. He'd no intention of seducing Marcella. Hadn't even given it a thought. Not that it wasn't a pleasant thought. It was quite a remarkably pleasant thought, actually. But not one he'd bloody well act upon. He'd just announced his vocation. What sort of vicar, what sort of man, for that matter, would she think him if he called at her hotel hoping to spend the night?

"You've the wrong idea, entirely, Bertie. Marcella and I are going to enjoy a drink and a friendly chat. That's all. I'm not anticipating anything more and neither is she. She's got quite a successful career in New York. We'll probably never get another opportunity to see each other again."

"Perfect then, isn't it?" Bertie persisted. "Nothing to stop you two from enjoying a bit of fun. She's far from home, on holiday of sorts. You really should be prepared, you know. She might be expecting a go. Wouldn't want to disappoint her." Sidling up to William, he nipped something into William's trousers' pocket.

William caught a flash of purple foil and pushed his brother off. Wedding guests milled all round them. William had a good idea of what might be contained inside that purple packet, but he wasn't about to whip it out and confirm his suspicions before an audience of friends and relatives.

Bertie wore a proud grin.

"You're appalling," William rebuked under his breath. "Was that a condom you just dropped in my pocket?"

Bertie was less discrete with the tone of his voice. "Well, you haven't very well brought any of your own, have you? I mean, you barely managed to get yourself dressed and to the church in time for the ceremony. Do you think you'll be needing another? Darcey carries extras in her bag."

"No, of course not. Only you, Bertie, would bring condoms to Aunt Lynne's wedding. I adore Marcella, but I've only just met her. She's just a friend. You really should speak of her with more respect."

Bertie took exception. "I'm very respectful of Aunt Lynne's friends, thank you. It's you she has to watch out for now, isn't it? Nothing sexual on your mind, then? Not even a bit of snogging? Then I suppose that's a halo pushing out your trousers, Your Reverence?"

As Bertie chuckled at his own pathetic humor, William sought to compose himself with a deep breath. He might try doggedly to resist thoughts of temptation, but unfortunately sometimes a bloke's body had a will of its own.

He scowled in disgust. "Just make certain you get the girls safely to their hotel, and for goodness sakes, Bertie, don't insult them with one of your rude outbursts."

Chapter 6

"Game for riding topless, ladies?" Bertie asked. He turned in the driver's seat to watch Marcella slide into the back of his red Saab convertible.

Marcella resisted a yawn, *ho-hum,* ignoring Bertie's leer as she scooted across the soft leather interior to make room for Sallie. All right, the kid was adorable in his own chubby-cheeked way, but his ogling did not impress her. Thanks to his brother, she'd experienced the ultimate in admiration. No man had ever gazed at her as William had when he walked Lynne down the aisle this morning dressed as a Regency lord. No man had ever stirred her to such excitement with just one glance. If she'd known at the time he was a vicar, well, she'd have . . . *hmm?*

She'd have been stunned.

Pretty much the way she was feeling now.

But was she any less attracted? Absolutely not. So William was a vicar. So what? To quote Sallie, a vicar was just a regular Joe. Tonight, she had a date with a regular Joe. No biggie. She'd dated regular Joes before. So what if she and William didn't lock lips afterwards? She'd get over the disappointment. No groping? No problem. Just being in William's presence was orgasmic. And clergyman or not, had she actually expected him to conduct himself as anything less than a perfect gentlemen? Of course not. His good manners were an integral part of his appeal.

She'd get this all into perspective before the evening was

through. Meanwhile, Bertie's cocksure grin persisted. He raised one brow as though to ask, How 'bout it?

In your dreams, pretty boy. Marcella narrowed her eyes, challenging him with a diva stare, and flipped back her waves. "No, thank you, Bertie. As beautiful a day as this is for a ride in a convertible, the truth is, Sallie and I are vain. We don't like getting our hair mussed."

Bertie continued to stare, his eyes glazing over dreamily. "Are you certain?" he asked softly. "You're totally hot, you know?" No sooner had the words left his mouth, when self-consciousness set in with a blush. "I mean," he stumbled, "it's totally hot . . . a totally hot day, that is. Quite a totally hot day, d'you-know-what-I-mean?"

"We know what you mean, Bertie, you randy git." Darcey settled into the seat beside him with a scowl. "I rather suppose they'd be more amenable to crawling on hands and knees back to their hotel than strip off their tops in front of you. Leave the car as it is, and pop on the air-conditioning. Otherwise, how d'you expect us to chat over all that wind?"

Without another word, Bertie straightened in his seat and started the engine.

Marcella reclined, exchanging a glance with Sallie, who hadn't stopped looking amused since she'd learned William was a vicar.

She's unusually quiet, Marcella noticed. Silence was less characteristic of Sallie than if she'd challenged Bertie and flashed him. Her friend seemed to be enjoying a private joke, and Marcella suspected whatever Sallie found so funny might have something to do with William. Something which might be better discussed in private, perhaps? Nah, William had been an open topic of discussion all day. "Okay, Sal, what's up?"

Sallie assumed an expression of innocence and shook her head. Marcella probed her with a you-can't-fool-me look.

Sallie considered, then as her grin began to grow, she giggled and quipped, "The vicar and the Tart."

Bertie drove the Saab off Rousham Park's lot onto Steeple Ashton. He gazed at Sallie through his rearview mirror like she'd gone bonkers.

Darcey turned around to ask, "Sorry, what d'you mean?"

But Marcella understood. *Amusing. Real cute.*

Sallie finger-combed her silky, dark honey hair off her face then leaned forward to clue in the others. "Back at our offices in New York, we sometimes refer to each other by last names. Marcella's last name is Tartaglia. She's 'Tart,' for short. She honked out a laugh and flourished a hand, indicating Marcella with open palm. "Pair her with William and we have . . ."

"Wicked!" Bertie howled.

Darcey's heavily glossed, deep rose lips parted in a gasp. "O-oh, sounds rather erotic, doesn't it? I mean, it's all quite lovely for Marcella and William. Like a bit of fate, or something. Who knows, perhaps tonight's the night for a private Vicars and Tarts party of their own, eh?"

"Exactly. And maybe Marcella'll even get her hair mussed." Sallie shot Marcella a hedonistic look from her baby blues. "You know, Tart, this occasion might just call for that little silk tunic number of yours." She winked, *hint-hint.*

Darcey frowned in confusion.

Sallie explained, "Marcella never travels without her silk tunic. It's this soft, yummy shade of strawberry with Georgette styling, a deep vee neckline, and long, sheer bell sleeves. Very romantic. In fact, it's the closest a girl can get to wearing a teddy without actually looking like a tart."

"Ha, ha. Very clever," Marcella jeered, even though she was loving Sallie's brain flash. She imagined a look of insane passion on William's face when he saw the single briolette bead from her garnet Y-necklace dangling between her breasts. A pair of fitted capris and her Isaac Mizrahi denim slides and she had an outfit for cocktails to rock his world.

"He's not some bloody shag toy," Bertie barked, startling Marcella out of her fashion trance.

"Um, excuse me?" she said.

Bertie glared at her in the rearview mirror. "Bloody unfair, it 'tis. We blokes invest quite a rather lot of time and energy into attracting you women. Can't get anywhere, can you, without some high-ranking job, an expensive car, or the proper chat-up line? William wears a bit of white round his neck and suddenly all you dead-gorgeous women fancy a bonk."

A 'bonk'? Marcella winced at Bertie's crude reaction to their harmless girl talk. "Hey, we're not talking sex," she corrected. "Just a little dressing to impress."

"Right." He nodded, both his expression and tone sarcastic. "Impress him with your breasts, that is. William's a weakness for breasts, you know. Rather like St. Paul."

"St. Paul had a weakness for breasts?" Darcey gave Bertie an incredulous gawk. "Dunno what you're on about."

"It's right there in the Bible, Darcey, isn't it? St. Paul said he was given a thorn in the flesh to buffet him. Well, women's breasts are William's thorn in the flesh."

Marcella looked to Sallie, who was obviously trying to hold it together. She lasted about a half-second before laughter burst out her firmly pressed lips.

Darcey eyed her boyfriend suspiciously. "You're the one, always goading William to have a go at the ladies. Are you jealous your brother has a date with Marcella?" Glancing behind, she confessed to Marcella, "Bertie's been admiring your chest all day."

"Sounds like a genetic predisposition." Sallie sighed dramatically. "Marcella, give the kid a break and show him your hooters. He was generous enough to give us a ride, after all."

Bertie's posture straightened. His swallow could be heard from the back seat of the car.

"As much as I appreciate the ride, Bertie, I'm never going to show you my hooters."

"Ingrate," he muttered.

Marcella stuck her tongue out at the back of his head. Then seriously, "Listen, Bertie. In William's defense, his being a vicar has absolutely nothing to do with his appeal. He wasn't wearing his clerical collar today. I had no idea he was a vicar. The fact is, William can handle a bike. He can mix a drink, burn up the dance floor, and conduct himself like a gentleman. He's charming, articulate, and looks hot in a tux. Did you ever consider that maybe, despite his being a vicar and not because of it, William is just the sort of man women find attractive?"

Bertie scoffed. "Is that what you believe, then? You fancy him a ladies' man? Well, you've got the wrong bloke if you're after a bit of casual fun. William's not looking for a date. He wants to fall in love."

Fall in love? *Wow.* Well, why not? William was a mature, sensitive, evolved male. His chosen profession entrusted him with the eternal destiny of an entire parish. It required him to join couples in the sacred, loving union of marriage. Later, he would baptize their babies. He consoled the bereaved and prayed for their dearly departed. Hey, Marcella reasoned, this guy did not shy from commitment. He embraced responsibility. Of course he wanted someone to share his life.

It wouldn't take long before some lucky woman snatched up the Honorable William. So, why couldn't she be lucky? She'd never felt this level of attraction or experienced the chemistry she shared with William. Maybe the timing wasn't quite right, but a man like William might never come her way again. Was she going to sit passively and let destiny pass her by? Let some other woman claim this prize catch?

Fifteen minutes later, as they drove through the misty and verdant old English countryside of the Cotswolds, Marcella still didn't know what she wanted. She hardly noticed Blenheim Palace, birthplace of Sir Winston Churchill, as the car rolled past. Bertie pulled his Saab into the hotel's drive, slowing to a stop before the ivy-covered facade of The Bear.

Marcella and Sallie thanked Bertie and Darcey for the ride and hopped out. After the couple drove off, Marcella hurried inside to shower and change.

According to a brochure left in the suite she shared with Sallie, The Bear had been the favorite hideaway of Richard Burton and Elizabeth Taylor during the height of their love affair.

A love affair was the one thing sorely missing from Marcella's life. How many men had Liz been involved with by the time she'd reached Marcella's age of twenty-eight? Way more than the number of dates Marcella had gone on in the past few years.

The phone rang as she was reapplying her makeup. It was William. Marcella agreed to meet him downstairs.

Twenty minutes later, William entered the lounge still clad in wedding attire. His white winged collar shirt hung out his tux trousers, both somewhat rumpled and baggy. His chestnut hair was wavy and tousled, his face glowing from his bike ride. The effect was irresistibly casual and sexy.

Marcella silently lamented she wasn't the one making an entrance. She waved him over, and as he approached the table, she stood, not so much to be polite as to leave an impression in her strawberry silk tunic and slim capris, which showcased her bronzed calves, thanks to a salon spray-mist tan.

She was probably trying too hard. Not a good thing, but then, how was a girl to continue attracting a man who easily looked sexy in a wrinkled tux and hairstyle that had survived several motorcycle jaunts?

"Hello," he greeted. His eyes shone with his smile, and as he stepped forward to place a kiss on her cheek, Marcella breathed a "Hi" in return.

William pulled away and skimmed his hands over his wrinkled shirt. "Didn't have time to nip home and change, I'm afraid. Aunt Lynne wanted me at her side to bid farewell to every last guest. Haven't kept you waiting long, I hope?"

"No, not at all."

"Great." He lingered admiringly over her body. "You look fabulous, by the way."

"Thank you." She watched William's Adam's apple bob with his swallow.

"Right then, let's have a seat, shall we?"

Marcella nodded, excited to get the evening under way.

William helped her resume her seat, then pulled out a curved ladderback chair for himself as he surveyed the lounge's tavern-style setting. The Bear had originally been built as a coaching inn in the thirteenth century, and although recently refurbished, it maintained its historic appeal. Marcella had chosen a small pedestal table before the open hearth. The shelf above displayed a row of large, antique pewter dishes.

"Rather cozy, isn't it?" he commented, folding his long, lean self into the seat beside her.

"Absolutely. Comfy and cozy, with lots of character and charm." And Marcella wasn't just referring to the atmosphere. She placed her forearms on the table and leaned forward.

William closed a large warm hand over her clasped fingers. "I'm really pleased you're here. Thank you for agreeing to meet me, privately, away from all the madness of Aunt Lynne's wedding." His voice was a warm, intimate baritone.

Marcella gazed into his beautifully intense, clear blue eyes and remembered to breathe. Oh boy, was she ever picking up some good vibrations. She found William pleasantly attentive and demonstrative, more so than she would have expected of a vicar, but then what she didn't know about vicars, about British men in general, was a real inconvenience.

William cocked a brow inquiringly. "You haven't brought along that gossiping work journal of yours, I hope?" He made a playful show of searching beneath their table.

She grinned. "Hey, if it wasn't for my organizer, I might not have nabbed your phone number."

He gave her hands a squeeze. "Not necessarily."

Marcella felt a pleasurable quivering in her belly. "Well, in answer to your question, no, I haven't brought my organizer. If all goes well, I won't need notes to remember this evening. I'm expecting tonight to be unforgettable."

Excitement flickered in the depths of William's aquamarine stare. His expression grew earnest, filling Marcella with anticipation as he opened his mouth to respond.

"Good evening, all. Would either of you care for a drink?"

Huh? The unfamiliar voice took Marcella unawares until she realized a waitress had arrived at their table. She glanced at William, who motioned for her to order.

"The house chardonnay for me, please," she said.

William leaned back in his seat and queried her with a puzzled frown. "Wine?" he mouthed. Then, turning to the waitress, he ordered, "A Guinness for me. And might we see a menu?" Addressing Marcella again, he asked, "D'you fancy a bite to eat? I'm feeling somewhat peckish, myself."

Since he'd asked for a menu, Marcella interpreted "peckish" as British-speak for hungry, with no suggestive inference. "Oh, sure. That'd be nice. The food here is great."

William thanked the waitress, who then left to fetch their drinks.

"So?" she asked, "Why the face when I ordered wine?"

William chuckled. "It's nothing, really. Just surprised to hear you order a proper beverage. No Potion for Passion this evening?"

Any number of witty comebacks would have been warranted, but Marcella played it straight. "Okay, I can take a little ribbing. But you really shouldn't poke fun until you've tried one for yourself."

"You're absolutely right, of course. And other than a sip from Sallie's today, I can't say I have, actually, tried a Potion for Passion. Which is odd, really, since I fancy myself somewhat of an expert in the field of mixed drinks, given my experience bartending. I have, however, sampled a Long, Hot Night and Sex on the Beach, but I never found them quite as enjoyable as that old favorite, you know. A Slow, Comfortable Screw up against the Wall."

Marcella dropped her jaw in mock horror. The words "wicked clergyman" came to mind, but she held her tongue, snapping her jaw quickly shut. She smiled and burst into flirtatious laughter. William laughed along with her, and Marcella gave his arm a playful shove, capitalizing on an opportunity to check out his bicep. Impressive. *Regular Joe, my ass,* she thought.

William cleared his throat. "I started all this silly business, I'm afraid, and now I find myself embarrassed by it. I should think you'd've had your fill of the Stafford family's awkward sense of humor, motoring with Bertie. Well, best you know my faults straightaway, I suppose, though I don't fancy you've got any of your own. No, you seem quite perfect."

It wasn't so much the flattery as his soft-spoken British delivery, combined with his humbleness and humor, that sent Marcella's libido skyrocketing. Maybe it was the adoration in William's eyes, but the waitress hadn't even brought her wine yet and already she felt a buzz. "Bertie tells me women are drawn to the novelty of your clerical collar. I disagree. I definitely think it's your charm."

He searched her face, uncertain. "I hope you don't think me insincere."

"Oh-no, William. Absolutely not. You ooze sincerity. That's part of what I find so charming."

He chuckled, relieved. "Oh, right. Very kind of you. Nothing worse than an insincere vicar, is there?"

Marcella laughed as he went on to explain, "For some odd reason, Bertie's got this ridiculous notion that since becoming ordained I've an advantage attracting the opposite sex. I suppose, if you consider the elderly ladies of my parish who seem to go out of their way to escort their unattached granddaughters and grandnieces to Sunday service an advantage, then yes, women are drawn to me. Although, 'dragged' might be a bit more precise."

Marcella eyed him shrewdly. He was far too modest. "Well, even if they are dragged to church initially, I bet they're thrilled when they discover the reason why. I bet they return week after week without grandma's encouragement. Why, I wouldn't be surprised if you've single-handedly reformed the female population of Bramble Moor by giving them something to look forward to come Sunday morning."

"Generally, it's not the women who need reforming."

His inquisitive stare prompted Marcella to quickly change the subject lest it be discovered she was a woman in need of reforming as far as her own church attendance.

"So, anyone ever catch your eye?" she asked. "There must have been someone special."

"It's quite obvious, isn't it, Marcella? Someone did catch my eye. This morning."

"Ah, yes. Thank goodness for that, but I think you're avoiding my question. What I meant was—"

"Yes, of course, I understand perfectly what you meant. The truth is, there was someone, once. We were engaged, but that was quite some years ago. We were both far too young and ambitious to make a go of marriage. But mature enough, fortunately, to call the whole thing off and pursue our separate paths before we made a terrible mistake and ruined a long-standing friendship we've maintained to this day. There's been no one to speak of since, really."

Meanwhile, Marcella, inside her obsessive and oftentimes insecure psyche, wondered what William was feeling when he unloaded that mouthful so quickly. Was he simply getting an inevitable dating question out of the way or had she touched on a sensitive subject? And why couldn't she be satisfied with the fact he was unattached and leave it at that? Why did she always have to scratch beneath the surface? It was mentally exhausting.

Before she could scratch further, however, the waitress arrived with their drinks and a menu.

William consulted her on his choice of munchies, and once the waitress had gone to fill their order, he turned to her. "It seems this conversation isn't going quite the way I'd hoped. All this talk about me. Although, I'm sure you've got all sorts of curious questions going round your head, as I have. I find I want to know everything about you. Have you a serious boyfriend in the States, Marcella?"

Fair enough, Marcella conceded. Better put his mind to rest on that score right away. "No boyfriend. Unfortunately, with my career, I haven't had much time to devote to a relationship. I've kinda been plugging for a promotion at the magazine. Early mornings, staying late, sometimes working ten- to twelve-hour days. Sometimes I even go in on weekends. You see, I'm hoping to step into your Aunt Lynne's position as Senior Editor now that she's resigned."

"Well . . . splendid. That's super for you," he said, although Marcella thought his expression registered disappointment. He recovered with an encouraging smile. "I wish you the best of luck. You're certainly well deserving, I'm sure."

Marcella worried she'd discouraged him, which she really didn't want to do at this tentative stage, not when she'd decided to turn on her game. Yes, she wanted to pursue a possible relationship, and hopefully, take this attraction to the next level.

She tried to compensate by adding, "I'm hoping things will calm down once I've actually been made Senior Editor. I'm looking forward to seriously devoting more time to a personal life."

He gave her an incredulous smile. "You mean, you expect you'll have less to do once you've been given more responsibility? I don't think it works that way, Marcella."

It did sound ridiculous, Marcella agreed, but she was determined to concentrate on the positive. "No problem. If there's one thing I've learned from Lynne, it's the power of delegation."

"Right," he allowed with a grin. "Unfortunately, you hardly impress me as the delegating type. You impress me as a perfectionist who'd rather tackle the job herself and see it done correctly than risk it to another's error. I admire your enthusiasm. So, tell me then, what goes on at your American magazine that has you so inspired?"

He was perceptive. Best she tread carefully, Marcella thought. She didn't want to bore him with the details of her day-to-day and make herself sound inaccessible by divulging the wide range of responsibilities that kept her creative processes churning well into the night.

Instead, she explained how she sought out and researched ideas for articles that embodied the magazine's mission, which was to applaud the lives of self-starting, enterprising women and offer readers the most tasteful of creative and romantic ideas on everything from decorating and entertaining to gardening and home comforts. She supervised each of her stories—

text, photos, and layout—to bring together a finished piece for Lynne's approval.

The food arrived, and as they dug into a variety of appetizers, not the least of which was an impressive pressed leek and wild mushroom terrine, William's questions turned to her family.

Marcella brought him back to her humble beginnings in Providence, Rhode Island. Her parents divorced when she was eight years old, and thereafter, life for herself, her mother, and younger brother centered around the family business—her grandfather's Italian restaurant on Federal Hill. By age eleven, Marcella could julienne as swiftly and efficiently as the best of them. She learned to cook everything from simple ethnic fare to fine cuisine and developed a flair for food styling and entertaining.

Family and friends expected she'd attend culinary school, but Marcella chose a career in the media when she was accepted into Providence's Brown University. It was her experience in the restaurant business, however, which gave her the edge she needed after graduation to land a job with a local food magazine. Which eventually led to a position at *Gracious Living* and her big move to New York.

They ordered a round of sodas. Marcella sipped her ginger ale, waiting until the waitress was out of earshot, then turned the topic of conversation back to William with the question of the day. How was it, she asked, that a vibrant, energetic blue blood with William's looks and charisma had been drawn to the clergy?

William paused thoughtfully from behind the rim of his glass before drinking his cola. "Not entirely comfortable with the knowledge I'm a vicar, are you?"

"No . . . I mean, yes. I'm completely cool with you being a vicar. Really. This is just me being nosey." Marcella inched her chair a little closer. "C'mon, Will," she pleaded. "I know you gotta have a story."

Lowering his glass, he met her gaze with a teasing smirk. "Not a particularly interesting one, no."

"Let's hear it anyway."

"Well, I'm not quite certain what it is you're expecting, Marcella. I've never been struck blind in the middle of the road or received guidance from an audible voice booming out the heavens."

"Maybe not, but from what I hear, you do have something in common with the Apostle Paul."

Marcella cracked up at his baffled expression, which grew more baffled the more she laughed. "You'll have to ask Bertie," she told him. "Now, tell me. Why'd you become a vicar?"

William eyed her shrewdly, then smiled and gave her a look of fond indulgence. Setting down his drink, he leaned forward and began by pointing out that unlike herself, who'd been earning her keep since childhood, he'd been born into quite a rather privileged life.

And like so many other children of fortune, he was unappreciative. The ease and convenience of having everything he could want or need at his disposal bred boredom. Sports entertained him most of the time, but with his natural ability, they never sufficiently challenged him. He grew restless easily and rebelled as a teen.

Marcella tried to visualize William as a rowdy kid, and unlike that of William the vicar, she found the image not altogether impossible to conjure.

He was disciplined, William explained, sent away to his godfather here in the Cotswolds, the Reverend Ernest Matheson, where he was forced to work, tending the vicarage garden and helping with odd duties round the church.

In the country, isolated from his friends and with no sporting events to amuse him, life slowed down considerably. His godfather proved a kind and patient guardian, always lending an ear to William's gripes. He encouraged William to look outward, to focus his energies on others rather than on himself and the self-centered entertainments that filled his young world.

William admitted he was resistant and angry. The only reason he attended services was to chat up the young church organist. But he stayed out of trouble, completed his chores, and gradually, a change was effected in him. William began to enjoy his visits and his work at the church. He'd discovered in himself a love for people. He recognized his need for a more responsible, yet simpler existence. A thirst he never knew he had began to be assuaged. By the end of his first term at Oxford, his future became clear. He made the decision to study theology.

They were now seated so close their heads nearly touched. The conviction in William's voice, the passion in his eyes, was infectious, and Marcella smiled in her surge of pride towards him.

Here she was, listening to a guy get enthused about becoming a priest, and she was getting turned on. What was wrong with her?

William loved his work, obviously. He enjoyed the church in the same way she enjoyed the magazine. More so, she was inclined to believe. He'd found purpose, and she envied him, because the truth was, there were times she still felt she was searching.

She caught William gazing at her quizzically. Before he could ask what she was thinking about, she asked him, "So, I don't suppose you get much time away from Bramble Moor, then, huh? To, you know," she waggled her brows up and down, "maybe visit New York sometime?"

Judging by his instant and wide grin, he understood her meaning and was flattered. His happiness waned as he pondered her question. "Er . . . it would be difficult, that."

"Not even long weekends?"

"Sundays are my busiest day, I'm afraid."

"Yes, of course. How silly of me. And tomorrow's Sunday. You probably have lots to do."

He nodded.

There didn't seem to be much of a prospect for them, did there? Marcella fretted. How was she going to see him again?

"Have you any plans for tomorrow?" he asked.

"Sallie and I thought we'd go to the Savoy for tea."

A light went out at the bar. The hours had flown much too fast, and now the lounge was preparing to close for the night.

"Well, I'm grateful we had tonight," Marcella said dejectedly.

William took her hand. He looked disheartened, more somber than she would have thought possible for someone with such a cheerful disposition. "For two people who seem incapable of arranging a way to see each other, I don't think I've ever enjoyed a woman's company more."

"Me too," Marcella agreed, suddenly at a loss for words. Her thoughts reeled. What to do? What to say? She didn't want this to be the end, but William looked as uncertain as she.

"I'll ring you here at the hotel before you leave, shall I?" he suggested brightly to Marcella's great relief. "Tomorrow night, if you're about. At the very least, perhaps we could be friends, or something. If not, I understand. You're quite busy. Anyway, you have my address and phone numbers if you ever want to ring me up or send a card. A Christmas card would be lovely. Or a birthday card, perhaps? A birthday card would do just as nicely. You could send both greetings with one card, in fact. My birthdate's December twenty-fourth, you see. Very thoughtful of me to time my entrance into the world so others could save on postage, don't you think? Anyway, the date is easy enough to remember, I s'pose, but just in case, perhaps you'd better dash upstairs and write it down in your journal."

Marcella had been chuckling through his speech, but now she sobered. "Don't worry. I will definitely remember. And, aw, what the hell? I'm not very economical. I'll send both cards."

Oops, she'd nearly forgotten. With her free hand she reached into her purse and produced her business card on which she had also written her home and cell phone numbers. "And this is for you."

William looked hopeful, but as he accepted the card and proceeded to stare thoughtfully at her neat scrawl, a frown formed a crease between his brows. "I'd love to see you again, Marcella, but tell me the truth. Is there any chance we can honestly continue with a relationship?"

Another couple of lights went out in the lounge. They sat in the dim glow, the only two patrons remaining. It was obvious the staff was giving them the signal to *adiós.*

A relationship with the honorable, mega-hunk William? Marcella's heart sang a joyous *Yes!* but William was expecting an honest response and the best she could offer was, "You know, there's a good chance I may not get that promotion, after all."

"That's not a very pleasant solution, is it?"

"Email?" Marcella suggested.

William looked skeptical. "The Church tends to frown upon priests who rely on a computer for socialization . . . might raise all sorts of suspicions, you know."

"Ah," Marcella acknowledged, as they shared a chuckle.

"Right. Well," William began, "we'd better clear out before that large and angry-looking waitperson over there decides to bodily remove us."

"Let me walk you outside," Marcella offered.

"I'd like that very much, thank you."

As much as she'd have liked to, Marcella didn't think it appropriate to ask William up to her room, nor did she think he'd accept the invitation.

Gazing into each other's eyes, they slowly rose to their feet.

William smiled at her as he dug in his pockets for a tip, tossing it down absently on the table as they prepared to leave. It landed with an odd snap, and the curious sound made Marcella turn.

There, on the table, among their empty glasses, crumpled cocktail napkins and a few pound notes, something bright and shiny caught her eye.

A purple-packaged condom.

Chapter 7

Giggles bubbled inside her. *What the . . . ?*

Call her naive. Unsophisticated. A tourist unfamiliar with British custom, but Marcella couldn't resist asking what might be considered an obvious question. "Hey, isn't that a condom?"

Yeah, it was definitely a condom. She recognized the packaging, because earlier this morning she'd mistaken several similar packets as perfume samples. They'd been scattered among Darcey's makeup during their quick beauty session in the ladies' room.

"Sorry?" With a shake of his head, William implied he must've heard incorrectly. "What did you say?"

Marcella cupped a hand to her mouth and enunciated in a quiet voice, "Prophylactic."

She pointed to their table.

William's gaze followed. There, in the flickering glow of candlelight, beneath the exposed oak beams of the dimly lit tavern, the amethyst foil square reflected like a jewel against the mahogany of the tabletop.

"Bloody hell!"

He lunged for the condom, but Marcella beat him to it, snatching up the glossy packet before William had the chance.

Giddy with laughter, assisted by the afternoon's cocktails and her recent glass of chardonnay, she dangled the condom between thumb and forefinger for his inspection.

"I'm sure you have a good explanation, but I just gotta say—

you really keep a girl on her toes, you know that? Man-oh-man, it's just one surprise after another with you. Naturally, as a young clergyman, I'd expect you to be progressive in your religious approach, but you're even more of a maverick than I imagined. Tipping in bars with condoms? Now that's liberal. What I don't get is," she pulled a clueless face, "why purple?"

William had endured her ribbing with quiet dignity, expressionless, but now his growing smile told her he was beginning to see the humor.

"I can see where you'd find this amusing," he said, "but it's really quite simple. Purple is the color of royalty. Crown Jewels, or so the expression goes."

He was goofing, right? The Honorable William sheathed in a purple condom in observance of his royal lineage? The image was erotically satisfying, she did have to admit. But, nah. Not William. He'd never . . . would he?

Obviously, William never meant to deposit a condom on the table. Question was, why had he been carrying one in the first place?

"Mind you, I'm not speaking of myself," he explained. "No, royal purple is Bertie's preference, the nutter. Make of it what you will, the truth is, *that,*" he said, indicating the foil packet, "is not mine. Really, Bertie slipped it in my pocket as he was leaving the reception. Another of his daft jokes. I'd completely forgotten about it until just now when I assumed I was reaching for a few pound notes. Sorry to disappoint you, Marcella, if you've a heart set on a maverick vicar. Let's, um . . . not mention a word of this to Bertie, shall we? I'd never hear the end of it."

"Having met Bertie, I do believe you. Okay, my lips are sealed. Still, you must have been very distracted, 'cause this soft, squishy, little love packet doesn't feel anything like a pound note."

William's grin was affectionate. "Right. Your fault, that, distracting me. Here, you've had your laugh. Hand over that ghastly purple shield and let's push off, shall we? As I recall, you were going to escort me out."

His warm tone held a hint of innuendo. Marcella was excited about what might happen once they got outside, even if it were no more than a goodnight kiss, but she closed her fingers protectively around the foil packet. Actually, she wasn't finished teasing.

"So, why would Bertie slip you a condom, d'you suppose?"

"Because he's a wanker."

"Because he thought you might get lucky tonight and need one?" With the delicate lift of a brow, she invited his response.

William had the grace to look humbled. His smile turned apologetic as he said, "Quite the arrogant bloke, isn't he? I mean, you've only known Bertie one afternoon, and already you've got his number. Imagine my horror. There I was, surrounded by family and friends, when quite suddenly I found myself with Bertie's hand down my trousers' pocket. Very awkward, that."

Then, on a more serious note, he added, "You do know, don't you, Marcella, I'd never make any such assumptions about tonight?"

Vulnerability shone from his clear blue eyes, willing her to believe him. For a moment, Marcella was overcome by a sense of the most excellent karma she'd ever experienced.

Desire thrust through her lower belly. The condom was burning a hole in her palm.

"William, would you like to come up to my room?"

The invitation glided off her tongue before she knew it, sounding as though it had come from someone more sexually liberated than she. She'd extended the invite, and now there it was, out in the open for them both to confront. Vicar or not, what were they going to do about this overwhelming physical attraction?

She'd gone heady with wanting him, but when a pause became silence, and William merely stared back, noncommittal with a slightly awed gawk, she began to lose her moxie. A moment ago, she'd thought it inappropriate to ask him up to her room. Damn, what had possessed her to do a complete one-eighty?

Suddenly, she felt it necessary to explain. "I thought maybe we could . . . um, talk some more. Drink coffee. Whatever. We don't have to use the condom, necessarily. Don't get me wrong, we absolutely do have to use it, if things get that far. I am in no way suggesting we should go that far."

"Of course not," he agreed with a grin.

His humor had returned. He smiled into her eyes with tenderness and affection, then gave a low chuckle as though she had just said something especially heartwarming.

William captured her waist in his big hands and pulled her to him. Excitement rushed through her at his hungry gaze. She'd obviously said something right, but what? What? What had she said? Was he relieved she wasn't expecting a romp in the sheets? Or maybe he was relieved to discover she wasn't some foreign nymph out to shag the vicar? He probably got enough of them locally. The subject had come up more than once today.

As William lowered his mouth to hers, Marcella parted her lips and let the questions float out her brain. She rose onto the balls of her feet to meet him, and as their lips locked, she reached her arms around his neck and gave herself over to the moment.

William's kisses were sensual nirvana. Some deep and lingering, others soft and sweet. He tasted her mouth, he kissed her face, he rubbed his slightly whiskered cheek against the side of her face. Marcella rubbed against him and nuzzled the strong sinew at the curve of his neck. She breathed his clean scent.

William returned to her mouth for another, this time more urgent, kiss. His hands explored her back through the thin, sheer silk of her tunic until she grew limp in his arms. He urged her closer and Marcella pressed against him, closer . . . closer, until her groin met with the hard length of his arousal.

Oh, vicar.

William emitted a low, sexy moan.

"Lounge is closing, mates!"

His lips stiffened above her own. He jerked his head back, let out a breath. Eye level with his nose, Marcella peeped up under her lashes into his aquamarine eyes, dazed and breathless. Slowly, she returned to awareness. Had that loud shout been directed at them?

Apparently. William set her back on her feet and breathed. He ran his fingers through his thick, chestnut hair, then gestured towards the exit. Time to go. Marcella managed a nod, then allowed him to take her firmly by the hand.

As William escorted her from the lounge, a waiter stood waiting in the foyer. He surged forward to hold the door for them, bidding them good night with a stiff, plastered smile.

Marcella thought she heard the words, "That's what we have rooms for," muttered behind them as they exited into the lobby.

As they walked along, William steered her towards the main entrance. Marcella stopped, drawing them both to a halt. "Elevators are this way," she pointed out.

He stole a wistful glance down the hallway which would lead them to her suite, then turned to meet her gaze.

"Let's talk outside," he suggested.

Disappointment seeped into her veins. *Aw . . . shit.* Her Latin blood was freakin' boiling and he was going to call it a night?

William's eyes pleaded with her to understand. "As much as

I do desire to be alone with you, Marcella, I can't risk popping up to your room. You see, I can't make love to you." He started in horror, then quickly amended, "I mean, I bloody well can, don't get me wrong. But I choose not to. D'you understand?"

Her lower lip trembled slightly. Nope, she wasn't quite catching his drift. 'Course it didn't help matters that he seemed to have changed his mind at a particularly vulnerable moment.

"I'm making a complete bollocks of an explanation, aren't I?" He shook his head, then attempted a smile. "Please, don't take what I've said the wrong way. I do fancy you, Marcella. Adore you, in fact." He gave her fingers a little squeeze. "I'm totally and hopelessly smitten, no question. But you see . . . well, purple's not really my color. Doesn't do a thing for me, I'm afraid."

Marcella snapped out of her self-pitying funk and narrowed him a glare. His dry wit never took a break, did it? "Ha, ha," she jeered. "You'd better be joking."

"Kidding about the purple, yes. It's no joke, however, how very much I find myself caring for you after only so short a time. But seriously, Marcella, I'm a vicar. The church is my way of life. My responsibility, actually. I've certain moral obligations to uphold. I am duty bound to set a proper example. You see, I don't believe in intimacy outside of a serious, committed relationship. And even though your invitation could just as well turn out to be nothing more than a perfectly innocent cup of coffee, with the way I'm feeling right now . . . and my current physical state, I don't believe it wise to tempt fate."

"Oh!" Only a man comfortable with honesty could have made such a frank admission. She was impressed. She hadn't misread him. It was just that being a vicar meant more to William than a paycheck. He really took his job seriously. She'd sensed this from the beginning. Unfortunately for her, those senses had been momentarily suspended in a fog of lust.

"Oh," she reiterated, this time with clarity.

Here she stood, head over heels for a tall, virile, handsome man, on what promised to be the most romantic evening of her life. Two single, healthy, red-blooded, consenting adults, with nothing standing between them and a night of earth-shattering sex but God.

So, where did this leave them? She couldn't promise William a relationship because of her job, and he couldn't agree to a simple romantic weekend because of his.

Suddenly, she remembered the condom and relaxed her grip until she felt the small packet unfurl in her palm.

"So, then, you've never . . . ?" Midsentence Marcella worried the question might be too personal.

William's gaze never wavered. "Not since I was ordained, no. Can't speak for what I did before that. Had to test out the goods, didn't I?"

Marcella returned his grin. So, he wasn't a virgin, then. She quickly pressed her memory for the evening's stats. William let her know during their conversation he was twenty-nine. He'd been a priest for six years.

Six years of abstinence. All that highborn testosterone bottled up inside his tall, gorgeous bod for seventy-two months and counting, aging like a fine imported wine. What she wouldn't give to be the lucky girl who popped his cork.

"Um . . . ya' know, you might want to watch yourself," she warned. "You sounded like Bertie just then."

"Well, I suppose I was rather a bit like Bertie, once upon a time. I was a randy fourteen, mad for the church organist in my godfather's church. We were together nine years. We'd rather become a comfortable, old habit by the time I was ready to join the clergy. When I explained to Emma we'd have to marry if our relationship were to continue, she started on arrangements for our wedding. Unfortunately, I was too busy with my own clerical preparations at the time to take an active part in the planning. If I had, I'd have noticed she was having doubts. In hindsight, I should have realized Emma was never the sort to be content with a comfortable, old habit. Not that there's anything wrong with being a vicar's wife, mind. Don't want you thinking it's terribly dull, or anything. Personally, I highly recommend my life in the country. Emma was just the wrong woman to share it with, you see. In the end, she decided to make a go of London in pursuit of fame and fortune."

He gave a little shrug. "So, there you have it. My romantic history . . . or lack thereof, as it were. Perhaps I should have mentioned something straightaway, but I simply couldn't wait another moment to kiss you."

Marcella waved off his apology. "Hell, no, you'd already waited long enough. I'm the one who should apologize. I was raised better than to offer temptation to a priest."

William laughed. "You are proving quite the test of my faith, I must say." Stepping closer, he cupped her chin and smiled longingly into her eyes. With the pad of his thumb, he caressed the underside of her jaw. His gaze dropped to her lips. "I don't believe I've ever been so entirely tempted."

Marcella swallowed the lump in her throat. He'd told her no, yet everything else about him seemed to signal her with a screeching *Yes,* and speaking for herself . . . well, she'd never felt so horny in her life.

William moved in for the kiss, but could she close her eyes, pucker her lips, and let nature take its course? Oh-no. Her brain had been scrambling like crazy to absorb Emma. Nine years. Nine years he'd been testing his goods out on Emma.

She stepped back, jerking her chin from his hand. There was something she just had to know.

William started. He searched her face, alarmed and confused. His eyes held a wounded "what'd I do?" look.

What'd he do? He'd done his country bumpkin church organist for nine years, yet here he was refusing to lay a finger on her sexy chic cosmopolitan self.

She was being unreasonable, of course. It was great William was being so open with her. Then what had caused this sudden anxiety over a woman she'd never met?

"You're still close friends with your ex, right?" Jealousy prevented her from referring to the woman by name.

"Huh? Oh . . . right," he drawled, his tone wary. "Yes. I believe I did mention that earlier, yes."

Obviously, he was wondering where this was all going, so Marcella got straight to the point. "Any chance you two might get back together? I'd just like to know. Honestly. Is it really over?"

His face flooded with relief. "Back with Emma? Not bloody likely, Marcella. Emma and I are . . . we're all very casual, really. Why, we're sort of childhood chums, I suppose you could say. Nothing more. It's completely over romantically. Totally. Absolutely."

Ha, the kind of childhood chums who enjoyed playing doctor!

Okay, she was cool with this. She smiled and gave him a nod of understanding. After all, what right did she have to question his past? She had no claim on William. They weren't even a couple. Except that she couldn't helping wondering. Emma had been the one to dump William, which would naturally come as a crushing blow in the middle of planning a wedding . . .

She searched his face for any hidden emotion. Was he hiding his pain behind that confident smile?

He gestured to the condom in her hand. "Well, now, what are we to do with that?"

The change of subject snapped Marcella's attention from the

past to the future. "I was thinking of hanging on to it as a souvenir."

"A souvenir? Are you mad? Really? Bertie's purple condom? Blimey. If you want a souvenir, Marcella, I could get you an outdated Queen's anniversary mug, or something. Certainly, we can find something slightly less ridiculous. Why, I'm not entirely sure that crumpled bit of suspicious-looking foil will make it through Customs. I must say, I am feeling a bit insecure. I hope you've no intention of using it."

Ah-ha, so she wasn't the only one vulnerable to jealousy. With a sexy smile, she walked her fingers up William's lean, hard chest, then toyed with the open neckline of his shirt. She peeked inside. Smooth and hairless from what she could tell. Very nice. With a celibate vicar, a girl had to sneak a thrill any way she could.

"Who knows, maybe someday you might be persuaded to fly to New York for a visit. In fact, I am hereby extending you an open invitation. In which case, I'm gonna save this for 'someday' "

She raised the condom package to eye level.

William gaped at it, horrified. "D'you really intend to nick that back to America?" He turned to study her with a pensive look, then slowly, his lips twisted in a grin.

"Well, that's all very promising, then, isn't it?" he asked, sweeping her into his arms. "Does this mean you've given some consideration to becoming a vicar's wife?"

What . . . whoa . . . wife? She'd only known him a day. The very idea was absurd. When she'd set herself a goal of stepping into Lynne Graham's shoes, marriage to a vicar was not what she'd had in mind. But then her subconscious interrupted. *Who are you kidding? You have so considered William as the One. You can't think of anything else.*

"Are you asking me to marry you?" she ventured to tease.

William brought his aristocratic nose in direct alignment with her own and made like an Eskimo. "Don't be surprised if before you leave, I do just that."

What was it about a corny nose rub that triggered a sensual response? Maybe the face-to-face aspect. William's eyes were dazzling. And he was looking so amused, Marcella felt sure he'd been kidding. Of course, he'd been kidding. But as they gazed into each other's eyes, she felt something pass between them that took her breath away.

William straightened. They jumped apart and simultaneously took a step backwards. Marcella felt shaken.

William chuckled, gathering himself. "Well, what am I doing, eh? It's quite late. I should be home polishing my sermon for tomorrow. I've a special service to prepare for. Got this early start. Got to be on form. I'll ring you tomorrow afternoon, shall I?"

Marcella nodded mutely.

"All right then, up to your room," he said with a nod towards the elevators. "I'll watch from here to make certain you get safely to the lifts."

Marcella realized she wasn't ready to let him out of her sight. "But I promised to walk you outside, remember?"

"Right." He smiled gratefully, but once they'd stepped outdoors, he left her with no more than a kiss on the cheek before turning to go.

She stood longingly in the warm bath of lamplight pouring out the black-paned windows of The Bear's ivy-covered facade and watched as William disappeared down the long drive into the darkness beyond.

William's heart pounded heavily in his chest as he headed for the car park.

"Ciao!" he heard her call from behind. He halted at the sound

of her voice and for a moment considered turning round and running back to her.

Her dark, sexy eyes. Those lovely breasts. At no time since he'd joined the Church had the struggle with his desires been such bleedin' agony. The taste, the feel of her soft inner lip lingered on his mouth. Perhaps just one final snog. With her loose-fitting top, it'd be easy, really, to ease a hand up inside or simply touch her through that sheer, flimsy material.

It'd hardly be enough, though, would it? After all, he couldn't bloody well expect he'd be satisfied with just a bit of a feel, and leave it at that. A vision of himself sheathed in a bright purple condom sprang suddenly to mind. *God help him.*

William rallied his strength. He took a deep breath, then gave a final wave and continued to stride away, towards his bike. His footsteps echoed in the night.

His was a rewarding job, involved in the everyday lives of families in his parish, sharing their laughter, comforting them through their tears. He was loved, trusted, and respected. Welcome in every home and at every table. What a bitter disappointment, then, at the end of a day, to leave all that and return with Babette to an empty house. Sometimes the quiet was refreshing, but more often than he cared to dwell upon, the silence mocked him.

Weddings, baptisms, funerals. All intimate family gatherings of which he played a central part. He was surrounded by people who shared their lives with someone special. Was there no one special for him?

He must be barking to think he had a chance with Marcella. She had a lot in common with Emma, didn't she? Very posh, very much one of the "It" girls with her smart sense of style and exciting career in the city. Certainly, she wasn't any more interested in becoming a vicar's wife than Emma had been.

Perhaps he shouldn't call Marcella tomorrow. What would be

the point? They'd spend another fabulous evening together, and then she'd be gone, off to New York and her busy magazine. She'd quickly forget all about him. There were sure to be plenty of New York blokes competing for her attention.

One last date? Seemed a bit like dangling a carrot he couldn't reach before his own nose.

Marcella unlocked the door to her suite and noticed a dim, flickering light coming from inside Sallie's room. As she got closer, she heard the low hum of the television and popped in her head. "Sallie," she whispered.

Silence.

She tiptoed into the room. "Sal?"

Sallie lay prone in bed, head cocked to one side, hair spilled over the pillows, dead to the world. A vanilla spice candle burned in a travel tin at her bedside, illuminating the honey highlights in her light brown hair.

Marcella blew out the candle, then picked up the remote. Sallie had been watching a BBC fashion police show.

Marcella hung around a moment hoping Sallie would wake. She thought about accidentally turning up the volume, *oops!*, but got distracted watching a cute redhead in a flippy bob advise a confused housewife that black was not the most flattering nor slimming of color choices.

"Don't you dare give her that crap about brown being the new black," she protested to the screen in a slightly raised voice, then immediately turned to see if she'd roused Sallie.

Her friend continued to sleep soundly. With a sigh, Marcella switched off the set.

She kicked off her denim slides, scooped them off the floor, then padded to her own room where she immediately switched on the bedside lamp so she could jot William's birth date down in her organizer. She tucked the condom safely in a front pocket.

She felt wired, sexually charged, frustrated at being left at the door, but riding on a high of William, with all her senses alert. She needed to wind down or she'd never be able to sleep. She needed girl talk.

She undressed, washed her face, dabbed on some vitamin enriched eye gel, then slipped on a full-length satin nightgown. She went into the sitting area for a sparkling water from the minibar, and on her way back, peeked inside Sallie's room in case she'd regained consciousness.

"Sal? Hey, Sal."

Sallie rolled onto her side with a little moan.

Marcella swallowed her disappointment and carried her water bottle back to bed. After a while, she forced herself to lie down.

Eventually, she drifted off to sleep, only to wake a couple of hours later, and as she lay there in the darkness, suddenly it came to her.

The perfect solution to seeing William again.

Chapter 8

Early the next morning, Marcella grabbed her organizer and sprang out of bed. Inside, she was jumping with excitement as she padded into the sitting area.

"Nate, honey, do me a favor and put Henri on the line. Uh-huh, that's right. What? Yeah, I know the call is expensive, but it gets more expensive the longer you bitch. I want to talk to Henri."

Darn, Sallie had beaten her to the phone. Marcella was anxious to make a quick call so she could plan their day, but if Nate put Henri on the line . . . ah, well, no avoiding the inevitable.

Glancing up, Sallie waved her over with a smile. Into the phone, she told Nate, "Dude, don't argue with me, okay? It is not stupid. He needs to hear my voice. He gets separation anxiety. Just do it, Nate."

Marcella took a seat across the small table from where Sallie sat. She unzipped her organizer, found the number she wanted to call, then poured herself a cup of hot joe from the pot Sallie had already brewed in the room's automatic coffee maker.

Sallie's face lit up like a Christmas tree. "Henri, *mon ange!* It's Mommy, *chéri. Je t'aime.*" Her tone rose to a sickeningly sweet pitch, ad nauseum. "Mommy misses her *petit monsieur.*"

Marcella stirred powdered creamer into her coffee, fighting the urge to barf, while Sallie made kissing noises into the phone.

"Have you been a good boy for your Uncle Nate?"

Through the receiver, Marcella heard Nate comment in an unamused tone.

Marcella hid a smile behind the rim of her coffee cup. She knew better than to waste brain power trying to understand why any woman would send her lovin' across the Atlantic to her teacup poodle, meanwhile neglecting her boyfriend who was holding the phone to the dog's ear. When it came to small animals, Sallie was a total marshmallow.

Poor Nate. He was a good guy. He really didn't have anything against little fufu dogs. He just had a hard time warming up to a four-and-a-half pound, territorial hairball who nipped at his ass while he was trying to make love to his girlfriend.

Yeah, Nate and Henri had their issues.

Nate got back on the line. Sallie confirmed their time of arrival into Kennedy Airport tomorrow evening. Nate had agreed to pick them up. Sallie lingered on the line another few minutes saying goodbye, then hung up and gave Marcella her full attention. "So? How'd it go with you and William last night? I never heard you come in."

"I'll tell you everything, I promise. But mind if I make a quick phone call first?"

Sallie shrugged. "Sure. Go ahead."

"Change of plans," Marcella explained as she snatched up the receiver, then began to dial. "I have the most fantastic idea. It'll be so much fun."

Sallie eyed her curiously.

After several rings, an elderly woman greeted Marcella on the other end of the line.

"Good morning," Marcella said. "What time is service this morning?" She jotted the reply in her organizer. "Yup, a-huh, got it. And coffee served in the church hall immediately afterwards? Excellent. Yes, I will. Thank you very much."

Sallie's brow shot up. "Church hall? What's this about? We're spending the day in London, remember? We have reservations at the Savoy. We bought hats."

"Wear your hat to church. This morning we'll be attending service at St. Francis's in Bramble Moor. William's church. Where we'll get an insider's view of the dishy Reverend Stafford, doing his thing. Cool, huh? What d'you think?"

Sallie gave her a long, bored stare. "Marcella, I do so not want to spend my last and only free day in England sitting in a pew of some ancient church. We did that yesterday, if you recall. What brought on this brainstorm? Did William invite you?"

"Well . . . no. I thought we'd surprise him."

"Uh-huh. Did anything happen last night you'd like to share?"

Marcella nodded humbly. "Yes, I'd like to share. And no, nothing happened. Well, nothing that would keep me from holding my head up in church."

She refilled Sallie's cup, then got down to the details of her evening with William . . . the sparks, the intimate conversation, holding hands. The infamous purple condom sent Sallie into hysterics, interrupting the story for a full minute. Marcella confessed she'd invited William up to her room. She told Sallie about their hot kiss in the lounge, William's vow of celibacy, his ex-fiancée Emma, and the spontaneous marriage proposal.

"William promised to call me later this afternoon so we could get together again this evening," Marcella concluded, "but today is my one chance to get a feel for the life he leads. See what he's like at work. I already have a pretty good idea of what he's like at play."

"So you want me to help you put the moves on him?"

"We all need a little help from our friends," Marcella giggled. But when Sallie failed to lighten up, she narrowed her gaze and said in all seriousness, "Don't make me call you on those nights you dragged me to jazz clubs all over Manhattan trolling for

Nate. You owe me, and you know it. I'm only asking for one morning."

"This is not just any morning." With a sigh, Sallie took a sip from her cup. "All right, all right. So, what's the plan, Tart? Go up for Holy Communion and lick his fingers as he puts it in your mouth?" Sallie laughed at her own jibe, then sobered under Marcella's glare.

"Seriously, Marcella, you can't be interested in pursuing a relationship with a vicar. A couple of days ago you thought Lynn was either nuts or desperate for marrying Henry."

"Who's talking marriage? You're the one who preaches living in the moment."

"That was yesterday, before we knew William. Or his profession. Besides, what else is there for you two besides marriage? Vicars don't screw around, Marcella. From what you've told me, William couldn't have made himself any clearer."

Marcella sprang from her seat to pace nervously across the room. "I'm not sure what I want. That's the problem. I need to see William up on that altar doing what he does, in that damn collar I've been hearing so much about. Maybe it'll cure me of this love jones. Maybe I'll say, 'Hey, a priest? Gag! What was I thinking?' and that'll be the end of it. Now, get dressed. Service begins at ten. I don't want to be late."

"Hurry, Sallie. Our taxi's waiting."

An hour and a half later, Marcella was dressed and ready to go. She wore white from head to toe, except for the soles of her strappy sandals, which flashed a striking contrast of lipstick red when she walked.

Sallie poked her head out of her bedroom. "Have you seen my thong Birkies?"

"Here by the sofa." As Sallie came padding into the sitting area, Marcella gave her the once-over. "Uh . . . that's not the dress you bought for the Savoy."

"We're not going to the Savoy." Sallie slipped into her thongs, then turned in her long drawstring skirt of weathered denim for Marcella's inspection. On top, she wore a sleeveless, bright orange crocheted shell. "Nobody dresses for church anymore. Casual chic is the thing in all religious circles. I've been watching fashion on the BBC. If I were you, Marcella, I'd lose the hat."

"What're you talking about? The English are famous for wearing hats." Annoyed, Marcella double-checked her look in the foyer mirror. She felt confident in her Italian-inspired sun hat with its small crown and extra-wide brim that shaded her head like an umbrella. A hat was the perfect compliment to the clean lines of her ankle-length halter dress. A hat brought style and sophistication to her ensemble, yet lent her an air of mystery.

It was all about attitude. Men noticed women in hats. The hat stayed.

"William's giving a special service. I want to look pulled together."

Sallie's face appeared suddenly in the mirror behind her. "What kind of special service?"

"No idea." Turning around, Marcella ushered Sallie out the door. "I really wish you'd worn that watercolor pastel chiffon skirt you picked out for the Savoy. I don't think it's appropriate to show your navel in church."

"No? And is that more or less appropriate than inviting the vicar up to your hotel room to slip a purple condom on his penis?"

A woman passing in the hallway gasped, then hurriedly continued on her way.

Marcella blushed beneath her wide brim. So maybe she wouldn't be able to hold her head up in church, after all.

★ ★ ★ ★ ★

Bramble Moor was a quaint, rural community untouched by time. Marcella saw thatched roofs, green fields, and grazing cows. Church bells rang all through the village as their taxi rolled down a long country lane. She sat in the back of the cab with Sallie, watching a tall stone spire in the distance grow larger and larger until Marcella realized it was the church steeple.

St. Francis sat at a roundabout. A four-foot stone wall surrounded the grounds. The taxi followed the turn and slowed to a stop at an opened gateway. Sallie climbed out while Marcella paid the driver. Despite their best efforts, they were running late.

"Who knew a country church could be so impressive," Sallie said as Marcella joined her on the curb.

Marcella ascended the stone bell tower with her gaze, craning her neck when she got to the spire, which seemed to reach into the heavens. "It's bigger than I'd imagined."

"Be mindful of what you do in there, Marcella. Think only pure thoughts. God is watching."

Marcella rolled her eyes. "C'mon."

A lantern hung from a metal arch supported by two stone columns that formed a gateway. Marcella and Sallie walked through together, then followed a short path until they reached the front entrance of the church.

A black-faced hound the size of a small cow lounged in the grass. As they approached, the dog lumbered to his feet. Testacles the size of tennis balls hung from his groin.

Marcella froze and grabbed Sallie's arm. "Uh . . . do you think he's vicious?"

The heavy double doors were closed, and she didn't see anyone else around.

Sallie broke free and continued forward. "He's cool. But stop gawking, Marcella. You're scaring him."

Marcella averted her eyes and quickly followed.

They opened the door and entered the foyer. To their left, a small table held a collection of empty casseroles. Marcella puzzled over them for only a moment, then turned to her right, where a wall blocked the nave of the church from view. Service had already begun.

"I hate walking into church late," Sallie whispered.

"Shhh . . . that's him, listen."

William's voice, strong and clear with its refined British tones, carried into the foyer.

". . . reflect on the beauty of this world, I'm quite aware it's not our material means that fill our lives with love and purpose, but God and his creation. Our faith, our families, our friends, the flowers, birds, and trees. Nature.

"And truly, what more wonderful gift of nature than our pets. They bring us comfort, joy, and loyalty. They open our hearts and teach us how to love. As I look out over the congregation this morning, I see faces literally glowing with that love. Pets are a precious part of our lives. And so today, we gather not to give thanks for our families, or for the flowers and trees . . . but for our animals."

Animals, Marcella thought. He was preaching about pets. She turned to Sallie, whose eyes had grown wide and shone with excitement. She pushed Marcella forward until they found themselves at the back of the church.

Immediately, Marcella's gaze was drawn upwards, above the altar, to three stained-glass windows fashioned in blues and greens in an impressive modern design. An amber cross provided a striking burst of contrasting color in the center window.

"Scripture says, 'The soul of every living thing is in the hand of God, and the breath of all mankind.' "

William's voice drew her eye to the left. He stood at a pulpit nestled beneath an archway. At his side sat a fawn and white saluki. Babette? She was gorgeous, the canine equivalent of a high fashion model. Thin and blonde, with a somewhat anorexic appearance, and an air of superiority and elegance. Babette sat tall, her long narrow head held high. She gazed past the congregation to Marcella with large, intelligent brown eyes.

"It's an animal blessing," Sallie whispered in awe. "This is the special service?"

Marcella tore her gaze from Babette and realized the pews were filled, not only with people, but dogs of various breeds and sizes. She saw cats on shoulders, rabbits on laps, and even a few bird and hamster cages. All were unusually quiet and peaceful, as though they understood the significance of the gathering.

Sallie's elbow poked her side. Marcella startled, glancing up to find William peering over his round wire-framed glasses. He had stopped speaking. His stare registered surprise.

Marcella gave him a wave.

Slowly, William's lips curled until his whole face seemed to illuminate. "Welcome," he greeted in his clear vicar's voice across the rows and rows of pews. "Join us, please."

Joy radiated deep inside her. She was aware of Sallie's hand on her arm, trying to drag her into a rear pew, but Marcella hadn't braved this visit to William's church for a snooze in the back. *Oh-no,* not after that welcoming smile. She intended to sit front and center.

Slipping from Sallie's grasp, she proceeded up the aisle with the boldness of a runway model. Her heels clattered in the stillness, but she ignored the stares and fought any embarrassment over the glaringly obvious fact she had not come for the service, per se, as neither she nor Sallie had brought along an animal.

William had resumed his sermon. "It was St. Francis of Assisi who noted, 'There is no degradation in the dignity of human nature in claiming kinship with creatures so beautiful . . . so wonderful . . . who praise God in the forest even as the angels praise him in heaven.' St. Francis referred to animals as his brothers and sisters because he understood they have the same origin as man."

Third row from the pulpit, Marcella spied an opening and motioned for Sallie to follow.

"Excuse me." Marcella could tell immediately the couple on the end had no intention of giving up their aisle seat. The woman pressed her handful of a poodle to her full breasts and shifted her legs to one side.

"Thank you . . . sorry . . . so sorry, excuse us," Marcella apologized as she and Sallie climbed over the couple's laps. The little dog growled.

Meanwhile, in the pew before them, a young woman holding a long-haired gray cat had turned to stare. She eyeballed Marcella's button-front halter dress, up its princess seaming to its squared neckline, to her white straw hat.

Marcella could just imagine her thinking. *That poor girl has no clue. Doesn't she know you don't wear white to an animal blessing?*

So, I'm wearing white? Big ta-da. Marcella dismissed her with a turn of the head, dusting off the pew before folding herself onto the bench. Checking her dress to make certain all buttons were secure, she glanced over at Sallie, who had taken the seat beside her, and found her friend locked in a goggle with the rude cat girl. Cat Girl gave Sallie a poised, slightly amused smile, then returned her attention back to William.

"Most animals, unless of course they've been mistreated through the erring of man, live from a pure heart. The spirits of animals have never known separation from God. Animals know their creator, you see. God and nature are one. And because their spirits are one with His, animals are naturally inclined to give thanks and praise to God."

William smiled, then with a chuckle interjected, "Rather the way your own dog gives you a bit of praise every time you come home."

The parishioners laughed and nodded in appreciation, while a little voice behind Marcella whined, "Mummy, I can't see."

Marcella removed her hat and placed it carefully on her knee. She gave the top of her head a quick fluff, not wanting to draw further attention to herself when she'd already disrupted the service.

At last, she thought as she settled down to listen. She didn't want to miss a single word. But who was responsible for that annoying sneezing? It seemed to be coming from the choir. Did no one have a tissue?

William's educated British baritone immediately drew her back, and Marcella soaked him up with her gaze. Before today, she'd never truly appreciated the allure a little rim of white in a high black collar could inspire. William had removed his glasses. His chestnut hair curled over his forehead. Tall, handsome, and intelligent, he addressed his congregation, the picture of humility and grace. A perfect yum-yum. Those white vestments lent him an angelic air, which was quite the novelty, quite the unexpected turn-on.

Suddenly his eyes found hers and one side of his mouth crooked in a boyish grin before his gaze moved on.

He's excited I'm here! Marcella's heart danced with the angels up among the cathedral ceiling, and she thought, *Mom would be so proud. She always said she wished I'd meet a nice boy at church.*

Sallie nudged her and mouthed, "Fashion Nazi." She pointed to the back of Cat Girl's head.

Huh? Marcella shook her head no, she didn't understand, when suddenly a thought occurred to her. Sallie had obviously seen Cat Girl staring at Marcella's outfit. Was this her witty way of saying, "I told you so"?

"Okay, I get it," Marcella muttered out one side of her mouth. "I'm overdressed."

Sallie frowned. She shook her head, then pointed again and mouthed, "B-B-C."

BBC? Marcella threw up her hands as though to say, "I have no idea what you're talking about." And while Sallie was going on about nothing, Marcella was missing William's sermon. She shot Sallie a warning look.

Sallie gave Marcella a "you're hopeless" glare and turned away, disappointed.

What is with her? Marcella wondered, but as she stared at the back of that strawberry blonde head, styled with bouncy curls that didn't quite reach the shoulders, something stirred her memory. Cat girl's porcelain complexion and perky nose had seemed vaguely familiar. *Hmm.* Why? Nah, couldn't place her. Who did they know in Bramble Moor, anyway?

Marcella let it go and resumed listening.

"God is love. His love is the force that binds us together as His children. The giving of ourselves in caring for our animals is an expression of God's love. For if animals are loved and give us love in return, if they comprehend love and understand how to express love, then most certainly they are part of God's family indeed. Often, I find myself reflecting on the deep connection I feel with Babette and how it reminds me of God's presence in all creation."

Gazing down from his pulpit on his beautiful saluki, he announced, "Babes loves unconditionally and never tries to be anything but what she is."

Again, Sallie nudged Marcella. When Marcella turned, she whispered, "That's what he's looking for in a woman."

Marcella cocked a brow knowingly. "In a perfect world."

"Right then, if you'll take up your hymn books. Hymn

number ninety-one, 'All Things Bright and Beautiful.' "

As Marcella searched for a hymnal, she noticed a tall, craggy, gray-bearded man emerge from the choir and approach the organ in a fit of sneezing.

William gestured to a nearby altar boy, who immediately stepped forward and took up Babette's leash, while William strode up the chancel steps in his long black cassock, past the altar to the organist.

"All right, Angus?" He laid a hand on the man's shoulder. "Here, why don't we let someone else fill in at the organ, just for today, eh? You might want to get yourself some air."

William turned to the congregation and asked, "Would you mind, Miss Parker? Angus here is terribly allergic to cats, I'm afraid."

Marcella froze, taken aback. Um . . . was William speaking to her? Of course not. He'd said Miss Parker. Then why did he appear to be addressing her? He was, after all, staring straight at her.

Marcella stared back, clueless. She opened her mouth and worked it silently, not knowing how to respond, and when she shrugged, he implored her with a charming smile and a pleading twinkle in his eye.

Slowly, the redhead seated in the pew before Marcella rose with her armload of gray cat. Marcella watched in growing embarrassment as Cat Girl made her way out of the pew and approached William at the organ, where she handed him her cat, then took Angus's seat on the organ bench.

Sallie gasped. "I knew it. That's Emma Parker!"

"Who?" Marcella wanted nothing more than to put her hat back on her head and pull it down over her eyes.

Sallie leaned close to whisper, "I've been trying to tell you. That chick is Emma Parker. She's the host of a fashion makeover show on the BBC. I watched her last night. She's pretty cool. And funny. And she plays the organ, too? Imagine."

Data ticked off inside Marcella's brain, scrambling to be organized into a coherent thought. Cat Girl was the show host she'd watched briefly on the TV in Sallie's room. Emma Parker. Emma! A girl named Emma who just happened to know how to play a church organ. Coincidence?

I don't think so!

The bastard. William had assured her they were over. Over, huh? Then what was Emma doing in his church? Maybe she'd stopped in for the special service so William could bless her pussy. Oh, no, that's right. He already had!

She hated herself for the nastiness running rampant through her thoughts, but Marcella felt powerless to control this jealousy building inside her. She watched William reach over Emma's shoulder and turn the music page. Did no one else find the scene unnecessarily intimate? And what were they whispering about up there?

Something else occurred to her. When William called Emma forward, Marcella had foolishly assumed he'd been looking at her. Had she also been mistaken, thinking the smile he'd given during his sermon had been for her, when actually it was meant for Emma?

Her heart sunk.

Chapter 9

"You don't find her a bit glam for a vicar?"

Emma threw out the question quite casually, while Quincy, her wiry gray cat, clawed his way up William's surplice to curl his body round William's neck. Holding the feline in place with one hand, William reached with the other to flip a page of the music program. "I may have, at first," he admitted. "But now I find I rather fancy glam."

"Apparently." With the lift of a brow, Emma positioned her fingers at the keyboard. "We all saw you interrupt your sermon to give her a gawk. Really, I half expected your tongue to drop to the floor and crawl down the aisle after her."

William grew concerned. He hardly thought he'd been that obvious. No doubt Marcella had left an impression on his entire congregation, but because he'd known Emma longer than any of them, he sought her approval especially.

Her shoulders shook with a giggle, and William realized she was having him on.

"Seriously though, William. What would the bishop think?"

"I should hope he'd think me a very lucky man and be pleased I've taken enough interest in a woman to once again be considering marriage."

At Emma's short intake of breath, William wondered whether Emma might feel just a bit jealous, then decided, no, she was merely surprised he'd entertain the idea of marriage to a woman he'd only met the day before. With a grin, he straightened and projected, "Here we are, Miss Parker. 'All Things Bright and Beautiful.' "

"Hymn number ninety-one in your hymnals, please." He strode to the top of the chancel steps, pried Quincy from his collar. and cradled him in his arms like an infant about to be baptized. At the first groan of the organ pipes, he lifted his voice in song, along with the choir:

All things bright and beautiful,
All creatures great and small.

His gaze sought Marcella among the flock.

All things wise and wonderful,
The Lord God made them all.

Ah, easily spotted. She'd put the hat back on. Its brim obscured her lovely dark eyes as she gazed down on her opened hymnal.

Each little flower that opens.
Each little bird that sings.
God made their glowing colors.
And made their tiny wings.

He lingered a moment, hoping he'd catch her eye, and when she didn't lift her head, he experienced a twinge of disappointment. He got the odd impression something was wrong. But that couldn't possibly be true. No, he was being ridiculous.

The purple-headed mountains,
The river running by,
The sunset and the morning,
That brightens up the sky.

Her friend Sallie was watching him, he noticed. Beaming, she made a fist and pointed at him, rapper fashion, which he took as a sign of approval. He smiled, gave Sallie a nod. Turning, he scanned the congregation and his thoughts drifted back to Marcella.

The instant he'd glanced up from the pulpit and found her there, watching him from the back of the church in a long, white dress, his heart was lost.

He'd been utterly gobsmacked. It had felt quite surreal, actually, the way the sunlight poured down on her from a nearby stained-glass window, and she, standing there, in a hazy glow, all whiteness and pale skin. Had he been visited by an angel? Hardly. Rather, the posh American Marcella Tartaglia had graced his humble church in Bramble Moor. The outrageous cheek of her. His chest swelled with pride.

When she'd started down the aisle towards him, if she'd been holding a bouquet, he wouldn't have been surprised to have heard his own voice promising, "I do."

William shook off the memory, hit by a moment of clarity in which everything fell into place. It arrived as more of a gut reaction than a coherent thought. All humor aside, could Marcella quite possibly be the woman he'd been destined for?

Paralyzing fear, acute joy, nervous anticipation, and gagging lust all rolled together into one tidy lump of emotion that suddenly lodged in his throat. He'd never quite experienced yearning like this, not in all the years he'd been with Emma.

Last night he may have been prepared to chuck what he'd originally thought a silly infatuation and move on, but this morning William could not imagine letting these feelings go without exploring where they might lead.

At the close of service, the doors of St. Francis were thrown wide. A queue of churchgoers and their animals filed into the sunny courtyard where William waited with Babette to greet them. He shook hands, scratched furry heads, and wished everyone a good day.

With each face that passed, each smile he exchanged, his heart knocked a bit harder against his rib cage. Marcella couldn't have already slipped by, could she? Without a word of farewell? Certainly not.

He turned round for a peek into the church foyer, searching for a glimpse of her white hat, when suddenly he was knocked forward by a blow behind the knees.

"Vicar!" an aged voice shouted in alarm. Babette barked out a warning. As he staggered forward, a pink knitted cap swam before his field of vision. Quickly, William regained his balance and righted himself.

"Al'right there, Vicar?"

William straightened his cassock. "Yes, quite, Mrs. Wilbourne. But what was—?"

A downward glance confirmed his suspicions. He'd no need to ask when it was perfectly clear he'd just been bumped by over two hundred pounds of Old English mastiff, pure bred and dearly beloved of elderly Lydia Wilbourne of the parish council.

"Sorry, Vicar. Clumsy oaf, that one. Doesn't know his own size."

"That's quite all right, Mrs. Wilbourne. My fault, I'm afraid. Wasn't paying proper attention. No harm done, eh, Teddy?"

Teddy gazed up at him innocently. An enormous tongue lagged out one side of his sagging black jowls. William reached down to give him a scratch behind the ears, and as Teddy closed his eyes in contentment, a long stream of drool dripped to the ground.

Something caught his eye, and William realized what Mrs. Wilbourne held in her hands.

He straightened, and gave an inward sigh.

Another bloody casserole.

Puddings, bakes, curries, and casseroles. God bless his parish. They never ceased in their obsession to see him fed.

"I did so want to bake you a shepherd's pie, Vicar," Mrs. Wilbourne explained. "Yesterday morn, I fried up a nice bit of lamb with some lovely lovage and onion, then left it on the cooker to simmer. I wasn't gone a minute, checking the post, when I heard this loud crash. My Teddy here had jumped up and tipped the pan. Imagine, a beautiful lamb mince all over the kitchen floor. Teddy had himself a lovely feast, but I'd none left for your pie. I was ready to have m'self a good cry, I was. How could I bring a shepherd's pie to church without the lamb? But then I thought, I reckon the vicar might enjoy tucking into a plate of crispy mash all the same."

Accepting the dish, William peered down inside. The cold potatoes had been crusted over in a golden crisscross pattern, which he was certain Mrs. Wilbourne had taken great pains to score.

"Yes," he said. "Yes, I will enjoy it. Absolutely. You were quite right to bring it along, Mrs. Wilbourne. Thank you, that's very kind, very kind indeed."

She beamed at him, displaying a full set of dentures. Her sincerity touched him, leaving him quite ashamed of his earlier ungrateful thoughts. He gave her a warm smile in return.

Mrs. Wilbourne ducked her head bashfully. A feathery wreath of snow-white hair stuck out from beneath her pink cap.

"Will you and Teddy be joining us downstairs for coffee, Mrs. Wilbourne? We've treats for the pets as well."

William thought of the table of baked goods laid out in the church hall and braced himself for her reply. No sooner had service begun when Teddy had knocked down the lectern, then humiliated Laura Owens with his repeated attempts to nose his way up her choir robe. He'd been immediately removed to the outdoors.

Mrs. Wilbourne looked to Teddy and made her apologies. She and Teddy would have a walk about the church grounds, she explained, share a quick bit of gossip with some of the other pet owners, and then it was home for an afternoon nap.

William wished her a pleasant afternoon and watched in fond amusement as Mrs. Wilbourne and her unlikely companion shuffled off. Standing there, he thought he detected an airy feminine scent, a sort of woodsy vanilla fragrance, perhaps. Babette tugged on her leash, and when he glanced down at her, he found her sniffing a women's hat. Its white brim was clasped between the fingers of a long, elegant hand. His pulse quickened. His gaze lifted to alight on the shapely waist, then dashed up a slim column of white to a dead-gorgeous face with dark, exotic features. "Marcella!"

She greeted him with an amused grin, gesturing over her shoulder at the church's entry. "I was wondering what the deal was with all the Corningware." She nodded approval. "Now I get it. How sweet."

"Very. And just one of many, I'm afraid," he said with a display of the casserole dish. "The charitable ladies of St. Francis feel it their duty to prepare meals for a poor, bachelor vicar. I s'pose I'll have to either marry or resign myself to eating baked mash the rest of my life."

"I seriously doubt it will ever come to that."

"No?" he asked hopefully. With a will of its own, his gaze dropped to her full, glossy lips. He wanted to take Marcella in his arms so terribly that for a moment he forgot who and where he was and stood mutely, just staring, until he had the presence of mind to force himself to look into her dark, deep-set eyes.

Marcella's spine tingled. *Whoa.* All at once the moment had turned intimate, and she was uncertain how to respond. How crazy was she, huh? Enticing a priest? And how crazy was this priest? Enticing her? He'd just finished sprinkling holy water over a bunch of household pets, asking God to keep them safe. Little old ladies mashed potatoes for him, and all she could think was how much she wanted to see him naked.

And then there'd been the total shock of finding Emma here. *Ahhh!* Her shock had quickly turned to jealousy, jealousy so insane it dredged up all the insecurity Marcella had ever experienced and threw it back in her face to leave her feeling inadequate.

Suddenly, her confidence level had regressed back to junior high. William was a major hunk and she was *Ragno,* the freakishly tall girl with skinny spider legs that stretched all the way up to her breasts. Back then, she'd worn only flat, thin-soled shoes, but instead of taking the emphasis off her height, all they ever did was accentuate her long, narrow feet. What chance did she have against William's high school sweetheart, Emma Parker, now a BBC celebrity?

She might have bolted if not for Sallie's clear thinking. Sallie had told her, "You are so totally overreacting. He explained they're just friends. And like, why would he lie? Why? Because he wants to get you into bed? Hello! And if he and Emma are a couple, then how come he pulled a solo at the wedding?"

Sallie's wisdom had done a slow absorb until it all came flooding back to her. Sanity. Calm.

William exuded calm. Marcella could feel that calmness even now, simply staring into his guileless, watercolor eyes. Tranquility and self-possession oozed from his pores. And behind that tranquility, she sensed strength, a strength so absolute he could afford to be kind. All her compulsive, perfectionist, control-freak tendencies chilled in his presence. She allowed herself to soak up his peaceful aura and relaxed with a smile.

"Look, I'm really pleased you're here," William told her.

"Me too," she confessed. "I'm glad I came. That was quite a service. Fun," she added, then chuckled at the memory. "Not what I was expecting, but definitely enjoyable."

"Fantastic," Sallie cheered, springing up from a crouch beside Babette. "You rock, William. Hey, thanks again for blessing the photo of my dog."

"I'm sorry I didn't get the opportunity to meet Henri in person. Speaking of which . . ." William shifted the potatoes to one hand, then leaned down with the other to brush the top of Babette's long narrow head. "This, ladies, as you've probably guessed, is Babette."

Babette the saluki stood tall and dignified by his side and wore a gentle expression in her deep brown eyes.

Sallie leaned forward. "We've met, haven't we, Babes?" she gushed in a voice as thick as maple syrup. "You're a beautiful girl. Yes, you are."

Babette wagged her curled, feathery tail.

"She is beautiful, William," Marcella had to agree. "She's well behaved and obviously devoted to you. I haven't seen her move from your side once."

William's face glowed with pride. He glanced down and ruffled one of Babette's long, silky ears. "Well, you see, she is a champion. Quite literally."

"A champion?" Marcella prodded.

Sallie straightened with interest.

"Absolutely," William confirmed with a nod. "Babes knows her way around the dog show ring, don't you, girl? Used to show her myself, in fact. One of my hobbies until the church took over our lives. Top in her breed, three years in a row, at Crufts. She celebrated her last year of competition with a win in her group."

This was news to Marcella. Dogs and dog shows. Another facet of William. And a subject she was not conversant on. Still, she was no idiot. She'd learned a thing or two hanging around Sallie and Henri, and she recognized the critical importance of this moment. If she was seriously going to get anywhere with William, she'd have to bond with his dog.

"Wow, I'm impressed." She reached out a shaky hand while Sallie and William looked on. Babette gave it an aloof sniff. "Hiya, girl," she said, thinking this was permission to move closer. She attempted to pet Babette, but the saluki jerked her head out of reach, then stepped back behind the shelter of William's cassock.

Crap. What a bust. Here, she'd been internalizing Emma as major competition when all along her real challenge had been this anorexic hound.

"Um . . . excuse me, Vicar." The soft, fragile voice saved her further embarrassment, as they all turned in unison towards a blonde girl of no more than twelve.

The girl looked to William expectantly, while in her hands, she clutched a small basket of cherry tomatoes.

"Chloe," William greeted in surprise. "Hello."

"Hello, Vicar. Mum asked me to bring these over." She raised her thin arms, extending him the basket. Green polish colored Chloe's short, stubby nails, and she wore a different silver ring on each finger and thumb.

Marcella watched with interest as William stepped forward to accept the tomatoes. As she'd hoped, this morning was shaping up to be one big eavesdrop into a day in the life of the Honorable Will. What she'd failed to foresee was that she'd be sharing his attention with an entire village.

"Thank you, Chloe," he acknowledged.

Chloe pressed her lips together nervously and mumbled, "Mum and I'd been shopping at the farmer's market yesterday and we wanted to bring something for . . . uh, you know, you blessing our Sting and all, and well, we know how you fancy tomatoes."

"Oh, absolutely. I'm mad for tomatoes." He popped one in his mouth and munched. "Very thoughtful of you and your mum."

Chloe's smile widened as she watched William swallow. Wrapping one sneaker around the foot of her other ankle, she told him, "They're from Sting, as well."

"Yes, of course. And what a precious little dog he is." William leaned closer and asked in a conspiratorial whisper which Marcella strained to hear, "So, d'you think Sting enjoyed the service? I got the impression from his growl he wasn't quite keen on the holy water."

Chloe giggled. "I think it reminded him of having a bath."

"Right. Exactly. Good point. I hadn't considered that." William straightened. "Well, I certainly do appreciate the tomatoes, Chloe. Pass my thanks along to your mum and Sting, will you?"

"I will." She turned and dashed off, shouting, "TTFN!"

"Bye, Chloe," William called after her.

When he turned back around, Marcella was waiting with a smile.

"Oh. You find this amusing, do you?"

Marcella glanced at Sallie for a second opinion. No sooner had they made eye contact when Sallie's face split in a grin.

Marcella returned her attention to William and nodded. "Well . . . yeah!"

"And do neither of you see the downside to all this Christian goodwill?" William asked them.

"The, uh, downside?" Marcella echoed blankly. "What downside? Cherry tomatoes are an excellent food source for the complexion."

Sallie's eyes gleamed with laughter. "I think it's incredibly sweet. These people adore you."

"Thank you, Sallie. It is sweet. Very sweet. It'd be a terrible waste not to eat every bit of this food, but s'pose I'm not in the mood for a Sunday lunch of cold mash and cherry tomatoes?"

"Stick it in the fridge?" Sallie offered. "You might wake up tonight with the munchies."

"I'm just curious." With a self-assured tilt of her chin, Marcella lifted her foot and set the bright red sole of her sandal one step closer to William. "What are you in the mood for?"

He hesitated. Meanwhile, his gaze melted into hers and his expression turned pensive. "Sadly, in this instance, it's not a question of being in the mood, as it is a matter of being responsible."

A hot rush spouted like a geyser up through Marcella's center, part arousal, part discomposure. She was toying with forbidden fruit. Any intelligent woman would have learned her lesson last night and let it go. But for some ungodly reason she couldn't stop throwing temptation his way.

Crazy as she obviously was, she wanted him.

"Whoa," Sallie whooped. "Why do I get the impression you two are not speaking of food?"

William cleared his throat. He gave a cool smile, then glanced away.

Marcella centered herself, ready with a cool smile of her own, when a flash exploded in her face. She was blinking away the blindness when she heard an unfamiliar British voice say, "Sorry. Just testing the flash. All these shade trees, you know? Vicar, would you mind posing for a photo with my iguana?"

"Oh, hello, Neil," William greeted. " 'Course, I wouldn't mind. Actually, what d'you say you hold your iguana while Babette and I stand alongside? Sallie here is a professional photographer. Perhaps she'd be kind enough to do the honors."

William handed Marcella his armload of free eats to hold. So, while he posed and Sallie shot, Marcella's eyes refocused until she could see clear enough to notice someone else about to join them.

Emma.

Immediately, Marcella straightened, doing her best to look glamorous and chic while holding a casserole of cold potatoes.

With such a clear view, she couldn't help but give Emma the once-over. She was dressed in a gray A-line skirt that ended at the knee and a fine-gauged knit top of pastel blue. Neat, conservative, ho-hum, but then in all fairness, the woman was dressed for church. Her figure wasn't half bad. But of course, anyone with an ounce of fashion sense knew a wrap top was breast-enhancing. She guessed Emma to be about . . . hmm, in those kitten heels, five-foot-seven or thereabouts.

Emma caught her staring and met the gaze undaunted. With each step she drew closer, her red hair gleamed with golden highlights. Definitely color enhanced. She wore a side part, bangs swept across one eye.

At last, they stood face to face.

Overall, Emma's were simple features, but packaged with her confident air, a sexy hairstyle and pretty green eyes, she could hardly be written off as unattractive. Not the sophisticate Marcella was, but Emma definitely had something, her own *je ne sais quoi* that a girl couldn't help but twinge with jealousy over.

In an attempt to be magnanimous, Marcella greeted Emma with a cheery, "Hi!"

In return, Emma gave her no more than an amused nod before turning away. "Well, William, I'm off. I've Quincy in his cat carrier waiting in the car, but I didn't want to leave without saying a proper goodbye." She reached on tiptoes and dropped a peck on his cheek.

Marcella was hoping she'd make an uneventful exit, but Emma stepped back and turned an appraising gaze on her and Sallie. "Aren't you going to introduce us, William? I'm dying to meet your new friends."

"It'd be my pleasure." William did the honors, playing up the magazine and Marcella's and Sallie's "posh" careers in New York, then briefly explaining how they'd all met yesterday at his Aunt Lynne's wedding.

Marcella shifted her culinary burden to one side and offered Emma her hand. "It's really nice to meet you." Which was totally true, because otherwise, she might have gone on wondering forever.

"I'm a fan," Sallie interjected.

Marcella wanted to roll her eyes. *Pleease.* As far as she knew, Sallie had tuned in to Emma's style makeover show for the first time last night and she'd fallen asleep halfway through.

Emma sent Sallie a warm, appreciative smile. "Thank you, Sallie. So, you've only a short holiday here in England, then? With all the shops and sights around London, William must have made quite the impression, for you and Marcella to come visit his church."

She turned pointedly to Marcella for an answer.

Marcella felt William's eyes on her as well, and she turned to him with her response. "Originally, we did have other plans, for tea at the Savoy."

"The Savoy?" Emma cried. "How fab! I know their head chef."

"Marcella made reservations months ago," Sallie added with a note of longing. "We bought hats."

"Hats?" Emma's gaze darted to the large hat hanging by Marcella's side and understanding seemed to dawn. She gave a slow grin. "Oh, I see."

Clutching her Italian-inspired designer millinery proudly, Marcella continued, "Yes, well, after meeting William yesterday, Sallie and I changed our minds. I couldn't imagine leaving England without—"

"William, you old bastard! It's been yonks!"

The shout cut across the churchyard. Midsentence, Marcella whirled towards the voice, along with the others. Addressing one's vicar as a bastard on Sunday morning was about as decorous as . . . well, as her tempting him with a purple condom the Saturday night before.

A husky, chisel-faced blonde with a buzz cut was fast approaching their little group in what was proving to be one interruption after another.

Catching her eye, William consoled her with an apologetic smile before turning his attention to the man whom he was straining to recognize. "Derek?"

"Will Stafford! Good to see you, mate." Derek grabbed hold of the hand William extended and pumped like a maniac.

"It has been a long time, hasn't it?"

As they drew apart, Derek gave William the once-over. "Bugger me, look at you. You really are a vicar, aren't you? I've a post with the Foreign Service, myself. Was in the neighborhood, visiting my sister Judy and her family. Judy Chadwick of your parish. You know the Chadwicks. When she mentioned the name of her vicar, I had to pop round and see for myself. So, the Anglicans have really accepted you as one of their leaders, have they?"

"Six years now. Marcella, Sallie, this is Derek Granger, an old mate of mine from university. We rowed on the same team. Derek, you remember Emma?"

"Emma Parker? 'Course, I do." With a slightly confused frown, he ping-ponged his gaze between Emma and William, eventually settling on Emma. "You two never married? No, didn't think so. Oh well, hello, Emma. Good to see you. Say, I heard you're on the telly now. D'you know Nigella Lawson, then?"

Emma gave him a dull stare. "Uh-no, I'm afraid we've never

actually met."

Snorting a laugh, Derek shot William a look. "Here, who needs Nigella when you've got beauties like this lot by your side, yeah?"

William gave a strained smile. *Hmm, tough one,* Marcella thought. As a vicar, it would be crude to agree. William hadn't joined the church to seduce women with his clerical collar. But, as a man who'd been romantic with two of the three so-called beauties, how could he honestly say no?

Lucky for William, Derek was a high-energy kind of guy, a windbag who talked so fast William didn't have time to gather breath for a verbal response before he was jabbering again.

"Not that Will here was one to chase the girls. Nah, didn't need to. They sort of gravitated to him, d'you know what I mean? Then he switched to theology. Wants to be a vicar, he says. We thought he'd gone mad. Barking. Reckon you thought so, too, yeah, Emma?"

Brows drawn, Emma opened her mouth. Derek gave William a knowing wink without pausing for her reply and said, "Knew what you were doing all along, didn't you, mate? Always were more clever than the lot of us, you old bugger. Hey, nice dog. Hi, doggie."

Marcella felt exhausted listening to him. Out the corner of one eye, she spotted someone hurrying towards them.

A woman in a ponytail stepped up beside Derek and offered William a breathless greeting. "Vicar."

"Judy, hello." Relief poured over William's features.

She gave him a small, embarrassed smile.

Derek peeked at her over his shoulder before punching William on the arm. "Say, come for dinner, Will? Judy doesn't mind one more, d'you, love?" He snatched a cherry tomato off the top of the basket Marcella was still holding and popped it into his mouth, then flicked his brows at her while he chewed.

"The vicar knows he's always welcome in our home, Derek," Judy said firmly, imploring William with an apologetic look.

"Thank you, Judy, that's very kind, but I rather think I already have plans for lunch," William begged off, casting Marcella a hopeful glance.

Moi? Marcella thought excitedly and beamed him back a *you-most-certainly-do* smile.

"Perhaps another time, then, Derek?" William wrapped an arm around his old classmate and started to walk him off. "We've a lot to catch up on. Excuse us a moment please, ladies."

Marcella watched them stride off, Babette keeping pace in a weightless gait alongside, and breathed a sigh of relief. "Man, the characters a vicar has to put up with, huh?"

"A vicar's wife, as well, I'd imagine," Emma announced to no one in particular, but of course Marcella knew she was directing the remark at her. "If you fancy life with a vicar, best to find out beforehand what you're in for."

Marcella could hardly believe what she was hearing. Her ears rang with the audacity. "I beg your pardon."

Emma maintained an aloof, nonchalant manner. "Just surmising here, but I've got the impression you and William are quite interested in each other. Am I correct?"

Marcella looked straight into Emma's cool green eyes. "Not subtle, are you?"

"You've never seen my show?"

"I have," Sallie said.

Marcella remained undecided about Emma. Although any vibes she sensed were definitely nonthreatening. Sallie seemed to like her. All right, she thought. What-the-hey? What did she have to lose by being honest?

"Okay, I know William and I only met yesterday, but I really, really like him. He's very special. He told me you two were once engaged, but it's totally over, right?"

"Oh, totally. Nothing romantic going on, but we have remained friends, obviously. I'm certain William must've told you so himself. But then, of course, I understand your need to hear it from me."

"So like, not to be rude or anything, but what are you doing here?"

"Marcella, that is rude." Sallie shook her head.

Emma merely grinned with a twinkle in her eye. "Quite simply, I'm a very great animal lover."

"Me too," Sallie said.

Emma turned a smile on Sallie, and Marcella thought she witnessed a certain kinship ignite between them.

"I'm also a vegetarian. I s'pose you could call me somewhat of an advocate."

"I know exactly what you mean," Sallie said. "I'm a vegetarian, too."

"Ah, sorry Emma," Marcella interrupted before she and Sallie started swapping recipes, "but I'm not exactly clear on what this has to do with you and William?"

"Long ago, I encouraged William, should he ever have a church of his own, to include a blessing of the animals as part of his services. I come every year to help out and lend my support. To the cause of animals, of course. Nothing more."

"I think Emma has a point, Marcella," Sallie said.

"Ah . . . which is?"

"Which is, if you are falling for William, it's now or never to discover the kind of life you'd be in for."

"He'd make the most wonderful husband. Loyal and attentive. If you've got what it takes to be a vicar's wife, that is," Emma challenged. "The role does come with its own responsibilities."

"Marcella's a crack at responsibility," Sallie championed. "She'd make an excellent vicar's wife."

Emma looked intrigued. "Would she really, Sallie? And why is that, d'you s'pose?"

"Hey," Marcella started to protest, then on second thought, held her tongue. She was reeling at the turn this absurd discussion had taken, but she was even more fascinated to hear what Sallie intended to say.

"Marcella was raised in a small Italian neighborhood with strong family values. Where she's from, gathering with family and friends is a big deal. She may have left home for the big city, but she's based her career on the domestic arts—food, entertaining, decorating. She was practically raised in a restaurant; she can handle the masses. She has the cooking skills to put a new spin on church suppers. Not to mention the creativity and editing skills to kick a church newsletter up to new heights. One of the things that makes Marcella such a great editor is her ability to always remain prepared for anything and stay in control. Marcella's all about organization, and when she needs to, believe me, she can be a total bitch on the phone."

This was why she loved her best friend. "Thank you, Sallie," Marcella said, completely blown away, "that was beautiful."

"Well, she certainly has the skills, but is becoming a vicar's wife something Marcella cares to do with her life?" Emma turned to her pointedly and left the challenge hanging in the air.

Excellent question, Marcella thought. Selfishly, she had to admit, she'd been feeling a tad impatient with everyone demanding William's attention. Was she being unreasonable to want him all to herself? She was quickly beginning to realize that being a part of William's life would require sacrifice.

Chapter 10

The moment Marcella saw William returning she welcomed him with a smile.

Like, the guy was dressed in a long black cassock, and still, he came off as an irresistible hottie. Go figure. Nothing, and surprisingly not even those vestments, detracted from his appeal. If anything, they lent him a regal, mysterious air. The skirt of his cassock flowed around his legs as he walked, and that whole, dark monochromatic look accentuated his striking height and bearing. Sexiest of all was his pleasantly approachable aura. A faithful dog at his side didn't hurt either.

Whatever she'd been expecting, watching William play out his vicar's role this morning had not, to any degree, cooled down her love jones.

Yes, Emma's question rattled her brain. Yes, she found the challenge of a serious relationship with a vicar daunting, but it wasn't anything that hadn't been acknowledged in her earlier conversation with Sallie.

As he approached, William held out his hands to relieve her of the casserole and basket of tomatoes. "Sorry to have left you with this haul."

"No problem." They exchanged a smile as Marcella passed him her burden, soaking up his masculine chi, like warmth from the sun.

As far as she was concerned, it was way too premature to freak. Not when she and William hadn't been able to agree on a solution for working out a long-distance relationship. What they needed was time alone.

William apologized for the interruption. "So, what did you ladies find to talk about, then, while I was off?" His eyes glittered affectionately over Marcella's face.

She shrugged one bare shoulder. "Nothing."

William dipped his head closer to hers. "Er, you didn't happen to mention me . . . while you were saying nothing?"

She felt her flesh warm under his gaze. They were making inane small talk. Yet something in William's tone and the intense look in his eyes made her skin prickle. "I might have."

" 'Course, I can't speak for you, Sallie," came Emma's voice in a sharp tone, "but I don't find it the least bit awkward watching William and Marcella eye each other up as though we weren't standing here a'tall."

William's head snapped up with a start. Marcella shook herself, then watched as William turned an embarrassed grin on Emma and Sallie. "Sorry, didn't mean to be rude."

"Hey, I was enjoying the show," Sallie admitted with a giggle. She stole a secretive smile at Marcella. "You guys really make a striking couple. Look at you, William. All in black. Marcella's decked out in white. William, you've got classic features. Marcella's are more exotic. You're very yin and yang-y together."

"Oh, right," Emma said thoughtfully. "A bit like two extremely tall chess pieces, aren't they?"

William shot her a glare, which seemed to amuse Emma. Marcella smiled. It was becoming increasingly clear she didn't have anything to worry about where Emma was concerned. Whatever Emma and William may have shared in the past, their current relationship was no more intimate than a pair of clowning siblings.

"Uh, shouldn't you be off, Em?" William queried. "You've Quincy waiting in the car, as I recall."

"He'll be fine for another minute or so."

"Right." William's tone was resigned, but turning, he brightened considerably. "So, Marcella, Sallie . . . since you've chucked your plans to attend service instead, I hope I can convince you both to stick round a bit longer and accompany me home for Sunday lunch. I've a pot of mash and cherry tomatoes. Totally vegetarian, Sal."

Marcella had been expecting an offer like this ever since William had turned down Derek's invitation. Lunch at William's bachelor pad. Or to quote his mom, that "beautiful stone cottage where he lived with no wife." *Perfetto. Yes!* She couldn't wait to check it out. "We'd love to join you for lunch, wouldn't we, Sallie?"

She cast Sallie a stony stare in hopes her friend would show enthusiasm. William was, after all, making an effort to assure Sallie didn't feel like a third wheel.

"Yeah . . . sure," Sallie responded on cue. "We'd love it."

It was obvious from her dull expression, she was ready to bolt.

Marcella was prepared. "I have an idea. Forget the reheated hash. I'll cook. Pasta!" Sallie loved pasta.

Sallie's eyes gleamed and Marcella complimented herself on her quick creative thinking, before turning to see William's reaction. He looked a little . . . dazed. Could he be overwhelmed by her generosity? "You did say you have a vegetable garden, right?"

He nodded cautiously. But hey, was that a grin forming on those delicious lips?

"I make a mean pasta primavera," she boasted.

"Excellent. Pasta primavera." He all but drooled. "I mean, fantastic, Marcella, but I couldn't ask you to—"

"Of course you can! It sounds brilliant, smashing, but shall I offer one additional suggestion?"

All eyes turned to Emma, who beamed back confidently, Marcella wondering what she could possibly have in mind when she hadn't even been invited.

Emma focused on Sallie. "What say you and I pop over to the Savoy, and leave these two singletons alone to spend the afternoon cooking up . . . um, whatever? You do have reservations, I believe. Bloody shame to waste them. We'll natter over a pot of tea, maybe hit the shops. I have a car. I can drop you round your hotel afterwards. What'd you say, Sallie?"

Sallie's face blossomed with joy. "Awesome! You wouldn't mind? Er, I wouldn't want to put you out or anything." She eyed Emma skeptically. "I mean, you hardly know me."

"Well, yes, I s'pose it's true we've only just met, but I know William and you know Marcella. Surely, that's worth a good gossip?"

Sallie's smile returned. "Okay, let's dish! Thanks, Emma, I'd love to come shopping with you. Uh, you don't mind, do you, Marcella?"

"No, of course not, Sal."

And why should she mind? This meant she'd have William all to herself. A dream come true. *Good going, Emma,* she thought. Marcella had been outclassed by a better offer, but so what? C'mon, what fashion-conscious female in her right mind would choose pasta primavera over an afternoon of shopping in London with a British celebrity escort?

Marcella would. She just had.

"Go! Have fun," she said. "Enjoy yourselves."

"We will, thanks." Sallie beamed. She gave William one final appraisal, caught Marcella's eye, and bounced her brows. "You, too."

Emma jangled her car keys. "Super! We'll need to pop round my flat in Earl's Court to drop off Quincy. I live walking distance from Knotting Hill. Just five minutes to the nearest tube stop, if you'd fancy a look round."

"I'd love a tour," Sallie said.

"Great. We're off, then."

It all happened so fast. They exchanged goodbyes and soon Marcella found herself watching her best friend head out with William's ex.

She'd made those reservations herself. The Savoy had been her brainstorm. Marcella had been looking forward to it for months. But who needed the Savoy, right? She was with William, dressed to the nines, and ready for their date. Starting now. At church. In a quiet country village. Out in the middle of nowhere.

He stepped up beside her. "It's not too late to join them. It's all right, you know. I'd understand."

He sounded so defeated, Marcella felt herself flush. Had she insulted William with her longing glances after Sallie and Emma? Sure, William might claim to understand if she left now, but he'd be hurt.

As she turned to face him, she saw the hope and expectancy in his eyes and felt her heart melt from deep inside.

"I want to be here."

"After meeting me, you couldn't imagine leaving England without what?"

She blanked, so he reiterated, "Before Derek arrived, you were about to tell Emma that you couldn't imagine leaving England without . . . something. What was it you wanted to say?"

"Oh . . . yeah, that."

"Yes, that." He quirked a brow slightly. "Well?"

"I was going to say, without taking every chance to get to know you better."

His stare lingered, searching her eyes, then suddenly he burst into a big, boyish grin. "Right. Splendid, then." With a jerk of his head, he indicated the church. "Er, would you like a coffee?"

"I'd love one."

Who needs tea, she thought.

Marcella gave a small gasp of appreciation as she drifted into William's office behind William and Babette. The decor bore a strong Victorian influence. Dark paneling, ornate moldings, an entire wall of dusty old books, and its central focus—a massive mahogany desk.

She skimmed her fingers over its leather desktop. "This is a beautiful piece. Is it antique?"

"It is, yes. Purchased at auction sale by a former clergy."

Marcella nodded, soaking up the ambience. "So this is the vicar's office, huh?" She dropped into the leather upholstered seat of a wood-carved chair opposite the desk and kicked off her sandals. "And this, I assume, is where people sit when they confront their eternal destinies? Maybe confess a dirty little secret or two?"

Stretching her tired feet on the carpet, she wiggled her toes and watched as William perched on the edge of his desk. He'd changed from his vestments into a pair of khaki trousers and a short-sleeved, periwinkle shirt tailored to accommodate his dog collar. The color intensified the blue in his eyes.

He folded his hands serenely before him. "Have you come to confront your eternal destiny?"

"No. My devout Italian mother set me straight at a very young age, and what she didn't cover, the nuns in the Catholic School I was sent to did."

William winced. "Right, I've heard stories about those Catholic nuns."

Marcella laughed lightheartedly. "Ah, but those are stories for another time."

"Very well, but while you're in that chair, feel free, of course,"

William said, leaning closer, "to discuss any dirty little secret you wish."

He grinned, she giggled back, and they held the gaze. Marcella could only imagine what he was thinking.

Or could she?

Was it possible over two hours had passed since that first cup of coffee in the church hall? Frankly, she was feeling a little beat. There'd been an hour of mix and mingle, smiling, shaking hands, making a fuss over all sorts of furry creatures, and pouring coffee for the more elderly parishioners.

There was also the occasional canine accident. Marcella had been moved to see that William was not above dropping to the floor with a handful of paper towels.

When the gathering broke, she lent a hand by sweeping the hall, not something she ever wanted to do in a white halter dress again. When at last they returned to the sanctuary, she helped William gather hymnals, then waited as he locked up his vestments. Never had she spent such a long morning at church.

Nor enjoyed herself more in a man's company.

Thinking about it, she gave William another smile before directing her attention elsewhere. "Why is there a bicycle in your office?"

"It's my transport to work, actually."

"Really?"

"Absolutely. Around the village, I find a bike is much more personable. It really is the best way of getting round. I'm visible; people see me. It's great. I'm always riding by and saying hello."

Marcella's smile was full of admiration. But wait . . . suddenly, she had a thought. "You mean the only way we have of getting to your house is a bicycle? So like, what exactly did you have in mind, huh? Riding me on the handlebars?"

As Marcella soon discovered, a bike was not their only means of travel. Turned out, William had something a little more accommodating in mind, and twenty minutes later, they loaded up the seniors' minibus. William in the driver's seat, Babette directly behind him, Marcella across the aisle with her hat and the morning's charitable foodstuffs, and the bike propped in front of the seat in back of hers.

She felt hot and sweaty. No air conditioning, but it was a quiet ride through the village, past the square, a pharmacy, a tiny post office, The Crown pub.

"They make a decent ploughman's lunch," William commented as they drove past, "if you've second thoughts about cooking."

When Marcella told him no, she had her heart set on preparing a home-cooked meal, William admitted he wasn't crazy enough to talk her out of it, but suggested they could always pop round later for a pint and some of his favorite Smoky Bacon crisps.

Marcella smiled from her seat and turned to admire more of the view. She liked the rustic style of the houses. "Now, there's something you don't see in New York," she said as they passed a field of grazing sheep.

"Right, there it is. Just ahead," William said a few minutes later. "Home sweet home."

As he slowed the bus to a stop, Marcella was welcomed by the sight of a stone cottage cradled in soothing woodland greens beneath a serene English sky. The picture of coziness, and it all sat on a compact, lovingly manicured lawn.

William opened the door and Marcella stepped outside for a closer look. A yellowish-green vine crawled up the right side of the cottage. Darker greens grew with abandon, low and hedge-like, along the foundation.

She saw small diamond-paned windows and a steep-pitched roof. On either side of the cottage door hung a lantern. Lacy wooden trim formed a border around the eaves, gingerbread style. Windows, door, lanterns and trim were all painted Dutch blue in striking detail against the pale gray stone.

Marcella felt like she'd stepped into a storybook. She turned, stepped aside as Babette came bounding past into the yard, then watched as William carried his bike off the bus.

As their eyes met, she dropped her jaw in a show of awe, then burst into a grin. "It's charming. I don't know what I was expecting. Maybe something a little more formal. But this. This is timeless. This is totally relaxed and absolutely quintessential. I mean . . . what can I say? Wow!"

"Thank you." He grinned, and Marcella wasn't sure if he was just pleased with her reaction or if he had something else on his mind.

"So, how was the ride? Not too bumpy, I hope?"

"The ride was fine," she said. "I enjoyed the ride."

"Yes, well, I s'pose if the seniors manage, so can you."

"Yeah, I survived, but I don't know about my dress, though." She peered down at herself, where a tiny doggie paw print had been stamped on her bodice and a smudge of strawberry jam stained her lap. Looking behind to access any booty damage, she was horrified at what she found. "Is that dirt? Ah, am I filthy?" She dusted her seat.

Something in the atmosphere changed. She sensed it immediately. Suddenly all the gaiety had been sucked out of the air and everything had gone quiet.

Marcella glanced up to find William's gaze intent on her backside. When he noticed her watching him, watching her, his eyes widened. Embarrassment flashed across his handsome features.

"Uh, no. It's, er, quite lovely, actually."

As Marcella straightened, her smile grew and grew. "It's refreshing to see you're not totally immune to me."

William's expression turned reproving. " 'Course I'm not immune to you." He hooked a finger inside his clerical collar and tugged. "This isn't some sort of compulsory halo, you know. I'd thought by now it was quite obvious. My feelings for you, that is."

She took a step closer. "What are your feelings for me?"

Gazing into her eyes, William walked the bike forward, where it remained between them as his gaze skimmed down the length of her body. When he again looked her in the face, he seemed a little shaken. "I can't stop thinking about you."

He regarded her with a worried crease between his brows. "Perhaps it wasn't such a ripping idea, after all, asking Emma to invite Sallie along shopping."

Marcella jumped in her skin. She let his words sink in a moment, then replayed them in her head, and still she couldn't move her brain past the shock. "You? You mean you put the whole thing in motion for Sallie and Emma to spend the day together? Using my reservation at the Savoy? That was your idea? Whoa, I can't believe this." Her amusement grew the more she thought about it, until she couldn't help but laugh. "You set up poor Sallie."

"No offense, but Sallie didn't seem very keen on your pasta primavera." With a tilt of his head, William shot her a give-me-a-break frown. "Poor Sallie, indeed. Oh, I really like Sallie, I truly do, don't mistake me. That's why I'm hoping it won't prove too much of a hardship for her, visiting London with a television fashion personality. Retailers generally can't do enough for Emma when she drops round their shops. They'll do anything to be featured on her show. Perhaps even slip all sorts of complimentary items into Emma's and Sallie's carrier bags. Makeup, fashions, accessories. And not the cheap stuff, mind. Do you think Sallie will be able to bear it?"

Marcella had a hard time containing her grin. "All right,

already. Easy on the sarcasm. I know Sallie will have a blast. She's a lucky girl. And as for me, I'm a pretty lucky girl, myself. I'm flattered you arranged for us to have this time alone, and I'm grateful to Emma for making it happen, but William . . ." She eyed him carefully as she asked in a conspiratorially low voice, "Whatever made you do it?"

He started to walk along with the bike, and Marcella fell in step beside him, following him up a gravel path to his door. "I was quite pleasantly surprised when I noticed you at service this morning and quickly realized I'd been given a chance." He turned to look at her. "I couldn't imagine letting you leave England without taking every opportunity to get to know you better."

Marcella grinned. "My words exactly."

"Exactly."

"Then we're on the same page?"

He beamed back. "I'd like to think so, yes."

Nothing, Marcella thought, *could cinch this moment more perfectly than a kiss.*

William lifted his bike and hurriedly pushed it against the side of the house. Marcella waited behind him with a flutter in her belly, watching the muscles flex in his arms. She moistened her dry lips and tried to sneak a peak through the cottage door window, but sunlight reflected off the diamond panes into her eyes.

She blinked, and when she turned, William was standing directly in front of her. There they stood at the entrance to his cottage, staring into one another's eyes.

Marcella didn't dare move. Neither did he, which after a moment led her to believe he was waiting for her to . . . to . . . what? Make the first move? She hadn't a clue and froze in mid-grin as William cupped her jaw in his hand, leaned slowly forward, and opened his mouth over hers.

Her hat slipped from her fingers as Marcella closed her eyes and allowed her senses to be carried away. She could feel the fire burning inside him. A girl had to wonder if a man who kissed this slowly, this passionately, had serious hopes of making love later.

Well, with any other guy she might wonder, but William had made his position pretty clear last night. He could be weakening, however. In which case, should she be strong for him and fend him off?

Yeah, right.

Finally, Marcella got honest with herself and ended the madness. She told herself not to be such an idiot. *Quit thinking and enjoy this moment, because it might be all you're going to get.* She let her eyes roll back in her head in mindless desire. She luxuriated in each demand William made on her, the melding of their mouths, every soft peck, and the taste of his lips. Adrenalin pumped excitement through her veins. And just as they were really, really getting into it, William softly pulled his lips from hers, coming up for air.

Gosh, he was strong. He must've had divine assistance.

He breathed, then smiled into her eyes with his watercolor-blue gaze. "We may have gone a bit off the page there."

"Oh, I don't think so. In fact, I think that page may deserve a bookmark. You know . . . in case we want to go back to it later."

They laughed like two silly school kids, then William picked her hat up off the ground and reached across to open the door.

He stepped aside, and with a jerk of his head, gestured for her to enter. "Welcome."

Marcella smiled as she ducked inside, elated with the way the day was progressing. Her gaze darted around the small entrance hall, from its polished stone floor, to the pale yellow striped wallpaper, to a row of etchings hanging to her right. On the opposite wall a shelf doubled as a coat rack. On the floor below sat a large rectangular wicker basket. Inside were gardening tools, shears, empty planters, gloves. A pair of muddy Wellingtons had been tucked behind the door.

Right away she liked the simplicity of what she saw. Her design sense told her functional, tasteful, welcoming, but deep inside Marcella was struck with a feeling of good, old-fashioned hominess.

William entered behind her with Babette, who disappeared into the house. "Originally, this was built as a home for an estate gamekeeper, in eighteen forty-six."

"Well it certainly looks good, for more than a hundred and fifty years old."

"Right, well, that is actually rather modern by British standards," William quipped with a wise-ass grin. "Fortunate for me, the previous owners did a serious amount of work restoring it. Replacing floors and the windows, raising ceilings, installing a proper heating system."

With a hand to her back, he escorted her farther inside for a tour. "I'd been living in the vicarage originally, but I'd some money of my own and jumped at this property when it came up for sale. I may have driven them out, actually, thinking back. You won't believe the number of times I rode past to have a look, imagining what I'd do with the gardens if I ever got my hands on them."

Lucky gardens, Marcella thought before directing her attention to an intimate dining area decorated in spring greens and barely large enough to accommodate its corner baker's rack, a round table, and four high-backed chairs. From there they moved to a cozy parlor with a bay window overlooking the back gardens. A shelf built high around the ceiling wrapped around three walls and held antiques, books, teapots, and other pieces of china. The furniture was a collection of older pieces, reupholstered in muted fabrics.

There was a beautiful claw-foot tub in the bath and painted furniture in William's bedroom.

The rooms had a mellow ambiance. *Very shabby chic,* she thought. She was impressed and told William so, over and over. "You did this all yourself?"

He shook his head and confessed in a low voice, "Mum's decorators."

"Lady Wiltshire." Marcella smiled in memory of their impromptu meeting after the wedding ceremony. "I guess it's not surprising the wife of a viscount would have such talented decorators."

"They did a splendid job of designing around the means of a vicar, don't you think?"

"I think it's a house anyone would feel comfortable in."

She was growing unusually fond of the space, and as they stood in the study, Marcella envisioned herself seated in the paisley club chair on a chilly evening, scribbling in her organizer beneath the reading lamp. There'd be a tartan throw over her legs as she reached for a cuppa off the antique tea cart.

Something very cosmic was happening to her inside this little house. The cottage had a personality all its own that kept drawing her in with its charm, and Marcella realized she was falling in love with it. The feeling seemed to parallel something else she was experiencing. The more time she spent with William, not only did he grow more powerfully attractive, but the deeper Marcella found herself caring for him.

Suddenly she needed a moment alone and excused herself to freshen up. William told her he'd be outside, rescuing the cherry tomatoes and Mrs. Wilbourne's mash from the minibus. When Marcella was ready, she should meet him in the kitchen.

A splash of cool water, a fluff of her dark waves, a little lip gloss, and Marcella couldn't understand how she'd let her feelings for William scare her.

She found him popping the cork off a bottle of wine and joined him at the small butcher-block island in the center of the kitchen.

"I thought you might be thirsty," he said.

"I am." Marcella tilted the bottle to read its label. A German riesling. Very nice. She held the glasses while William poured, then handed one off to him and clinked hers against it. *"Salute."*

"Cheers."

They watched each other over the rim of their glasses as they sipped. The wine eased down Marcella's throat, luscious, honeyed—lightly sweet. She could feel herself relaxing by the minute.

"I should start thinking about lunch," she ventured, turning to take stock of the rest of William's kitchen. She found it bachelor-friendly in a nonthreatening sort of way. Compact, yet more efficient than what she had in her small New York apartment. "It's spotless."

"One of the perks of not doing much cooking, I s'pose. A really tidy kitchen."

The cabinets were of light oak. The stainless steel stove had a backsplash of black tile where the pots and pans hung. But . . . *hmm,* no refrigerator?

William directed her attention beneath the counter next to the sink. Marcella opened the door, only to be struck with amusement at what she found inside. "I don't know why I thought it would be bare." The fridge was packed with casseroles.

"I imagine your refrigerator must be well stocked."

"It's pathetic. Even the best chefs don't necessarily enjoy cooking for themselves. No, if I'm lucky, dinners for me are usually experimental recipes left over from the magazine's test kitchen."

"Sounds a bit adventuresome. Well, I'll go out and gather the veggies, shall I? Feel free to go through the cupboards and make a list of any other ingredients you might need. I'll pop down to the grocer's and pick them up. Here, you might want to don this."

He handed her a folded square of navy blue fabric.

Marcella eyed it curiously before shaking it open. It was an apron. Across the front, it read, "The Naked Chef."

"All I have, I'm afraid. A housewarming gift from Bertie. Really," he argued, when she shot him a comical look. "It's the name of a television cooking program. It's not a suggestion or anything."

Marcella thought he looked extremely amused with himself as he headed out the back door. She slipped the apron over her head, muttering wryly to herself, "I'm not the one who refused to take off his clothes."

William paused in the doorway. "What's that?"

"Zucchini. I'll need some zucchini."

"Here in England, we call them courgettes." He was smiling in such a way that Marcella suspected he'd heard her correctly the first time.

"Fine then, courgettes. And garlic and peppers and whatever else you've got."

"I think you'll be really pleased with my courgettes. Right, well, if I haven't returned in ten minutes, you'll likely find me in the garden taking my clothes off for my role as the Naked Chef's assistant."

"Tease," she shouted as he chuckled out the door.

He came back minutes later, fully clothed and carrying an armload of produce which he dumped on the counter. Marcella handed him her list. William kissed her goodbye, and while he went to buy bread, cheeses, and pasta, Marcella prepared the vegetables.

She was really enjoying herself, feeling right at home, getting into a domestic swing. She'd organized her ingredients and decided she had enough to make not only the pasta primavera, but a roasted eggplant spread and a smashed cherry tomato and olive bruschetta.

She was peeling and chopping, thinking how incredibly great this weekend had turned out, how lucky she was to have met a terrific and totally fun guy like William, blissful in the romance of cooking dinner for him, loving his home, when Marcella realized what she was doing. She was fantasizing. Fantasizing about this relationship working out.

Was that what she wanted? She didn't know. Just thinking about it gave her heart palpitations. William's world was so far removed from her life in New York, so foreign. Was she willing to do whatever it took to be with him? Living in the English countryside with a vicar? It was almost . . . bizarre.

Suddenly everything seemed too quiet. The house was too quiet. Bramble Moor was too quiet.

She couldn't breathe.

Chapter 11

Marcella threw open the back door and stuck out her head. She fanned her face with her hand, but it didn't help. She couldn't get the warm afternoon air into her lungs fast enough, so she stumbled out onto the terrace, gasping in the shade of an aged, ivy-covered stone wall about ten feet tall.

Oh God. She was starting to hyperventilate.

All around her grew a dense, woodland garden. Ferns, hostas, shrubbery, and herbs mingled with an explosion of blooms and rose bushes, all jostling each other for space. Everything sort of spilled over everything else. You'd think with all the oxygen being generated she'd be able to breathe.

But this anxiety attack wasn't about to be calmed by a deep breath.

Some crazy, hopelessly romantic part of her was enjoying the role of domestic diva, which wasn't so much an issue except it brought to mind Sallie's little speech outside the church and made Marcella realize she was seriously beginning to want to give a future with William a real shot—vicar, English countryside, and all. Well, why not? For love, she'd do anything.

Whoa, hold on Betty Crocker homemaker. Not that simple. Oh, no, no, no, no, no. She had a life in New York. She had a fantastic career and, hopefully, a promotion waiting in the wings. And although it might work for some women, in this instance, having it all just wasn't an option.

It all came down to location, location, location.

Marcella heard her name being called and snapped-to in fear of being exposed. She pulled herself together and arranged her features into a smile. "I'm out here."

Babette loped out onto the terrace. William stood in the doorway gazing at her adoringly for a moment with a silly grin on his face. "I reckon I've got everything you asked. They'd some wonderfully fresh strawberries I brought home as well." He gestured indoors with a jerk of his head and said, "I popped the lot in the fridge." Then he stepped out, letting the door slam behind him. "Been out here long?"

"A few minutes. I was just admiring your garden. *Gracious Living* runs a series on gardening. I don't cover the stories myself, of course," she said as he came to stand beside her, "but I know enough to recognize a traditional English cottage garden when I see one. It takes real talent to tuck so many plants into a contained area and have it come out looking this spontaneous and natural. It's beautiful."

"Thank you. Admittedly, gardening is sort of an obsession with me. I love mucking about. Keeps me grounded. Literally," he added with a twinkle. "When I'm in the garden, I lose the need to control everything. You see, no matter how meticulous I may be in the planning, it never quite turns out the way I thought it would. Sort of like life, really. Sometimes the best things are just happy accidents." He grinned.

Suddenly, for no explainable reason, Marcella's vision blurred behind a sheen of tears. She blinked furiously to clear it.

"Er . . . is something wrong, Marcella?"

"What? No, of course not. Nothing."

William frowned, and the longer he regarded her, the deeper his brow creased. "Is it . . . me? Have I done something? Forgotten to do something? Here you were, serving coffee in the church hall all morning, and now I've brought you home to prepare my lunch. Damn, I've been a feckless sod, haven't I? Or is it the dress? Please, let me pay to have it cleaned."

Marcella couldn't help but smile. "A sod? You? Please, no," she scoffed with a roll of her eyes. "No, I'm fine. And you've been great. Don't worry about the dress. The dress is fine, too. Really, William, it's nothing. Nothing," she reiterated, trying to keep her voice upbeat. "It's silly. I'd be ashamed to mention it, it's so ridiculous."

"Ah, but as you've pointed out yourself, I'm the one people round here turn to when they've a confession to make. It's all part of what I do, isn't it, being sympathetic to what others are feeling? Actually, I was a really keen listener long before I was ordained. Hey, if it's the collar that bothers you, here's a thought. I'll nick inside, fetch you a glass of wine, pull a Guinness t-shirt over my head, and you can pretend you're talking to a bartender. And you would be, in fact. In a manner of speaking. You'd be talking with a retired bartender, what d'you say?"

A giggle bubbled out of her at the imploring look on his face.

"Trust me, Marcella, there's nothing you could say that I'd dismiss as silly."

She was smiling now, and *oh crap,* what was the use? It would've been easier to lie to her mother. How was she to jive this handsome vicar with his clear blue, see-right-through-to-your-soul, compassionate eyes? Besides, this had escalated into way too big a deal. She couldn't let him think he'd done something to put her off.

"Okay. The truth is . . . I-I'm having such a good time, I hate to see it end," she admitted, quickly averting her eyes while she took a breath. "See? Now, tell me that wasn't silly? Oh God, I'm so embarrassed."

But when she glanced up again all the humor was gone from William's expression. He stared blankly, until gradually, Marcella began to notice something raw and vulnerable burn in his eyes.

"You're not having me on?" He reached for her upper arms and drew her close. "It's not just happening to me?"

Marcella pressed her hands to his chest and let his meaning sink in. *What-d'ya-know?* They were on the same page again. She smiled, then shook her head, no. She definitely wasn't having him on.

"This is really happening, isn't it?" he asked again. "You and me? I mean, I'm sensing there could be something special between us. Absolutely. And I think you feel it as well. Am I right?"

She nodded.

"Well then, it's quite simple, really. I won't let you go until we sort this out. Surely, there's some way we can keep in touch."

"Oh, sure, we can keep in touch. But if you're talking about a relationship, that's not so simple. Maybe we're just kidding ourselves. Tomorrow I'm going home to my career in New York and you'll still be here with yours. How's that going to work?"

"I'm prepared to do whatever it takes."

"That wouldn't include a relocation to New York, would it?" *You could live with me,* she was thinking. Fantasizing, rather.

He looked stricken at the idea.

"No, I didn't think so. Not unless you could bring your entire congregation, right?" Marcella grinned, giving him the cue to relax. She understood how deeply he was rooted here. People depended on him. His church, this little village, a homey cottage, they all defined the Honorable Will.

It would be so simple if she could just pack him in her suitcase, smuggle him home, then carry him around all day in a PuchiBag like Sallie did with her teacup poodle.

"But you," he ventured. "Perhaps you could . . ."

He trailed off at the appalled look on her face.

"What? I could . . . what? Move here? And what sort of employment would an urban girly girl like myself find in

Bramble Moor? Um, you're not suggesting I pin a scarlet letter to my chest and shack up with the local vicar?"

"The cheek," he lamented. "Er, no. I wasn't, actually."

She did have her pride. Marcella considered herself more secure in her role as a single, professional woman than to change citizenship for the opportunity of dating someone. Manhattan, after all, was swarming with available men. Granted, it was nearly impossible to find love. But a date? A date was feasible. If she had the time, energy, or, for that matter, level of desire she felt with William.

But all was not lost. She sensed the wheels turning in his head.

"Right, well, I, on the other hand, I could perhaps ask the bishop to send me a curate. Yes, with a bit of training, a curate could share in the responsibilities. Then I'd be free to take a mini-break every now and then, what d'you think? I could come to New York."

"Well . . . yeah!" she rejoiced, thrilled he'd actually hit on something that offered them hope. "It's a start. It's a great start. Okay, so, let's enjoy the day and take it from there."

"Come, walk in the garden with me."

He was halfway to offering her his hand when suddenly there came a distant look in his eyes.

"Be back in a flash," he said before disappearing into the house.

Moments later Marcella heard him call out her name. She spied him through the screen door with a wine glass in each hand and a bowl of strawberries cradled against his chest.

She pulled a how-sweet-are-you face and walked over to swing open the door. "Are we going on a picnic?"

"Er, would you mind?" He indicated the berries with a nod.

"Oh sure." She grabbed for the bowl and he stepped out to

join her on the terrace, making a beeline for a wall of clipped boxwoods.

"Right, just this way," he said.

Her curiosity piqued, Marcella followed him behind the hedgerow where a garden walkway lay hidden from view. It took her aback, the sight was so beautiful. Flowering plants bordered either side of a lush carpet of grass in a progression of color. Blue yielded to gray-blue then lavender then faded to pale pinks and finally off-white blooms. And there, waiting for them at the end of this grassy aisle was a white-painted wooden lawn bench for two.

A strikingly modern focal point in such an old fashioned, tousled garden. Its high back was made of wavy, horizontal slats that gave the illusion the loveseat was swaying with the breeze.

"William, you dawg! Your mom was right. Aren't you the accomplished gardener? I've never seen anything so romantic."

Babette lay sprawled across the seat. William gestured for her to get down. "Babes and I spend quite a bit of time here, you see. I'm usually reading, writing sermons, sometimes just sitting. I don't recall ever feeling particularly romantic. But mind, a young couple from my parish did request to take their vows here recently. So perhaps you have something there, Marcella." Turning, he smiled into her eyes. "Perhaps it is rather romantic. Shall we have a seat and give it a go?"

Inside, she felt a fizz of excitement. Who was he kidding? He had this all planned. "Yes, let's."

She didn't hesitate to be seated even though Marcella knew she'd now be adding dog hairs to the collection of smudges and stains defacing her once-chic, summer-white booty. She balanced the bowl of berries on the armrest and accepted a glass of wine from William.

He folded himself into the seat beside her, relaxed back with a sigh, and swung an arm around her shoulders. His legs fell open. The denseness of his quads pressed against her slim thigh.

Behind them, the flowers faded into the forest. A whiff of honeysuckle scented the air.

Marcella plucked up a strawberry, dipped it in her wine, and fed it to William.

"Did you grow up in a mansion?" The question had just popped into her head. She wanted to know everything about him. It was a start.

He glanced at her quizzically, then admitted, "Well . . . um, yeah . . . the manor house where my parents still reside," he mumbled between chews.

"What was, um, is it like?" She watched him lick the wine-berry juice from his lips.

After a thoughtful pause, he made a frown of distaste. "Drafty." He was looking out across the garden and there was laughter in his eyes.

"Funny, you don't look like a man who's survived the trauma of childhood drafts."

He turned into her gaze. "I'll take you there sometime, if you don't believe me. The formal dining room still has no electric lighting."

Marcella wondered if that day would actually come. "And so how did you guys see what you were eating? Or was that the whole point."

He laughed. "Mum prefers to make do with a roaring fire and candlelight."

"Hmm, sounds wonderful."

"Oh, it is. Until the drafts snuff out the candles."

She gave him a playful slap on the forearm. "Seriously, I know people in New York who've built careers around buying and maintaining a country home. They slave to afford one, then either put up with the commute or spend their weeknights in the City away from their families, all for the pleasure of enjoying a peaceful environment on the weekends. But for you, this is your everyday life."

"That's true. I am fortunate, absolutely. But in all fairness, it was a bit difficult getting used to all the peacefulness. Too bloody quiet. Too far away from my mates. I arrived here and nearly everyone my own age was married, busy starting families. I was mad with loneliness." He reached down to where his dog lay at his feet and scratched her behind the ears. "Dunno how I'd have survived without Babes."

"But then the ladies of my parish started welcoming me with cottage pies and toffee tarts." He reclined back with a sigh. "As time went on, I began to value the time I had to focus on people, rather than having to rush from one appointment to the next. And the countryside does have its own way of embracing you. I mean, there's the sunsets and starry nights and changing seasons. And, of course, my gardens. I don't believe I've ever felt more at home anywhere."

Whoever said nice guys weren't hot? Suddenly, Marcella didn't feel like talking anymore. It was all she could do not to crawl into his lap.

She could feel the heat rising off her body and snuggled closer. "So, you say you enjoy 'reading' out here?"

He stared. Puzzled at the suggestiveness in her tone, she assumed. Then, all at once, Marcella saw his eyes widen with understanding.

"Oh, I do. You, er, did remember to bookmark our page?"

She answered with a nod, closing her eyes as he lowered his mouth to hers for a long, deep kiss.

He pulled away slowly, tugging on her bottom lip. "Was that where we left off, d'you s'pose?" His voice had dropped to a hoarse whisper.

"Uh-huh," Marcella managed before their mouths collided again. Endorphins released in her brain, sending feel-good signals all through her system.

They did nothing but kiss. Literally, nothing but kiss. No groping, grabbing, or pulling of clothing. Nothing but express their passion with mouths and tongues. Their kisses were everything, not just a prelude on the way to sex. It was the sex. And it was the most arousing experience of Marcella's sensual life. Small talk would've been an unnecessary interruption. Their lips said everything that needed to be said.

Marcella remained just barely unaware of time passing. Or later, the darkening sky. Or even the cool raindrops when they began to splatter on their warmed skin, until it was too late and they were caught in a downpour.

They hurried inside, and after drying off, Marcella prepared the appetizers and the pasta primavera, which they ate in the tiny dining room to the sound of rain pattering above. Later, they had coffee in the parlor and made out on the squashy sofa.

It was rather late by the time William got Marcella back to her hotel. Much too late to pop in for one final drink and a bit more time with her. Just as well, he supposed. She needed to get up first thing to catch her flight.

Rather than drop her at the door, he parked the seniors' minibus in the visitors' area and escorted her through the car park to the inn's entrance. Lanterns bathed their faces in golden light, which might have been quite romantic if not for a mosquito buzzing round his head.

He reached for her hand and gazed into her lovely, exotic face, swallowing back the lump in his throat. No putting it off any longer.

"We'll have to say our goodbyes here," he said. "I've an early funeral in the morning. Marcella, I'm really, really sorry I won't be able to see you off at the airport, but there's absolutely no way I can get out of it, you understand."

She seemed to understand perfectly. She seemed fine with it. He, on the other hand, was devastated. He wondered what she was thinking. He couldn't say, but he was fairly certain his own overly earnest stare was quite transparent. It was all he could do not to plead, *You won't forget me?*

He wouldn't forget *her.* First chance he got, he'd make a call to the bishop and ask to be assigned a curate. Surely, Bishop Laughton would understand how busy things were at St. Francis. And he'd be pleased to learn William had met a woman he'd taken serious interest in. 'Course, Bishop Laughton might not see the urgency in that, but then William didn't intend to mention the lady in question was from another country, much less another faith.

So this was it, then? Ms. Marcella Tartaglia had gotten what she needed for her magazine and was taking her cheeky wit and fabulous breasts back to New York. Blimey, he should have made love to her when he had the chance. Bertie's condom. Yes, she still had Bertie's purple condom. Perhaps he could—No, he couldn't. Bloody hell, what had come over him?

Focus, Will, focus.

At this very moment, dearly departed Mrs. Barker was resting in her coffin awaiting burial, and her family was depending on him to be on form. They'd need to lean on him for strength during their time of grief, even if the poor duck had been ninety-eight when she'd passed on, God bless her soul.

Already it was becoming sadly apparent that trying to build a relationship around his and Marcella's careers was going to prove quite the challenge.

Marcella returned to a darkened suite. A soft light shone from her room to illuminate her way, and as she tiptoed past Sallie's door, she saw her friend was fast asleep. Sallie lay on her side, cheek to pillow, long silky hair splayed across her face and over the edge of the mattress.

Marcella slipped quietly into her own room, her body a buzz of unreleased sexual energy, too wired to sleep. Her mind raced through the last two days, scrambling to preserve every moment with William in her memory. Who knew when she'd see him again.

She flopped onto the bed, leaning back into something that crumpled beneath her weight. Startled, she reached behind and pulled out a Harvey Nichols shopping bag. Harvey Nichols? *Harvey Nichols!* No. Had Sallie bought her a present during her shopping spree? Marcella dug inside, peeling back layers of tissue paper to expose a black satin evening purse covered in pink velvet roses.

She hooked a finger beneath its skinny strap and lifted out the bag, totally mesmerized. *Love it,* her fashion sense sang. *Love, love.* Inside, Marcella found more tissue paper and unwrapped a beautiful silk orchid hair clip embellished with Swarovski crystals.

And here she'd thought she'd have to go to bed alone.

Already, Marcella could feel herself begin to wind down. She got undressed and ready for bed, but when she slipped between the sheets, thoughts of William returned. As much as she loved the accessories, and she did love them, she couldn't help but wish she were spending the night with him. A fling might be just the thing to still this adrenaline rush through her system and set her head straight. But no, that only worked for men, didn't it?

Was this the force that drove Lynne Graham to leave New York and abandon her coveted senior editor position at *Gracious Living? Awesome.*

Suddenly, Marcella realized she hadn't opened her organizer since early Saturday, and that was only to jot down pertinent William facts. The concept was mind-blowing.

She thought of him for hours. Eventually, she did drift off, but come morning, Marcella awoke feeling groggy from lack of sleep. Inside, a battle of conflicting emotions raged. She felt excited about returning to work. She was looking forward to a bath in her own tub. But seriously bummed to be leaving. And, as a result, was left with little energy or desire to glam up her appearance.

She threw on a pair of skinny-legged crop pants and some round toe flats. Her dark Jackie-O sunglasses and a little lip gloss was all she needed to slip quietly out of the country. Really, what did it matter? No one ever looked their best on a return international flight.

Except for Sallie.

Marcella did a double take. Her friend was styling in a new look. Close-cut, knee-length, white silk shorts with a clingy beige tee and an ivory soft-shouldered jacket. Sallie's hair was pulled severely back from her clean-fresh face. The picture of chic. On her feet, Sallie wore a pair of pointy-toed mules with a kitten heel. Marcella had never seen her in anything other than Birkenstocks.

"Emma?" Marcella ventured.

With a nod, Sallie raved of Emma's style-guru coolness.

Feeling like a frump beside her, Marcella followed Sallie out of their suite and through the motions of checking out. Together they met their cab outside the inn.

Marcella handed the taxi driver her makeup case, the contents of which had gone untouched, as he began to load the trunk. She hoped to get to the airport and on the plane before anyone saw her.

"Okay, am I hallucinating or is that a hearse?"

Hearse? Did Sallie say a hearse? With a baffled shake of her head, Marcella went back to counting her suitcases. One large rolling case, garment bag, a carry-on . . .

"It is, Marcella, look! It's a hearse. Why would a funeral procession be passing through the parking lot of our hotel?"

This time, the significance behind Sallie's words clicked. Marcella's head shot up. Her heart felt suddenly lighter.

Sure enough, a hearse was rolling down the drive, but it didn't appear to be just passing through. No, it was headed straight for the hotel. A cavalcade of other vehicles followed, so slowly Marcella could hear the gravel crunch beneath their tires.

She whipped off her sunglasses. "Oh my God, Sallie, how do I look? Am I pale? Dammit, why didn't I at least use some blusher?" Marcella shook out her hair, threw back her shoulders and tugged her camisole a little lower on her bustline.

Sallie studied her with a suspicious grin. "What's going on?"

Marcella didn't dare jinx the moment by voicing an explanation, lest this didn't turn out to be what . . . or rather who, she hoped. Still, it was all she could do not to click her heels with joy as she watched the hearse and its motorcade crawl closer. The procession filed past their taxi and lined up along the front of the hotel. As the hearse eased to a stop, a black limousine broke behind it, followed by each successive car in turn.

There must have been at least thirty vehicles idling in the drive, blocking her taxi's exit. And was it her imagination, or did every face inside the cars seem to be gawking?

The taxi driver threw up his arms and swore in a language Marcella didn't recognize.

A door to the limo opened. Someone was stepping out. Marcella saw a black shoe, the hem of a black pants' leg. A tall figure began to unfold from the limousine, and a young, handsome, chestnut-haired vicar holding a long-stemmed red rose emerged.

Yeah!

Marcella beamed as he hurried towards her.

"I don't believe you," she squealed at his approach. "I have no idea how you pulled this off, but I'm happy you're here."

"Minor detour. When she was alive, Mrs. B. loved a good drive through the country. I suggested we might take her for one last spin past Blenheim Palace, and seeing as we were just across the street . . ." He trailed off with a shrug, looking boyishly pleased with himself. "Can't stay long, obviously." He offered her the rose.

Marcella accepted and smiled into the bloom as she inhaled its fragrance.

"Eeeow," Sallie squawked. "Marcella, you do realize that probably came off a funeral arrangement?"

William turned, his eyes widening as though noticing Sallie for the first time. "Sallie . . . oh! Look at you." He gave her a quick once-over, obviously pleased at what he saw. "Enjoyed your shopping, I see. You look fantastic."

"Thank you." Sallie shot him a sidelong grin as though affectionately to impart the opinion she thought him a little nuts.

William seemed to embrace that opinion with his smile. "Well, ladies, Godspeed. Have a safe trip home."

Sallie stepped forward and kissed him on the cheek.

A horn honked. William turned and signaled he was on his way. "Duty calls. It's off to the crematorium."

He winked at Sallie, then stepped up to Marcella and took her hand. "Goodbye, Marcella."

She felt her throat tighten. "See ya."

He leaned in for a kiss. Marcella clung to his lips in a long, bittersweet kiss. As they slowly parted, William gazed into her eyes, nuzzled the tip of her nose, and whispered, "Don't forget me." Then he released her and turned to walk away.

Her heart was breaking. Just as well she hadn't bothered with makeup. It'd only be running down her face now if she had. Marcella watched as William slipped back into the limo, surprised at how much it hurt to see him go. The passengers in those cars weren't the only ones grieving.

She'd come to England for business and to attend a wedding. She had never expected this. Love at first sight. With a goodbye in the midst of a funeral procession.

Chapter 12

"I'm going to be honest with you, Marcella. Word's out there's a senior editor post available here at *Gracious Living,* and every self-proclaimed domestic arts goddess from coast to coast with an ounce of ambition and a scrap of publishing experience has expressed an interest. Now, don't let on I've told you—it's supposed to be strictly confidential—but I've recently learned . . ."

Gracious Living's Editor-in-Chief, Catherine Klein, leaned over her Day-Timer, layout pages, samples, photographs, and all the other paperwork cluttering her large cherry desk and continued in a secretive tone, "Beth Anne had lunch with Jillian Navarro at the Four Seasons last week. Beth Anne has expressed some concern at your being so young, and, apparently, Jillian's looking to leave *Country Home and Gardens.*"

Okay, not good. Marcella felt a queasy lurch in the pit of her stomach. Beth Anne Copeland was *Gracious Living*'s Publisher. Was she seriously considering Jillian Navarro for Senior Decorating and Entertainment Editor? *Okay, really not good.* Jillian Navarro, with her faux French accent? *Please.* Sallie was more convincing speaking French to her dog. Jillian, with her condescending smile and tough-as-nails management style?

Marcella didn't think she could bear the nightmare of losing this promotion to Jillian Navarro and then being forced to work under the Valkyrie. It was all she could do to remain seated in the cream-upholstered, cherry side chair opposite Catherine's desk. She wanted to jump up and protest. *Oh no, this can't be.*

Beth Anne's making a terrible mistake. But, being a professional, she kept her expression impassive.

Midwesterner Jillian had studied at the American University of Paris and had ten years experience over Marcella, but did she possess the passion, the ingenuity, the design skills Marcella did?

Well, likely she did, or she wouldn't be where she was today. Ah, but perhaps her ambition exceeded her talent. And how did Catherine feel about all this? That's what Marcella needed to know. Surely, Catherine didn't believe Jillian could do a better job.

Marcella inclined her head as though she found the news mildly disconcerting. "Catherine, I—"

Catherine raised a hand to silence her. "Since learning of this private luncheon, I've sat down with Beth Anne, and despite Jillian's obvious experience, we both agree. She is not our first choice. You are, Marcella."

As the reality behind Catherine's words seeped into her consciousness, Marcella broke into a beaming, giddy grin.

Catherine had come through for her.

Marcella shrugged humbly. "Thank you, Catherine. As you can see, I'm thrilled. It means a lot to know that you believe in me."

Catherine looked pleased with her reaction. "We certainly do. I speak for the entire executive board when I say you've shown remarkable talent for articulating *Gracious Living*'s editorial message. No other candidate embraces the magazine's mission through her personality and her work quite like you. You have a skill for mastering new subject areas quickly and you always ask the right questions."

Marcella savored the moment. She was floating. She could have, in fact, floated right through Catherine's office windows overlooking a north view of the Manhattan skyline and walked on air sixteen floors above West 57th Street below.

Instead, she pulled herself from the clouds and kept her focus inside the room. Catherine's office featured a suite of furniture which would have just as easily complimented the parlor of a restored nineteenth-century Connecticut colonial.

Who knew? Marcella thought. At this rate, maybe someday this office would be hers.

She swelled with pride. "Thank you, Catherine."

Excitement sparked in Catherine's eyes as she sat on the edge of her seat. "Starting with the next issue, your name will appear as 'Marcella Tartaglia, Acting Senior Editor, Decorating and Entertainment.' "

Marcella was all ready to squeal with delight when a warning flashed in her brain and she realized what Catherine had said.

"Excuse me, Catherine, but I don't understand. Why *Acting* Senior Editor?"

Catherine gave a knowing smile, leaning back with a composure that reflected none of Marcella's concern. "Rest assured, I believe in your talent one hundred percent. Think of this trial period as a courtesy to Beth Anne. Give it, say, three months, and I'm confident by then Beth Anne will be satisfied with your ability to handle the responsibilities of the position, and the title will become permanent. Just continue to deliver the same excellence and quality of work you're famous for, Marcella, and the job will be yours."

Marcella was halfway to a smile, still digesting this bittersweet twist to her professional victory, when Catherine moved on with business.

"As of today, I want you in the boardroom with my other senior staffers for this issue's show meeting. And, of course, you'll need to save room in your calendar to meet with me one-on-one on a weekly basis. Now, have a look at this. Or better yet—taste."

Catherine pulled a decorative oval tin towards her and removed the lid. It reminded Marcella of a small Victorian hatbox. Velvet ribbons draped down the sides, left to hang untied.

The heavy scent of brandy wafted through the air as Catherine reached inside to remove a thick slice of . . . uh, something dark. No, it was fruitcake. She placed the fruitcake on a delicate Victoriana napkin and extended it across her desk to Marcella.

Marcella tucked her organizer under one arm and rose, stepping forward to accept the slice. From the moment Catherine dropped the fruitcake in her palm, Marcella could feel its moisture absorbing through the napkin.

She resumed her seat, staring at the fruit-and-nut laden slice. Catherine gestured for her to go ahead, and without breaking eye contact, Marcella bit into the wet cake. Between bites of soft, chewy cake, she crunched walnuts, chewed rich cherries, and rolled a lovely flavor around her tongue . . . sherry, oh! Enjoyable.

At her growing smile, Catherine commented, "Isn't it marvelous?"

Marcella's brows shot up in pleasant surprise. "Delish. I never knew fruitcake could be like this. My grandmother's was always kind of dry. This is decadent."

Catherine nodded her agreement. "It's baked by a company called Victoria Reed Cakes. Pippa Carlisle is a young British entrepreneur who has started a mail-order business based on the old English cake recipes passed down to her from her great-great grandmother, Victoria Reed. The company is founded on the traditions of Grandmother Reed, once a young serving girl who worked in London. Every year, for instance, she would bake her Victorian fruitcake and carry it home to her mother on Mothering Sunday. Or what we Americans prefer to call Mother's Day."

"Mmmm," Marcella mumbled while nodding her interest

and swallowing a second mouthful of cake.

"The company operates from a bakery in Gloucestershire."

"That's in the northern area of the Cotswolds, isn't it?"

"I believe so." Catherine passed her an order catalog. "It's all in here. The handmade cakes are packaged in attractive boxes, stylized for different occasions. They also fill orders for Marks and Spencer stores."

"Wow, that's impressive." Marcella lay aside what remained of her fruitcake and began to browse the brochure. She read that Pippa Carlisle ran her bakery from the village of Mickleton in Chipping Campden, Gloucestershire. That was . . . what? A half hour from Oxford? She wasn't certain, but it was close enough.

"The thing is, Marcella, *Gracious Living* needs to expand with more European articles, and our readers are especially curious about England. I'm very pleased with your coverage of Lynne's wedding, and as a result, we plan on sending more editors to the U.K. to cover stories, starting with this one. I'd like you to send an editor and a photographer to Gloucestershire A.S.A.P. Maybe we can make the Christmas issue. We'll do a four-page spread. Five hundred words. I wouldn't be surprised if our coverage generated American orders for Victoria Reed Cakes. I know I wouldn't be disappointed getting one of these delicious little treasures in the mail for Christmas."

Marcella was so excited she could hardly contain herself. Her mind worked furiously, but it wasn't a magazine article she envisioned. She never dreamed she'd be able to get back to William this soon. It was almost too good to be true.

"Catherine, why have me send anyone else? This story is perfect for me. I'd love to cover it myself. Plus, I'm already familiar with the area."

Catherine's smile grew. "I admire your dedication, Marcella. And I agree, you could do wonders with this story. I'd gladly assign it to you, but as Senior Editor you have more pressing responsibilities here. I'm afraid that means no traveling for a while. You're going to have your hands full pulling together our Christmas issue. Decorating and Entertainment will dominate the pages. This is your chance to prove yourself to Beth Anne, once and for all. Give us a spectacular holiday entertaining section, and Beth Anne won't be able to raise a single objection to making your title permanent. Now, open your organizer, go pour yourself a cup of coffee, and let's schedule some meetings. Oh, and there's a press launch I'd like you to attend."

Marcella obediently unzipped her organizer. As she turned to next week's calendar, she couldn't help but ask herself, what had she gained from this meeting? Well, for one thing, she'd gained the responsibility of a Senior Editor without any of the glory. And if she hadn't gotten "promoted," she'd now be free to accept Catherine's fruitcake assignment and fly back to England for a reunion with William.

But what was she thinking? She should be excited. This was cause for celebration. She was one step closer to her dream job. Senior Editor. Exactly what she'd always wanted, and today she'd climbed another rung up the ladder.

And slipped into a nonexistent social life.

How would William take the news? she wondered. Maybe it'd be wise not to mention this whole fruitcake scenario. She'd only been back in Manhattan a week, and already romance didn't seem to be in their stars. This was just the sort of complication that made balancing a career and a relationship damn near impossible.

Later that same day, Marcella gathered with a group of kitchen associates, assistants, and interns in the magazine's test kitchen to sample a batch of sticky toffee buns, warm from the oven, the recipe of which was to accompany an article on hosting an old-fashioned Southern tea. As usual, she expected every detail to shine.

M'Liss, as the test kitchen's director preferred to be called over her simple birth name of Melissa, served.

They look yummy, Marcella thought, thrilled with their presentation. She began envisioning the table setting she'd use to style the photo shoot. Something outdoors perhaps. Lots of white lace. Flowers.

She pulled out a tissue and wiped off her lip gloss so it wouldn't interfere with the flavor before biting into the soft, gooey bun, chewing slowly, tasting, tasting . . .

Mmm . . . yes! Rich, buttery, not too sweet. She listened to the buzz. Everyone agreed. They were scrumptious.

Ryan Patterson from Marketing double-dipped his roll in the baking pan, scraping up the last of the caramel sauce. "Awesome," he agreed.

Marcella reserved comment. Part of her job was to spot opportunities for improvement, and it would take more than kudos from Ryan Patterson to satisfy her discerning palate.

He hadn't even been invited. She'd bumped into Ryan in the hallway, and as she opened the door to enter the kitchen, he caught a whiff of the fresh-baked toffee buns and followed her inside. "I had to work through lunch," he'd said. "Think you can hook me up?"

Marcella couldn't quite wrap her taste buds around the problem, but she sensed something lacking. She sampled another bite, then suddenly she knew. "I think they could use a teensy bit of mace," she suggested.

Everyone stopped in mid-chew to gape.

"I disagree."

This came from M'Liss in her denim chef's coat and zebra-print skull cap. "I feel the recipe is perfect, as is."

Marcella didn't need a magnifying glass to see that M'Liss

thought she was being obsessive. *Whatever.* Marcella just hoped she wasn't going to get attitude over this. She didn't enjoy challenging the test kitchen's expertise. Their job involved more than testing recipes. They prepared some of the most excellent meals in the City for guests and special functions, served on china with crystal place settings in *Gracious Living*'s private dining room.

They knew their stuff, but any lack of perfection when the article went to print would ultimately reflect on the Food and Entertainment Department. And as Senior Editor, Marcella now had her ass on the line. She wasn't about to bite her tongue only to have some reader write in later and complain. No way would she allow even the minutest detail to slide if it meant jeopardizing her new status over something as minor as toffee sticky buns.

The more she thought about it, the firmer her resolve grew. "No, I'm sorry, M'Liss. I can't print this recipe when I'm not satisfied. Try them again with a quarter teaspoon of mace."

"Smart thinking, Tart," Ryan said. "Hey, would somebody mind buzzing me when the next batch is ready?"

M'Liss opened her mouth, but any snappy retort she had ready was intercepted by the opening of the door and the sound of a disturbance from without.

"Wait, please . . . hey! You really shouldn't be bringing a dog into the kitchen. It's not sanitary!"

There was desperation in the voice, which Marcella recognized as Lauren's from Reception. Everyone turned as Sallie breezed into the kitchen, shaking her head and muttering unappreciatively, "Since when did this establishment turn canine non grata?"

The door sealed shut behind her with a slam and no sign of Lauren, a conscientious Arizona native and relatively new employee, whom Marcella imagined still out in the hallway, fretting.

Flipping back her long honey-brown hair, Sallie resumed a pleasant expression and continued past the stainless steel refrigerators towards the group. "Hi guys, I was told I could find Marcella Tartag—"

"Over here, Sal." Marcella stepped out from behind Ryan to wave her over. "Come join us."

"What is Lauren's problem?" Ryan whispered to Marcella as his gaze combed Sallie's silk shantung A-line skirt with matching turquoise camisole and the glimpse of bare midriff that shown between. "She's no dog."

Choking back impatience, Marcella gestured to the fashion tote hanging by Sallie's side, a swirled vintage design of pink, brown, avocado, and red with silver hardware. The head of a tiny black poodle poked out an opening in the front, sniffing the air with increasing interest.

Ryan's eyes widened. "Is it real?"

"No, it's a bobble head. Everyone, I believe you all know Sallie. All except for Ryan. Sallie, this is Ryan Patterson. Ryan, meet Sallie Madigan. Oh, and that's Henri."

Henri sized up the group with intelligent, black obsidian eyes, his nose a shiny black gumdrop. He was immaculately groomed, with a smooth muzzle, long curly ears, and a topknot slightly larger than a cotton puff. He wore a Louis Vuitton collar from which dangled an eighteen-carat, engraved i.d. tag that read, "Scratch my butt."

Manhattan was a mecca of modern dog culture. The teacup craze especially had developed into something of a phenomenon, of strong women and their obsession with itsy-bitsy, needy bundles of fur, that unlike their boyfriends, they could lavish with love and attention twenty-four/seven and never fear rejection. And the most amazing part: Dogs were always up, always appreciative, and seemed completely incapable of showing indifference to someone they loved. A girl's fantasy.

And just one more relationship out of my reach, Marcella regretted as she forgot for a moment that Henri wasn't human. She watched the kitchen staff cluster around, talking baby talk, begging to hold him, and suffered a pang of envy before snapping back to sanity.

Sallie looked to the last traces of caramel sauce inside the empty bake pan. "Looks like I got here too late. What'd I miss?"

"You didn't miss anything," Ryan told her. "They needed a touch of mace anyway."

M'Liss turned on him, eyes narrowed. "Why are you still here?"

Marcella offered Sallie what remained of her roll. "Toffee sticky buns. Here, you're welcome to the rest of mine."

"Gee, a half-eaten roll," she said. "Thanks."

But as Marcella anticipated, the warm toffee smell was irresistible. Sallie snatched up the bun.

"I have something for you, too," Sallie said. She removed a small portfolio from the side pocket of Henri's carrier and handed it to Marcella.

"What's this?"

"Photos."

Marcella realized what they were immediately, and while Sallie shared her sticky bun with Henri, Marcella tucked the package beneath her arm and moved to the sink to wash her hands.

The kitchen staff got back to work, mixing up another batch of buns. Ryan gave Sallie one final ogle and excused himself to return to his office.

As Marcella dried her hands, she debated whether she should save the package for later when she could enjoy them in private. But already the suspense was driving her crazy, and she opened the portfolio, anxious for a peek.

Out slid a neat stack of eight-by-ten glossies, and there, right on top, the most perfect candid shot of William standing by his motorcycle with mussed hair, unsuspectingly tucking in his shirt when he thought no one was around.

Marcella recalled the moment with a smile, the first time she'd ever lain eyes on him. She switched to a second photo, this one of William shrugging into his frock coat. Then, William tying his cravat. William donning a pair of white gloves, the quintessential English gentleman in full morning dress.

Next was a close-up in which Sallie had captured William's earnest expression as he set his top hat to just the right angle. Over a week had passed since then. She traced his lips with a fingertip and longing swelled up inside until she felt the pain of missing William prick her behind the eyes.

"Who's the hottie?"

Marcella returned from her sentimental journey with a start.

Bree, another test kitchen associate, stood gawking over her shoulder. "Sexy costume. Is he like an actor or something?"

Others had begun to drift over, curious to see what the fuss was about, and before Marcella realized her intentions, Bree plucked another photograph from the back of the pile, holding it up for all to see.

"Look everyone, here he is cast in the role of a priest."

When had Sallie shot that? Marcella turned for a look at it herself, when M'Liss snatched away the remaining photos.

As images of William were shared around the room, Marcella felt a private part of her heart being violated.

M'Liss's curiosity turned into a sly smile the longer she browsed the photos. "Those eyes could melt your heart, but I seriously doubt he's an actor, Bree," she said. "Not unless Marcella has been moonlighting as his leading lady."

She raised a brow inquiringly. "You're in nearly every photo together, Marcella. So who is he? Does your hottie have a name?"

"Yeah," Marcella snapped. She was about to declare, *He's not my hottie!* when she caught herself. God forbid she give anyone the impression William was available.

"Yes, he has a name," she repeated, not sure why she was feeling so defensive. "He's the Honorable William John Anthony Grafton Stafford, third son of Lord Wiltshire, the Eighteenth Viscount of Wiltshire."

She had it memorized from her notes. "And you're absolutely right, M'Liss. He's not an actor. He's a vicar."

Eyes widened with intrigue and a collective "aah" filled the room. Marcella quickly plucked her photos from the sticky fingers of the kitchen staff and returned them to the portfolio. "Actually, these are pictures of Lynne's wedding."

"Really? I didn't notice Lynne in any of the photographs," M'Liss said dryly.

Marcella could think of no comment to prevent William's launch into the latest round of office gossip. It was already too late for damage control.

Averting her gaze, she made to leave. "If you'll excuse me, I need to take these to my office. Coming, Sal?"

On her way out, Marcella felt M'Liss's stare burn her back. She knew what M'Liss and the others were thinking. Lynne, as *Gracious Living*'s Senior Decorating and Entertainment Editor, had become involved with an English vicar. Here was Marcella, acting in the capacity of Lynne's replacement, her first morning on the job, and she'd literally stepped into the woman's persona, both professionally and socially, with a vicar of her own.

I am *not* Lynne Graham, Marcella chanted silently as she slipped from the kitchen. She had nothing in common with Lynne. Okay, so it was no secret she aspired to Lynne's title, but she was completely secure in her own identity. She was certainly not out to clone the woman's life. *Please.*

And just because she hadn't revealed them to the kitchen staff, didn't mean her feelings for William weren't genuine and unique and totally sincere. Although, to any outside observer, this would appear a bizarre case of déjà vu, wouldn't it?

"Mind telling me what that was about?" Sallie demanded as they walked the corridors. "And why're you suddenly so quiet? You're starting to freak me out."

Marcella waited until they were inside her office with the door closed before sharing the news of her promotion and its trial terms.

Sallie shone with excitement. "That is so cool. Congratulations." She jumped from her seat to give Marcella a hug.

"I'm really happy for you," she said, then pulled back, obviously sensing Marcella was not sharing her enthusiasm.

"This is good. Right?" Sallie searched her face. "But you're not excited. What am I missing?"

"I am excited; I am. I'm just not feeling the level of excitement I'd anticipated, that's all. And with good reason. This promotion is not official. I'm Acting Senior Editor. Acting. Believe me, there's plenty of anxiety to deal with in that respect, although I've been assured the job will be mine. And I was hoping I'd be able to arrange my schedule so I could visit William."

"Ah," Sallie said, nodding understanding. Without further comment, she lifted Henri from his carrier and set him loose on the floor.

Marcella meanwhile pulled out the photographs and began arranging them in a display across the top of her desk. "The way my future looks now, even if William lived right here in Manhattan, I still wouldn't have much time for him. I've worked my entire career for this opportunity—I'd be crazy not to give this shot at Senior Editor everything I've got. Oh, speaking of shots, these photos are really fantastic, Sal."

When Marcella first returned to Manhattan, she had wondered whether the City and her work would consume her, causing her time in the Cotswolds to somehow fade. Instead, she felt restless and out of place. William and his life had made an indelible impression on her.

She didn't know how many seconds had passed before she realized she was lost in a photo of William toasting the bride and groom.

Sallie sat on the opposite side of the desk, saying nothing.

Marcella caught herself and apologized to her friend, then said, "Say, you never told me what you and Emma dished about over tea at the Savoy. Did Emma have anything interesting to say?"

Sallie nodded impassively. "She told me a little about herself and William."

"And!?"

"And . . . FYI, Emma, it seems, comes from a strict, religious family. Very active in the church. She told me her childhood is filled with memories of practicing the church organ. So, one Sunday William shows up. The most beautiful boy she's ever seen. He's slouched in the pew, lots of attitude. Clearly, he didn't want to be there, which, of course, made him all the more intriguing to Emma. Her stares didn't go unnoticed, because after service when everyone else was headed out the door, William pushed his way through the congregation to the front of the church. They talked, started dating, and were pretty into each other. Emma said she thought she was losing her virginity to a bad boy, but he turned out to be an angel. As much as she cared for him, she didn't think she'd be happy as a vicar's wife. She said if you're half the domestic diva I claimed you were, you'd be lucky to spend your life with him."

Marcella absorbed this info in a state of numbness, not sure what she was feeling, or what she could do about her feelings even if she were to acknowledge them. "Why haven't you told me any of this before?"

"You never asked. Besides, what would have been the point. Like you said, you don't have time for him anyway, right?"

"Then why bring me these photos?"

Sallie rolled her eyes. "Shall I take them back? Maybe the girls in the kitchen would like to pin them on the recipe board."

Sallie was half off her seat, reaching for them, when Marcella splayed her arms across her desk and replied with an emphatic, "No!"

She took them home with her that night, only to toss them on the kitchen counter where they remained throughout the next week, because she was afraid if she opened Sallie's portfolio, she'd never be able to quit daydreaming.

Chapter 13

Several weeks later, at ten in the evening, about the time most New Yorkers were headed out to enjoy the City's night scene, Marcella returned to her apartment after a long day with nothing in her stomach but a sushi roll and three white chocolate martinis.

She switched on a light and kicked off her cotton-candy pink, pointy flats at the door. Dropping her organizer on the foyer table, she pressed a preset key on her cell and waited for the number to connect as she padded to the sofa.

She curled up against the cushions, bare feet tucked beneath her, and hugged the knees of her espresso skinny pants. By the fourth ring, the combo chocolate rush–vodka buzz was beginning to dull, and what moments ago seemed impulsively romantic was revealing itself to be nothing more than an act of neediness.

Needy? This was so not like her. She was so into maintaining a healthy sense of self and not depending on others for fulfillment. She had her career. Something she had reasonable control over. And hey, when had feeling in control ever been a bad thing? She'd learned to be cautious, as a child of divorce, and not rush into making emotional investments in the opposite sex. In other words, she didn't sit home waiting for the phone to ring.

She hardly ever stayed home. Just this evening, for instance, she'd been schmoozing with celebs and socialites and other members of the press at a media party to launch the opening of a hot new Manhattan lounge, co-owned by an ex–rock guitarist and an up-and-coming cookbook author.

She stayed busy and social and active. And if she did happen to have a little downtime, she switched on Oprah for some "spirit and self" empowerment. And okay, maybe also to check out the woman's jewelry. But generally speaking, Marcella followed the New Age teachings ascribed to a secure, single, professional woman for living her best life.

So like, where the hell had this neediness come from?

Suddenly, she felt ridiculous. She was halfway to pressing the End key, when a gruff, muffled greeting came through the earpiece.

"William, hi," she said, lifting the phone back to her ear. "I woke you, didn't I? The time difference, I totally forgot. It must be . . . um, three a.m. where you are. Ouch. I am so sorry."

"Marcella!? What's wrong? What's happened?"

His voice sounded thick and groggy. She envisioned him raised on one elbow, lids weighed down with sleep, chestnut hair mussed. She hadn't meant to alarm him, calling at this hour. They phoned each other regularly. At first they spoke every day, but lately, either she got busy with a project or William was tied up calling on a parishioner, and between the transcontinental time difference and their busy schedules, it was getting more and more difficult to make a connection.

"Nothing, nothing's happened. Everything's dandy. I just got in and thought I'd give you a ring," she confessed. "Bad idea. Stupid, I know, but I just wanted to hear your voice."

Oh God, had she actually said that?

Bad enough she felt needy. Did she have to verbalize it, too?

"You've just got in?" William sounded totally confused. "At three in the morning, you say?"

"This is the city that never sleeps. Ha-ha. No, seriously, it's only ten o'clock here."

"Ten, right," he repeated as though he were still trying to digest the whole phone call. "So where've you been off to, then, till ten in the morning?"

Rather than confuse him further, Marcella moved forward with a brief explanation of her work-related function, adding, "It's a chocolate-inspired cocktail lounge, appropriately called 'The Chocolate Bar.' Their motto is, 'Spend the night with us and we'll cover your cherry in chocolate.' "

"Is this a proper topic for a midnight call to a vicar, d'you s'pose?" He cleared his throat. "Okay, fully awake now. Er, . . . by cherry, they're referring to the kind you use to garnish a mixed drink?"

"Well, they wouldn't have much of a clientele if they were referring to any other."

"Yanks," he grumbled into the line. "You're all barking."

He followed with deep chuckles, which alone made the call worthwhile. Marcella giggled in response, feeling suddenly lighter, and asked, "So, how was your day?"

"My day? Bit premature to tell, but I must say, it's started off fantastically. It's good to hear your voice, too."

Marcella hugged her knees and smiled.

"Actually, I'm glad you called," he said. "I've some news. The bishop has agreed to consider my request for a curate."

"Great! So what happens now?"

"I wait to hear."

"How long do you think it will take?"

"Dunno. Few weeks, perhaps. I was going to ring you."

"It sounds encouraging," she chirped, although the thought did arise that now they'd have to wait on the bishop before they could even begin to plan when they'd see each other again.

"Hey, I'm gonna let you get back to sleep," she said. "We'll talk more later. I'm really happy about your news, William."

"I'll ring you," he assured.

Marcella tried to remain upbeat as they hung up.

She considered phoning Sallie, but Sallie worked full-time, plus she had a live-in boyfriend and a small dog, speaking of needy, who both demanded her attention. She didn't need to be dumped with Marcella's angst at this late hour.

Still, Marcella couldn't help but feel concern that, despite their best efforts to stay connected, hers and William's lives and careers would take them in different directions.

As the weeks passed, Marcella threw herself further into her work to avoid watching the calendar. The summer ebbed away, and still there'd been no official word on William's curate. She'd fallen for a great guy in an impossible situation and was feeling more lonely and vulnerable than she had in a long time, when one morning Ryan Patterson stopped by her office.

He sank into the rocking chair opposite her desk before Marcella had the chance to offer him a seat.

The creative atmosphere of the magazine invited individual expression in the offices of its staff. Marcella surrounded her environment with homey touches, like a hand-crocheted afghan draped over the back of a rocker. She often wondered whether it was her cozy decor, and not her personally, that drew Ryan to her door.

"So, how's it going, Tart?"

"Um . . . fine."

She didn't ask, and Ryan didn't offer to tell her, why he'd come. He just rocked in the chair wearing a smug expression.

Marcella didn't have time for games. In a few minutes, she was due in the Art Department to look over some photographs. With a shake of her head, she returned to the sample layout pages she'd been going over before Ryan arrived.

"You're probably wondering why I'm here."

Duh, Marcella thought.

"It's like this, Tart. I believe we're in a position to do each other a big favor."

She glanced up. Ryan grinned back, still rocking.

"Okay, how's this for a favor?" she offered. "You leave now, and I'll forget you interrupted my busy morning."

"Gotta love that sharp wit." He chuckled to himself as though he couldn't be more pleased with her sarcasm. "Jack likes a woman with a sense of humor."

"Jack?" she exploded. "Who's Jack?"

"See, I knew you'd be curious."

"The only thing I'm curious about is why the men in the white coats haven't come for you yet."

Ryan raised a hand to silence her protests, then leaned forward as though he were about to reveal some great secret. "Jack Linney," he said. "One of the most respected attorneys in Providence. Your hometown. He's a good friend of mine, and he happens to be in the City today. We'd planned to meet for lunch, but suddenly I've got this emergency Marketing meeting. Then I thought, hey, Jack isn't seeing anyone at the moment. Marcella's unattached. Who knows, they might hit it off? So, how 'bout it, Tart? Do me a favor and have lunch with my buddy, Jack? You can catch up on all the news from home."

A blind date? Was he kidding? Marcella didn't even attempt to hide her disgust.

"Yeah, all right, I know what you're thinking, but he's a great guy. Good-looking, clean-cut. Really. There's no way I'd set you up with some loser when I have to face you at the office every day."

"I appreciate that, Ryan, but I can't help you. I've got too much going on."

"Did I mention Jack works out? And he's tall." Ryan raised his brows in invitation. "Six-two."

He was trying to work her weakness for tall men to his advantage. You had to admire his persistence. "I wouldn't care if Jack had a giant beanstalk. I'm not interested."

"Whoa. Well, as a matter of fact—"

"Look, why me? Why not ask someone from Fashion? There's Roxanne. She just broke up with her latest boyfriend. Or, hey . . . how about Holly?"

Ryan shook his head. "I've kinda been working on Holly for myself. No, it has to be you. I can't think of a better match. C'mon, one hour, two at the max, and everyone's happy. Jack doesn't have to eat alone, and you get a glimpse of what it's like to have a social life."

"Oh, well, since you put it that way . . ." She tapped her pencil on the desk, thinking. "No!"

Ryan's amusement deflated.

"Okay, if you must know," she said. "I'm seeing someone."

He looked shell-shocked. "Since when? Why haven't you ever mentioned him before? Who is he?"

Marcella told him of how she met William at Lynne's wedding, giving Ryan as few details as possible and completely skimming over the whole vicar issue.

Ryan leaned back in the rocker and listened, elbows on the armrest. He'd gone uncharacteristically quiet.

"So, you're dating Lynne's nephew," he commented at length. "Some English dude. Couldn't find anyone local, huh? And here I thought Jack being from Providence might present a problem if you two decided you wanted to see each other again." He considered a moment, then nodded defeat. "Okay, so like, tell me, Busy Girl, how often do you have time to visit England?"

Marcella felt her defenses rise, knowing there was no way she could answer that question honestly and still expect Ryan to understand the unique connection she'd made with William during the short time they'd been together.

"I haven't had a chance to get away," she admitted. "I've got three major food stories in this issue alone, not to mention the holiday issues coming up. I've been in overdrive since taking over Lynne's responsibilities."

Marcella heard the whine in her voice and quieted.

Ryan studied her. "Oh . . . so, this boyfriend of yours flies to New York regularly? He must work for some sort of international corporation, then? How come I've never seen him around?"

Marcella looked down at her hands. "Unfortunately, William hasn't managed to get away either," she mumbled.

When Ryan didn't comment, she glanced up, only to find he had rebounded with a smirk.

"Lynne's wedding was three months ago. Are you telling me you guys haven't seen each other since?"

"Well," Marcella balked, but before she could think of anything to say in her defense, Ryan stood.

"Do I really need to state the obvious?" Rolling his eyes, he said, "Like, if the guy really cared for you, he'd make time. I know it's none of my business—"

"Took the words right out of my mouth."

"—but I really think you owe it to yourself to date someone in the same country, at least. I'm only talking lunch. And if for no other reason, go as a point of reference. For comparison. To be sure that what you think you have going with this guy is the real thing and not your way of coping with loneliness."

"I am not lonely, okay? I'm busy."

"Whatever. Did I mention Jack has reservations at Le Cirque."

Okay, now she was impressed. "Your friend got into Le Cirque?"

Ryan scoffed. "You didn't think I was talking a quickie hot dog on the corner, did you? I told you, I'm looking out for you. And here's something else to consider. As a potential senior staffer, you owe it to the magazine to be more social. When it comes time to naming Lynne's permanent replacement, you don't want Beth Anne thinking you're not accessible. Jillian Navarro has been known to lunch at Le Cirque."

Marcella narrowed her eyes. "Now you're fighting dirty."

"Yeah, but I do have a point."

He did have a point. At her hesitation, Ryan stepped in for the kill. "Think chocolate souffle."

Oh man. Marcella could almost taste the chocolate melting on her tongue.

Ryan laughed at her expression, and Marcella quickly composed her features before she began to drool.

"Look," he said, "I'll ring Jack right now and let him know you've only got an hour to spare. In one hour, if you're not having the time of your life, you return to the office, no excuses necessary."

Marcella found herself considering his offer. Blind date aside, this could be a good thing.

Lunch at Le Cirque. An opportunity for her to see and be seen in one of the City's most fashionable restaurants. No telling how many business and social luncheons of interest would be taking place all around her. She'd show *Gracious Living* she could network as well as Jillian Navarro. And the best part was, today more so than usual, she was dressed to make an impression, even if she was pushing autumn a bit in her new, fabulous tweed outfit.

God knew, she could use a break from the office. And meeting Ryan's friend really might help her figure out if William was "the one" or if she simply continued to care for him because it was easy. Not actually being together, they'd never faced the challenges of a normal relationship.

And William. How long before he got tired of waiting for her to free up her schedule? How long before another woman caught his eye? Even more likely, how long before he caught some deserving woman's eye and she pursued him?

He'd already been more than patient. He'd been an angel, but even once the bishop assigned William a curate, how often would he be able to travel to New York? Maybe a relationship between them was never meant to be. Maybe she needed to take a step towards moving on rather than hanging on.

"Oh, all right," she told Ryan. "I'll do it. I'll meet Jack for one hour, but I'm not sticking around for the chocolate souffle."

Ryan gave a whoop. "Deal."

Marcella arrived at the restaurant with a queasy stomach and the premonition she shouldn't have come.

Why not? the left side of her brain demanded. It was a good arrangement. Not so much a date as two people who needed to stretch their social skills with only an hour to spare. It was lunch, and then she was outta there.

With a deep breath, she turned her focus outward to Le Cirque's Renaissance decor as she followed the maitre d' into the main dining room. Carved, walnut paneling. Red and cream color scheme. If this were a date, she'd be impressed. And oh-my-gosh wasn't that Joan Rivers at the table they'd just passed?

If she only had time, she'd love to go over and tell Ms. Rivers she was wearing a Joan Rivers watch she'd purchased off the QVC shopping channel. But they were fast approaching a table for two where a dark-haired, impeccably dressed man in a navy pinstripe anxiously awaited. Not so bad, she thought, for first impressions. Not bad, at all. The receding hairline suited his face.

Marcella checked her posture. She straightened her belted tweed jacket and smoothed down the hips of her brown pencil skirt.

"Your guest has arrived, sir," the maitre d' announced.

Her host rose in greeting and offered his hand. "Marcella? Jack. Jack Linney. Thank you for joining me. I can't imagine what Ryan said to convince you to come on such short notice, but it's nice to have you here."

He smiled so warm and inviting, Marcella's discomfort ebbed. "Thanks, Jack. It's nice to be here."

As they shook hands, his dark brown eyes dropped the length of her body to linger briefly at her shoes before once again meeting her gaze. "Good to meet a fellow Rhode Islander," he said, "even if I had to travel to New York to do it."

Together, they laughed off their nerves. And who knew? She might even be able to work up an appetite. The way his eyes twinkled with attraction was a total ego booster.

The maitre d' assisted Marcella into her seat, and Jack resumed his.

"What are you drinking?" Jack was already calling over the waiter. Once Marcella had given her order, he gestured to her outfit and said, "You look beautiful. And since you had no idea this morning you'd be having lunch with someone new, can I assume you're into fashion? Aren't those Rafe New York shoes?"

He pointed to the floor and together they leaned over the table to admire Marcella's latest splurge. A pair of rose-and-brown-houndstooth plaid, peep-toe slingbacks.

"Well, yes, they are," she said, at first shocked and then impressed at his astute observation. But how many straight guys would know something like that? Could Jack be gay? And Ryan not be aware of it? Highly unlikely.

She chuckled away the thought. "Wow, that was good. You certainly know shoes."

He shrugged, gave a humble grin. "I hope I'm not being too forward, but those shoes are very sexy on you."

Marcella corrected herself. No, not gay. A player. Or else, trying really hard to please.

She grinned, sipped her water, and looked over the menu. She decided on the lobster salad. Jack ordered sea bass.

The food was delicious, and as they ate, they talked a little bit about his work, a little bit about hers, but not enough to bore one another. They discussed their favorite movies, the foods they liked, the restaurants they frequented. Marcella couldn't resist name-dropping her grandfather's place on Federal Hill.

"Smithy's?" Jack asked. "Smithy's is your grandfather's restaurant?"

"Named for the blacksmith's shop that operated in the same building during the nineteenth century."

"Yes, I know. I go there often. If your grandfather owns the place, then you must know the pretty redheaded hostess."

Marcella was already nodding. "That's my mom."

"Teresa is your mom? No kidding. Now I know where you get your looks. Say, know what I love best about Smithy's? The meatballs. Those suckers are big." He kissed his fingers. *"Benissimo!"*

It made her laugh. "My grandfather rolls them himself, every day. He taught me everything I know about cooking." Marcella lay her fork down with a sigh. "You're making me feel homesick."

Marcella's family were all back in Providence. Her grandfather, mother, and not-so-little brother, Rocco. Rocco was the only family member who'd never actually worked in the restaurant, but he lived in the apartment above and ate dinner there almost every night.

Being with Jack was a totally different experience than being with William, Marcella realized. With Jack, everything was familiar, and in the midst of all her insecurity lately, that felt comforting.

"Do you get back to visit often?" Jack asked.

Something in his tone, the warmth in his eyes, warned Marcella to prepare herself. He was going to mention seeing each other again. And why not? They were having a great time. If there wasn't so much else going on in her life—that is, her feelings for William—Marcella might enjoy a second date. But although Jack was sweet, he was no substitute for the Honorable William. Hers was more than a cosmic attraction. William was a cut above. In charm, in character, in trustworthiness. How could she ever move past him? What she needed was to get serious about working something out with William, once and for all. They couldn't continue in this limbo state.

But getting back to Jack's question, she said, "I don't visit Providence as often as I'd like, no."

"Well, it's not all that far away. Consider a trip home some weekend." Jack leaned a forearm on the table and strained closer. "I'd really like to get together with you again, Marcella. Can I call you sometime?"

Marcella wrung her hands in her lap as she considered her answer. "I really enjoyed meeting you, Jack. This was fun . . . but, you see . . . there's this certain guy I really care for, and I'm hoping what we have will lead to a serious relationship. I'm sorry."

"Oh." His brow wrinkled in disappointment. "No, don't apologize. I'm not surprised there's someone else. But if things change, or if you're ever in Rhode Island and need a friend, or just a familiar face across the table, I hope you'll think about giving me a call." He reached into the vest pocket of his suit jacket and offered her his business card.

Marcella slipped the card into her purse. Accepting it was the only polite thing to do.

The waiter arrived to clear away their plates. "Well, since we may never see each other again," Jack said, "at least we should part over dessert. Let me guess? Chocolate souffle?"

Had Ryan tipped him off about her passion for chocolate? Still . . . "Oh-no, I couldn't, really. Thank you, but I need to get back to work."

"Tell you what? I'm gonna take the initiative here and order us a couple of souffles anyway." He glanced up at the waiter who acknowledged him with a nod. "And two coffees, please." Jack watched as he departed, then turned back to Marcella. "Go if you must," he told her, "but later this afternoon, when your stomach starts to rumble and that midday slump has you tempted to buy a candy bar from the vending machine, you'll be wishing you stayed a few more minutes."

Marcella laughed. She couldn't help but wonder, what would it hurt? Jack had been the perfect lunch partner. He seemed a really nice guy. He'd been kind. He wasn't putting any pressure on her. And hadn't Sallie taught her the value of living in the moment? Well, for the moment, chocolate souffle was available when William wasn't.

Marcella rolled her eyes with a giggle. "Okay-okay. You argue a good case, Counselor. I'll stay."

"Thank you," Jack whispered. His shoulders seemed to slump in relief with his smile.

The souffle was everything Marcella imagined. And even once she felt totally stuffed, she continued to layer spoonful after spoonful of the rich chocolate into her mouth. She stopped to sip her coffee, and when she lowered the cup, Jack reached across the table to cover her hand.

Marcella grinned, slightly alarmed, not quite sure how to react, when Jack said, "Before you leave, Marcella, do you think you might let me smell your feet?"

She felt like she'd been hit with a brick. Everything sort of went dark and still inside her head. She was so weirded out, she couldn't remember how to speak. Then survival instincts kicked in, and Marcella jerked her hand from beneath his. "You're kidding, right?"

Jack's earnest expression never wavered. "I like women's feet," he said simply. "The delicate bone structure, their smooth sleekness. Put them in a pair of beautiful shoes and . . ." He lifted the tablecloth for a glimpse at her houndstooth sling-backs, then straightened and burned a seductive gaze into her eyes. "Your feet have been turning me on since you walked up to our table." He practically salivated.

A jolt of fear hit her. Marcella lowered her eyes and announced, "I think I'd better leave now." She reached for her purse and rose.

Jack jumped up to head her off. "Please, just one little sniff?"

Marcella turned on her heel and hurried off, as fast as her pencil skirt would allow. Jack called out her name. Her skin crawled at the sound of his voice. She bumped into an empty seat and stumbled, tripping out of a shoe. Then, suddenly, he was there, beside her, helping her regain her balance. Marcella pulled away, and Jack bent down to retrieve the shoe. He lifted it carefully in both hands as though he held Cinderella's glass slipper.

Marcella watched in disbelief as he brought it to his nose and inhaled deeply. A look of bliss washed over his face and then . . . *oh . . . oh God, no . . . yuck!* He stuck his tongue into the peep-toe and French-kissed her shoe.

That freak was sexually molesting her shoe! It was more than she could bear. She wrenched it away, resisting the urge to take out an eye with the heel, and hobbled out the restaurant as fast as she could without a backwards glance.

Out on the Madison Avenue sidewalk, she scrambled to the curb, screaming, "Emergency!" as she practically hurled herself into a taxi that had been hailed by a young couple. Inside the cab, she struggled to catch her breath before directing the driver to West 57th.

She limped into her office building, nodded to the security guard, and hurried up the elevators to *Gracious Living*, trying to ignore the stares of those who were probably wondering why she wore only one shoe, while holding the other as far away from her as possible, as if it were contaminated.

Finally, Marcella reached the safe haven of her office. She was almost tempted to sneak a whiff of the shoe Jack had licked. Did her feet smell? Had that freak Jack been attracted to her smelly feet when all the while she thought he'd been charmed by her looks and personality? The memory repulsed her. She wanted to hurl. Instead, she dropped the shoe into a waste basket, then kicked off its mate to the corner of the room.

She took a seat behind her desk, opened her purse, and ripped Jack Linney's business card to shreds. She felt violated, disgusted with all men and dating in general.

Well, not all men. There was this one guy. The catch of a lifetime. A prince of a guy, and yet they weren't together. But she loved him. *L.O.V.E.* loved him. How desperately she wanted to be with him now, but he lived an ocean away and unfortunately that would require a long swim.

Chapter 14

Smack in the middle of Marcella's pity party, Lauren from Reception buzzed. "Marcella, there's someone here to see you."

"Unless they have an appointment, which I seriously doubt, I don't want to see anyone."

She had to pull herself together. Psyche herself up and refocus her energy into the magazine and the million and one things yet to be done. Come morning, Catherine, Beth Anne, and the entire executive board would be meeting to discuss the Senior Decorating and Entertainment Editor position. As Acting Senior Editor—and a successful one at that, if she did say so herself—Marcella expected this meeting was just a formality. The board was going to offer her the position. She knew it.

She owned that job.

Although, lately life seemed to be chipping away at her confidence. Especially after this afternoon's fiasco, Marcella felt there was so much bad karma surrounding her, she couldn't be certain of anything anymore.

"He doesn't have an appointment," came Lauren's voice through the speakerphone. "But I think it might be important."

Lauren's voice lowered to a whisper. "He's a priest."

Priest? Marcella's hopes soared. But Lauren had spoken so softly, she wasn't sure she'd heard correctly and moved closer to the receiver. "Did he give a name?"

"The Reverend William Stafford."

"I'll be right there. Tell him I'll be right there."

William! William was here. How was that possible? Suddenly, her heart felt light enough to float.

Adrenalin shot through her body and Marcella jumped from her seat only to realize her feet were bare.

Her shoes. She had nothing to wear.

Anger flared inside her. No way could she greet William like this. There by the door, hooked over the rim of her wastebasket, where it hung from its three-inch heel, was her houndstooth slingback. God only knew what germs the sole of her foot had come in contact with on the City's sidewalks. She'd take her chances. But under no circumstance would she ever again wear that saliva-contaminated shoe.

She calmed herself with a deep breath, then in a moment of inspiration picked up the phone and called Holly in Fashion.

She was desperate, she told Holly. Shoe emergency. No time for details. Did the Fashion Department have anything in a size nine, preferably brown? Holly promised to come through with something pronto. After all, what woman couldn't sympathize at being stuck without the appropriate shoe? Reassured, Marcella pulled a mirror from her side desk drawer to freshen her makeup while she waited.

Moments later, the sound of approaching footsteps echoed from down the hall and she rose, expecting Holly.

Ryan Patterson, buddy to the smelly foot man and the last person Marcella wanted to see, popped his head in her door, holding a pair of snakeskin and green suede Mary Janes with a stiletto heel.

"What are *you* doing here?" she demanded with all the bitchiness the sight of him inspired, while the fashion conscious part of her brain silently screeched, *Snakeskin?#@!*

"Uh, hi. I was hanging out in Fashion, talking to Holly when you called." He gestured with the shoes and smiled apologetically. "Nothing in brown."

"Do you ever spend any time actually working?"

Ryan didn't react to that, but simply strode inside to place the shoes on her desk. "Look, Tart, you have every reason to be angry. I heard what happened, and I want you to know I feel terrible."

"What!? What did you hear? Did your friend tell you he sexually molested my shoe?"

Ryan looked like he was going to be sick. "Look, Jack's really sorry about that. I mean, I figured he was attracted to women's feet 'cause he used to paint his ex-girlfriend's toenails. But I never thought—"

"You knew and yet you begged me to meet him anyway?" Marcella pointed an accusing finger. "You! You owe me a pair of shoes. And not just any designer. Rafe New York."

"Whatever." Ryan raised his hands in defeat. "I'll pay for the shoes."

"First chance I get, I've got to call my brother Rocco and tell him to keep an eye out for Jack at the restaurant. Do you know, that freak has been eyeing my mother?"

"Jack is harmless, Marcella. I swear to you."

"Harmless, huh? Tell that to my shoes."

She snatched up the Mary Janes, then sat down to strap them on, her thoughts turning to William. William was a breast man, but he'd never asked if he could pop one in his mouth as an after-dinner mint.

Her eyes narrowed at Ryan. "You are never to mention this to anyone. Understand? Not even Holly. God, I hope no one saw me at Le Cirque. If this gets out, I swear, I'm calling my Italian uncles."

"Whoa, don't bring in the uncles. I won't say a word, I promise."

She deepened the threat with a glare, because truth was, Marcella had no Italian uncles. "You'll have to excuse me now," she said. "I'm expecting someone."

"Okay, fine." Ryan backed out of her office. "We're cool then, right? Oh, and Holly says she needs the shoes back for a fashion shoot tomorrow."

He left and Marcella stood in the Mary Janes. If not for the snakeskin, which totally clashed with her tweed jacket, the green suede might have worked. She turned, suddenly sensing a presence, and found Lynne Graham in the doorway, looking fabulous in a purple mandarin collar pants suit.

For a moment, surprise knocked the breath from her body. "Lynne, hi. Good to see you."

Lynne Graham was second only to Ryan on the list of people Marcella didn't wish to see. But she forced a smile and walked awkwardly around her desk in the uncomfortable Mary Janes as Lynne strode inside. They grasped hands and exchanged a quick peck on the cheek.

"What brings you to New York?" Marcella asked as they stepped apart. "Have you come with William?"

"Er, no, actually. William came with me."

Marcella stared back, confused, to which Lynne said, "I'll let him explain. You were taking so long, I decided to escort him in myself. We ran into M'Liss and Bree, who absolutely insisted he visit the test kitchen. He's with them now. Too polite to refuse. Besides, seems he's something of a celebrity with the female chefs. I don't recall ever mentioning my nephew to the kitchen staff. How did they know who he was, d'you s'pose?"

Marcella's memory flashed back three months earlier to the day Sallie delivered Lynne's wedding photos. Enlargements of William were passed around and ogled. Marcella decided to keep the memory to herself.

Lynne's gaze meanwhile busily roamed the office. She paused at the slingback in the wastebasket, briefly fixed upon a second discarded shoe in the corner, then glanced down at Marcella's reptile and green suede shod feet.

Her nose wrinkled in distaste. “Seems I’ve caught you in a bit of a shoe crisis. I rather fancy the pair in the bin. But then, these hellish style preferences are why you don’t work in the Fashion Department, I s’pose.”

“These shoes are not my fault!” Chalk it up to a rotten afternoon or the fact Lynne’s sarcasm hadn’t taken a break since the wedding, but something inside Marcella snapped. No longer could she hold her tongue and pretend the jibes didn’t sting.

“What’s going on, Lynne? What’s the deal with all the shots you’ve taken at me since the wedding? You’re obviously upset over something, but for the life of me, I don’t know what. Have I done something to offend you?”

Lynne’s eyes sparked angrily. Then slowly, her glare softened and she folded her arms with a sigh. Marcella thought she caught the glimpse of a smile.

“Well, if you must know, the fact is, I quite admire you, Marcella. I’ve come to give the board my recommendation for promoting you to Senior Editor. But that’s hardly enough for you now, is it? You want my nephew, too. Well, you’ll soon realize, if you haven’t already, you can’t have both.”

“You made me feel I wasn’t good enough for him.”

“It’s nothing personal, dear.”

“Nothing personal? C’mon, Lynne. It’s totally personal. We care for each other.”

“You must understand, Marcella, I don’t want William falling in love with you, when it’s a career in New York you really want. He’s been passed over for a career once before, and I won’t stand by and watch him get hurt again.”

“Lynne, the last thing I want is to see William hurt.”

“You say that now, but the truth is, he *is* going to get hurt, isn’t he? Congratulations, Marcella. Tomorrow morning the board is going to offer you my old job, and when it comes down to making a choice, it's senior editor of a major New York magazine you want, isn't it?"

Senior Editor! I'm going to be Senior Editor. Excitement surged through Marcella's core, happiness beyond belief.

"Oh, don't bother to say anything," Lynne continued. "I know the answer. From the day you arrived, I knew you were after my position. But you're bright and professional, and I accepted ours as a healthy, competitive, working relationship. Well, take some advice from me, you've no idea the pressure. Oh, it'll be fantastic for a while. You'll feel on top of world, relaxing and enjoying your success. Then, one day, perhaps sooner than you realize, someone younger, thinner, beautiful and talented, will arrive. She'll be the magazine's new little darling, on her way to the top. She'll always be about, so bloody helpful, wanting to learn, willing to do anything for the experience. What she's really after is your title, and she'll make life hell in the knowledge that all you have to make is one little cock-up and you could be replaced."

Lynne's confession blew her away, and for a moment, Marcella didn't quite know how to react. "You're saying I was that 'new little darling'?"

Lynne nodded.

"I . . . I'm sorry, I had no idea you felt this way. I've always thought of you as the most secure woman I've ever known. Sure I want to be Senior Editor. Doesn't anyone who pursues a career with a magazine? But really, Lynne, this is absurd. I was never a threat to you. I mean, how could I be? You're one of the most admired editors in the business. I never had a hope of replacing you until the day you resigned."

Lynne seated herself on the edge of Marcella's desk, and for the first time in the four years she'd known her, Marcella saw Lynne's shoulders sag.

"It's a relief to be free of the pressure. I don't regret a thing. I adore Henry, but I do s'pose, there is a part of me that's as green as your shoes over your youth and success."

Marcella had the urge to wrap an arm around Lynne and give her a hug, which Lynne must've sensed, because she immediately rose from the desk and stepped away.

"I'm still quite cross at you for toying with my nephew."

"I am not toy—"

"And before you let flattery go to your head, you should know I've other business here at the magazine. At this point, I don't see the harm in telling you. Although, it has been kept rather hush-hush. *Gracious Living* has created a new London-based position, which they've offered me. They're prepared to arrange for me to work from home, if that's what I desire."

"Sounds great. You're going to take it, right?"

"Good heavens, no. I'm not interested in some minor features editor position when I've a CV to land a senior staffer's post virtually anywhere. We do have magazines in England, you know. No, for the present, I'm perfectly content to devote myself to Henry."

Marcella nodded, absorbing all this new info.

"Ciao bella," a familiar voice greeted from the doorway.

When she glanced up and saw him, Marcella's heart lurched. William, in black trousers, black shirt, and white clerical collar, standing tall and gorgeous right here in her office. And holding what appeared to be a tray of . . . uh, Christmas cookies?

His face illuminated in a smile. Marcella let loose an ecstatic squeal and rushed him, as fast as a pair of stilettos could carry a girl. He awkwardly shifted the cookie tray to make room for her in his arms, while with his free hand, he drew her close for a kiss. Marcella snaked her arms up around his neck and thought, God how she'd missed this man.

Several oblivious moments later, they were interrupted by

Lynne clearing her throat.

William lifted his head. "Aunt Lynne, oh, excuse us." As they drew apart, he ducked his head bashfully, then, with a grin, gave Marcella a wink.

Lynne approached. "William, dear, perhaps Marcella would care to join us for a late lunch." She cast Marcella a pointed look on her way out the door. " 'Course she'll need to change those shoes first."

Marcella endured William's smirk. "You do seem a bit taller."

"Sorry I didn't make it to Reception in time to greet you. I had a situation." Marcella peered down the hall to confirm Lynne was indeed gone, then pulled William inside and closed the door. "I had to borrow this pair from the Fashion Department."

His gaze had already found the wastebasket, and while he puzzled over the sight of her trashed shoe, Marcella relieved him of the cookie tray, saying, "Looks like the kitchen staff's been busy."

William stepped closer, scooping her back into his arms. "Friendly lot. Apparently, they've been experimenting for the Christmas issue. Insisted I take some of their cookies. I'd thought I'd never left St. Francis's."

The quickest way to a man's heart, Marcella mused. Later, she'd have a little chat with those chefs and make it clear the priest was off limits. But for now, she pushed everything but William to the back of her mind and closed her eyes to receive his kiss.

Months of longing flowed from their lips. They kissed till they were breathless, then stood with foreheads touching and stared into one another's eyes.

"I'm so happy you're here. I missed you."

"I've missed you, too," he said.

They straightened and Marcella reached up to trace his jawline. "So? What're you doing here? Not that that's a complaint."

"After that kiss, I'd have a difficult time believing it was. Anyway, right, as I recall, you did extend me an open invitation. It was back in the lounge at The Bear."

"But the last time we talked," which Marcella recalled had been exactly four days ago, "you still hadn't been assigned a curate. How'd you manage to get away? And why didn't you let me know you were coming? I would have met you at the airport."

"It was all so spur of the moment." He turned and began pacing the office. "Only yesterday, I learned Aunt Lynne was flying to New York on business to do with the magazine. The thought of her coming here, to where you worked . . . and me, stuck in England . . . it hardly seemed fair. I poured out my plight, and Henry, God bless him, took pity. Offered me his seat on the plane, then arranged for someone to look after my parish in my absence. I couldn't wait any longer to be with you, curate or not."

Music to Marcella's ears. But she was curious. "And Lynne went along with this?"

"Obviously," he said, and there was pride in his smile. "She adores you. Speaking of Aunt Lynne, mustn't keep her waiting long, she's been so kind. She wants to introduce me to some of her friends." He took Marcella's hands and gave them a gentle squeeze. "Join us?"

Another lunch? With Lynne and her friends? "I . . . oh . . . I can't right now. Too much to do. Besides, I've already been to lunch. If only I had known." And damn, if only she had. "But you go ahead. I'll finish up here so we can get an early start on this evening. You, ah, don't have other plans for tonight, I hope?"

His aquamarine eyes sparkled. "None that don't include you. We'll go to dinner. Somewhere special. Aunt Lynne's given me some suggestions."

"I have a better idea. It's been three months since we've seen each other. Tonight should be just the two of us. Alone. Why don't we have dinner at my place?"

He looked skeptical. Marcella imagined him wondering where an invitation to her place might lead.

Anywhere he wanted.

"Oh, but, I couldn't possibly ask you to cook," he argued. "Actually, I was looking forward to taking you on a real date."

She had to convince him. If she were busy serving, William wouldn't notice her lack of appetite. Whereas, if he took her out, he might be insulted to see her picking at her food. After that fiasco of a stomach-turning lunch and a belly stuffed with chocolate souffle, Marcella didn't feel up to another restaurant.

Besides, she wanted nothing more than to be alone with him.

"We can do the date thing tomorrow," she promised. "Tonight, I'll whip up something light and simple for dinner. A little wine. Some candlelight. Just a quiet dinner. It'll be fun. C'mon, I've seen your home. Aren't you a little curious to check out mine?"

"Curiosity has nothing to do with it. This isn't a good idea, Marcella. Especially not our first night together after months of separation."

Honorable Will. She couldn't help but sigh. With a tilt of her head, she gave him her best doe eyes. "I promise not to attack you."

Marcella could read in his eyes, he wanted to say yes.

Of course, he couldn't see her fingers crossed behind her back. Hey, didn't his crossing an ocean mean William was ready to step up to the next level? They had reached a point where something had to give, one way or the other. Either this relationship would grow or it would die. And it definitely wasn't going to be the latter.

She snatched a pad from her desk and scribbled down her Madison Avenue address, in case William wasn't as into remembering details as she was. "I'll stop at the market on my way home to get what I need. Meet me at my place around six. My building's right next door to a small barbershop." She tore off the sheet and presented it to him. "You can set the table while I fix dinner."

He stared at the sheet, unmoving, and swallowed.

"C'mon," she encouraged. "I was only kidding. I won't really make you set the table."

Her teasing finally coaxed a smile out of him, and with a shake of his head, he accepted the address. "As long as you're certain this is what you want. I'll bring the wine, then, shall I?"

"It'll be great. You'll see."

William stared helplessly into her eyes. "That's precisely what worries me."

Chapter 15

A few hours later, William stood before the door to Marcella's flat and reminded himself no matter what temptations lay beyond, he must remember who he was and what he represented. As an ordained parish priest of the Church of England, under supreme governorship of Her Majesty the Queen, he mustn't allow his desires to get the better of him, no matter how tightly Marcella's top clung to her breasts or how softly she gazed into his eyes.

Balancing his packages in one arm, he extended the other hand, but it trembled as he reached for the buzzer.

Blimey. He clenched his fist, shook it out, then tried again.

The bell sounded from within, and moments later, Marcella swung open the door, welcoming him with a sunny smile in a dress surprisingly more conservative than anything he'd seen her wear.

"Hi."

"Hi."

For a moment, he simply stared.

Her navy dot print ended at the knee and crossed beneath her breasts in a high waist. Over it, she wore a short red cardigan. Something he'd expect one might wear to church. Well, not Marcella specifically, but a dress another woman might wear to church.

Yet on Marcella, with her dark exotic eyes and lashes as thick and jet as her hair, the look reminded him of a young Sophia

Loren. Or possibly a farmer's daughter from the Tuscan countryside. Conservative perhaps, but she could have been wearing nothing a'tall and it would have had the same effect on him.

"You look absolutely . . . lovely."

Her eyes danced over him, widening as they dropped from his face. "And, whoa, look at you in a crew neck." Reaching forth, she snagged the neckline of his jumper and tugged. "I can actually see your throat. Very shag-a-delic."

She made a sound similar to a purr and stretched towards him for a kiss. William's lids closed heavily as her lips drew near, his eyes all but rolling back in his head as she pressed them to his. He kissed her tenderly, grew a bit more aggressive, and then impatient altogether, as he opened his mouth hungrily over hers. She curled into his body in response. Her fingers slipped inside his jumper to stroke the base of his throat, that spot usually guarded by the symbol of his calling. When he felt the packages in his arms begin to slip, he rallied strength and pulled away, lightheaded as he lifted his head, and he hadn't even gotten through the door yet, God help him.

With a giggle, she stepped back and pulled him into her flat by a handful of jumper. "Come in."

Releasing him, she turned to shut the door. William smoothed the wrinkles from his jumper and glanced round a large, open space of both front room and eat-in kitchen combined. Everywhere he looked featured some shade of white. From the high pearly ceilings to a glass coffee table through which he could see the plush, milky carpet beneath. A silver tray filled with sea shells functioned as a candle holder. Pale blue walls surrounded an ivory jacquard parlor set with cream knitted throws and frosty beaded cushions. The late afternoon sun shone through a row of windows above a small dining area onto the kitchen's white glass-fronted cabinets, counters, and appliances, making the entire area gleam.

"Home sweet home," Marcella quipped as she came to stand alongside him.

"Yes, it's all very . . . white," he said, unable to find a more appropriate word. "Posh, certainly. But quite lively. D'you s'pose heaven looks a bit like this, like the inside of a cloud?"

She gave his arm a playful whack, then turned her gaze about the room. "Okay, I hear ya. But I find a white-on-white palette quiet and comforting. Especially after a long day at work."

"Oh, absolutely. It's lovely, honest. I just hope I don't spill anything. Speaking of which, these are for you." He passed Marcella a tall paper sack. "White zin. I thought since you said you'd be cooking light . . ."

"White zinfandel is perfect."

"And here." He handed her a small pastry box. "Chocolate. My first instinct was to bring flowers. But then, flowers aren't really the thing anymore, are they? Chocolate is the more fashionable way to show affection, I've been told. You'd think a vicar wouldn't be versed in such things, but the woman behind the sweets counter assured me I couldn't go wrong with a Black Forest cheesecake. They've, er, arranged the cherries in the shape of a heart."

She beamed, looking quite amused, but William worried whether he'd sounded a bit like a spod. You'd think he'd never dated before. Actually, he couldn't remember feeling this nervous in his life.

He followed Marcella into the kitchen, watching as she popped the cheesecake into the fridge. Little did she know, his trip to the States was more than a visit. He'd come with a purpose. And though he was bursting with it, he'd only just arrived. Patience was wise, surely . . . at least until tomorrow.

"So, what's for supper, then?" Stuffing a hand into his trousers' pocket, he peered into a large skillet on the cooker.

Inside, chicken fillets and capers sauteed in butter and oil. Fresh lemons lay sliced on a cutting board.

"Chicken piccata," she announced, peeling the foil from the stem of the wine bottle. "And there's roasted balsamic vegetables in the oven."

"Smells fantastic." He'd already opened the door for a peek. "Here, let me help you with that."

William took the bottle from her and noticed that a pair of short, thick wine glasses had been set out. "Do I detect a rustic, country theme to this evening's meal?"

"What gave it away? The dress? Damn, and I was aiming for subtle."

She passed him a corkscrew, which he accepted with a raise of his brows. "That dress is the only thing subtle about you tonight, I'm afraid."

She smiled, eyeing him shrewdly. "Unlike your not wearing your dog collar, you mean?"

"To the contrary, I wasn't trying to imply anything by not wearing the collar. I simply wanted to dress attractively for our dinner date."

"A little too attractive for your own good." And the way she stared as she said it started his heart to pound. "I hope you're hungry."

"Believe it or not, I'm famished." He popped the cork and she held up a glass for him to fill.

"There was the long plane ride," he explained as he poured. "Then, I didn't eat much with Aunt Lynne and her girlfriends. We went to one of those really posh restaurants where the chefs are keen on garnish, but dreadfully economical when it comes to portions, d'you know what I mean? It seemed every time I'd start to take a bite someone would ask another question. What do you wear under your cassock? Or something equally ridiculous. What is it about an English vicar that poses such a novelty to you American women?"

"What do you wear under your cassock?" Her gaze skimmed down, well below his waist.

His hand trembled. The wine spilled.

"Just playing with you," she said as she stilled his hand and set down the bottle, moving closer. "But I thought we'd already gone over this. It's not so much the collar, as the man in the collar."

William took her in his arms. His fingers tightened round her small waist, and blimey, if the cool silk of her dress didn't feel as delicate as a negligee beneath the warmth of his hand.

She pressed closer. Her breath touched his lips as she softly whispered, "I can't believe you're really here."

William lost himself in her deep brown eyes. It felt as though these last three months had never separated them. The connection and sense of rightness were as keen as ever.

He kissed her then, his palm gliding down to knead the curve of her slim hip, where his thumb discovered the lace edge of her knickers through the fine silk. Very naive of him to think this dress conservative. His blood boiled with desire, and he clutched her tighter, unable to satisfy himself with a kiss alone. Marcella moaned beneath his lips, wrapping her arms around his neck, crushing her breasts to his chest. He caught a whiff of the woodsy vanilla fragrance she wore and his senses whirred. His body responded. His hands spread lower to cover her tight bottom, clasping her to him with all the wanting pulsing through his veins, until suddenly something inside him signaled a warning.

Jolting to his senses, William released her, pulling out of the kiss. He steadied his breath, somehow managed to smile.

"Er, what shall I do to help?" he asked.

He'd be first to admit, living up to one's principles was not an easy thing. Visions of her knickers danced in his brain.

Marcella's gaze had locked on his lips. She blinked and looked into his eyes with a dazed expression. "Wow," she mouthed.

"Wow, indeed. But dinner," he reminded her. "How shall I help?"

"Oh, dinner." At once, she'd regained composure. She backed away slowly, reached for her wine glass, then eyed him seductively over the rim as she took a sip. "So . . . when you said you were hungry just now, you were talking about food?"

Heat spread up his already quite warm neck, until he noticed the corner of her mouth twitch. "You're having quite a bit of fun with me tonight, aren't you?"

"Not half as much as I'd like to."

"Marcella, please," he begged.

"Okay, okay. Dinner's ready, anyway. Let me take the veggies out of the oven, then we can load up our plates and carry them out to the terrace."

"The terrace? Great." He could do with a bit of air.

"It's just through my bedroom."

For a moment, he wasn't sure whether she was having him on again. "Your bedroom?"

"That's right. The terrace is just outside my bedroom window. Climbing out is a small inconvenience, considering. And don't give me that look. I'm not trying to trick you."

"I'd never suggest you were," he balked.

" 'Cause like I'd ever have to trick a man into bed."

"I've no argument with that."

They exchanged smiles while Marcella slipped on a pair of oven mitts, and as she bent to reach inside the oven, William was tempted to give that bottom of hers a playful slap.

He resisted and focused rather on channeling the hunger in his body to the one organ he could satisfy—his stomach. He helped himself to a generous portion of the chicken piccata and roasted vegetables. And several of the cheese-stuffed figs wrapped in prosciutto Marcella had prepared as a starter.

He popped one in his mouth, chewing as he tucked the wine bottle under one arm. He balanced his dinner plate in his palm and followed Marcella into her bedroom, bracing himself as though he ridiculously expected to discover it some sort of seduction den. He found the room decidedly feminine and just as light-filled as the rest of her flat. Airy white linens edged in pale pink dressed an antique reproduction, white scroll, metal bed.

They walked round the foot of the bed and set their plates on a nightstand by the room's only window.

"Allow me," William volunteered, as Marcella stepped forward to raise the screen. "I'm feeling adventuresome. This is a first, you know. Climbing out a window for my supper."

"Well, then . . ." Marcella retrieved the wine glasses and handed one off to him. "To a night of firsts," she said, chinking his glass with hers.

She sipped, yet William hesitated. "I'm not entirely sure I should be drinking to that." Still, he downed a swallow, then handed back the glass, and raised the screen so he could poke his head out the window for a look.

Beneath a canvas awning and surrounded by greenery, a small, round table had been laid with a pink-checkered cloth and a centerpiece of fresh dahlias. A pair of garden chairs wore deeper pink slipcovers. Impatiens and hostas flourished in the sunlight, and a small herb garden scented the air.

William hooked a leg over the sill, then ducked his head and pulled himself through the window onto a decking of weathered cedar planking.

"Positively bucolic. Remind me again. Are we somewhere in the European countryside? This can't possibly be New York."

"Believe it or not, you are now standing on the roof of a

Madison Avenue barbershop."

"Fantastic." He saw rows of adjacent brownstone gardens, just as well maintained, verdant with potted plants and ivy crawling down their walls.

Certainly, this was more romantic than any inner-city restaurant he could have afforded. Amazing quality of Marcella's, her ability to take the simplest of life's pleasures and make them memorable. She'd started from humble beginnings, and with her God-given talents and a lot of hard work, made quite a success of herself. Coming from privilege, it was an accomplishment he greatly admired.

"Dinner's getting cold," she warned, shaking him from his musings.

"Right. Of course." He turned back to the window and transferred the plates and glassware she passed him to the table, then assisted her onto the terrace.

Awareness of her simmered inside him as he stood behind her, holding her chair. He watched her lovely little bottom settle into the seat and a question popped in his head. Were her knickers as pristine as her flat's decor? White virginal lace, perhaps? Or bright and bold, like her choice of table setting?

He took his place opposite her and admired the spread. She'd obviously gone to a great deal of effort to make this evening perfect, and on such short notice. As he said grace over the meal, he offered a special thanks for the good fortune that had made it possible for him to be with Marcella tonight.

She voiced an enthusiastic "Amen," then lifted her gaze to his.

With a wink, William tucked in to his supper. He'd been noshing for several minutes when he remembered his manners and complimented her on the meal. "And, how much longer, d'you s'pose you'll push that bit of carrot round your plate before you actually eat it. You haven't touched a nibble."

"I've been enjoying watching you eat."

"Happy to entertain you." He took a swallow of wine. "Aunt Lynne's told me about the promotion you're to be offered at tomorrow's meeting. Seems she's spoiled the surprise. Anyway, well done, Marcella." He raised his glass to her. "You must be excited."

She shrugged. "Yeah, it's a great opportunity. But let's not talk about work tonight, okay?"

William put his glass down and leaned forward. "I don't understand. I thought you'd be pleased. Isn't this promotion what you've always wanted?"

She nodded. "I know, I know. It is. I'm just saying, for tonight, I'd rather not talk about what's happening tomorrow, or our careers, or how much time we have before you go back to England. Tonight, let's be totally in the moment, right here and now, you and me, as though nothing in the world matters but . . . us."

William beamed. It sounded like a brilliant plan, except . . . there were all sorts of things that did matter. Like the fact that, if, or more likely when, Marcella accepted her promotion, there'd no longer be an "us," would there? What future did they have when their schedules didn't allow them to be together? Three months between visits was far too unbearable. Disturbing that she didn't want to discuss it.

He stared at what was left of the food on his plate. Suddenly, he'd lost his appetite.

She frowned. "What is it?"

Perhaps this was his opportunity to say the words he'd been rehearsing. Moments slipped by before William gazed into her eyes, dead serious. She sat poised on the edge of her seat, waiting. Then, as he began to open his mouth, she jumped up.

"Time for dessert."

"Dessert? But we've only started with dinner." She reached

for his plate, but William covered it with his hand.

"Suit yourself." He caught something devious in her smile before she turned and carried her own dinner back to the window.

"Marcella," he called after her, "is this some sort of gag?"

Ignoring him, she hiked up her skirt and swung a leg over the sill. She paused and glanced back, straddling the window's ledge and taunting him with a pale, slender thigh. Was the woman trying to drive him mad?

She disappeared with a giggle, leaving him totally in bits. William refilled his wine glass, then got up from the table and crossed to the edge of the terrace where he stared blankly at the Madison Avenue traffic below. With each sip of zinfandel, the sun sank lower in the Manhattan skyline and his reasons for not making love to Marcella swirled in a foggy mist that clouded his mind.

Moments later, he heard her return. She emerged from the window and approached him with something concealed behind her back. The smooth silk of her dress poured over her sylphlike figure and incredibly long legs to outline her hips and thighs with each saucy stride. William found himself in temptation up to the dog collar he wasn't wearing. He didn't trust himself.

He stepped away from the railing. "Marcella, I've no idea what this is about, but I'm not feeling like cheesecake at the moment."

"At the moment . . . neither do I." Her lips were full and moist, her tone sensual.

She presented him with a delicate china dessert plate. On it, a purple foil square rested on a lace doily. William stared. Bertie's condom? That hideous purple sheath she'd threatened to smuggle back to America.

Obviously, she'd succeeded.

And was he supposed to be amused? Was this some sort of

gag? No, he hardly thought so. Not if Marcella's amorous gaze were any indication. Her dark eyes were as intoxicating as any drug. Desire swam through his veins, stimulating his heartbeat, pumping all the blood to the lower half of his body so he'd none left in his head to form a coherent thought. His defenses crashed.

He'd absolutely no resistance left.

Marcella inched closer to William. "The cheesecake was really thoughtful and sweet. But, you know, as sensual as chocolate may be, indulging only gives me a quick high then leaves me kinda . . . empty. Nope, there's only one thing that will truly satisfy me. One man, is what I'm trying to say."

Marcella released a breath. There, she'd said it.

The plate trembled in her hand, which had nothing to do with the two glasses of wine she'd consumed or the slight buzz that resulted.

She'd lain her emotions bare, exposed all over her face for William to see. She'd missed him. Really missed him. And now that he was here, she wanted . . . no, needed to be close to him. As close as two consenting adults could possibly get. Was that so wrong?

His eyes blazed wolfishly. She took that as a no to her unspoken question and a definite yes to everything else. *Whoa,* the naughty side of Honorable William unleashed. The anticipation alone was enough to drive her to the brink of an orgasmic meltdown.

He reached for the plate. Marcella scooped up the condom before William could set it on the table with his wine glass. She clutched it protectively behind her back as he cupped her chin and gazed hungrily into her eyes. He yanked her close, angled his head. Her own eyes closed, lips parted . . .

His mouth slammed down on hers. Their kiss was insatiable, frantic. Marcella plunged the fingers of her free hand in his thick chestnut waves. William tugged on her sweater, pulling it off her shoulders.

She lowered her arms to let it fall. Already, his fingers were at her back searching for the zipper, while he guided her steps backwards towards the window. They broke apart, pausing to catch their breaths before they climbed through. Marcella went first, then William followed, moving so hastily he banged his head on the sill.

"Bugger."

"Ooh, sweetie. Here, let me see." As Marcella held her arms out to him, William ducked his head and she kissed the spot. She fluffed his hair and continued the kisses down the side of his face, skimming her soft lips across his abrasive jaw, then ran her tongue along the outer curve of his ear. "I know just how to make it better," she promised in a soft whisper.

She nibbled his earlobe and he expressed his pleasure in a painfully deep moan. When he raised his face to hers, his watercolor eyes were clouded with lust.

Later, they'd take their time, but for now Marcella didn't think either one of them could wait a moment longer.

William kicked off his shoes. Marcella pulled her zipper the remainder of the way down her back. He yanked his sweater over his head and tossed it to the floor. She slipped the dress off one shoulder, then followed with the next, hypnotized by his smooth, toned chest.

While William watched, Marcella glided the dress down her hips and let it crumble at her feet. Then she stepped from the silky puddle in nothing but a black lace plunge bra and a pair of matching boyshorts.

William swallowed, staring into the deep V of her bra with hunger and wanting. "So . . . black lace?"

Marcella giggled, moving closer. "Black lace, yes." His chest rose and fell heavily with his breathing. She stretched forth a hand and pressed her palm to his heart.

He encircled her waist and drew her close. "Suits you perfectly. But then, you'd look gorgeous in anything, I'd imagine . . . or better yet, nothing a'tall. You're incredibly beautiful."

She loved the soft, hoarse tone his voice had taken, the intense, hot look that glittered beneath his lashes. It took all her strength to pull away so she could turn down the ivory *matelassé* coverlet on her bed. She climbed on, making room for William beside her as they stretched upon the cool cotton sheets.

A breeze blew in off the terrace as they kissed. Long sweet kisses that lingered, while they sought nothing more than to hold each other. William caressed her hips, her buttocks, her thighs, then began to flutter tender pecks below her jaw and along the curve of her neck before he lowered his head to her bosom. He dipped his tongue in her cleavage, nuzzling as much of her as he could reach inside the plunging neckline of her bra.

When at last he lifted his head, Marcella placed both hands at his strong shoulders and pushed him off. She rolled over on top of him, straddling his body as she pinned him against the pillows. Her hands smoothed the tight muscle of his pecs, then caressed his lean ribs before she trailed her fingers down his flat stomach. She sat back on his legs and smiled.

His gaze had dropped to her panties.

"Does that look mean you approve of my boyshorts?"

"*Boy*-shorts? Is that what American women are calling their knickers these days?" Reaching, he slid his fingers inside the front of her panties where he began to stroke her with the back of his knuckles. "Bloody lie. Nope, sorry, can't find anything boylike in these shorts. Perhaps . . . if I explore a bit further."

She felt a giggle, but what escaped was a series of low moans as Marcella was swept up in the sweet, wonderful sensations he created.

"Oh-no, nothing male about that, is there?" She shuddered as his fingers probed deeper. "Are you certain you've got the correct name for your knickers? Oh, and what's this? Something entirely feminine, if I'm not mistaken. Lovely . . . yes, very lovely."

Any sense of control ebbed away. Her head lolled back. Her eyes drifted shut in intense concentration at what he was making her feel. William's soft British baritone, his sexy humor, the featherweight touch of his fingertip. Overwhelming. Relentless. She couldn't . . . couldn't take much more . . . couldn't bear the agony . . . *oh, God* . . . couldn't . . . hold on.

Passion rocketed through her body and she convulsed in spasms of release.

Slowly, Marcella came to, opening her eyes to William's naked chest. She lifted her gaze to his mussed chestnut hair against her white cotton pillows, his drowsy blue eyes and a smug smile that made him look almost as sated as she felt.

Raising a hand to her flushed face, she released a slow breath. "You have every reason to feel proud. That was awesome." She leaned forward, arms extended on either side of his head and hovered over him. "But don't you think it's time you shared in the pleasure?"

He looked deep into her eyes and groaned.

Marcella found the condom tucked beneath one corner of a pillow. She snatched it up, sticking the foil packet between her teeth while she reached for the waistband of William's pants with both hands. Carefully, she eased the zipper down over his bulging erection.

James Bond in an Aston Martin. Superman in a red cape. The Honorable William in a royal purple condom.

This was going to be so good!

She yanked open his fly.

"Wait!"

Marcella glanced at the strong fingers encircling her wrist, to the frown that creased William's forehead, to his alert gaze, which only seconds ago had been dreamy with desire.

"Wait," he softly repeated, loosening his grip. "I know you think this is clever, but I really don't want to recall our first time together wearing my wankish brother Bertie's purple condom."

Marcella spit out the packet. No problem. What'd she care if his penis was the color of a lollipop? "Okay, okay, that's cool. There's a drug store just around the—"

"No." With a pained expression, William struggled to rise. "Actually, I was thinking of something more in the way of a cold shower. I . . . We can't . . . do . . . this."

With trance-like movements, Marcella climbed off him.

William swung his legs over the edge of the bed and sat up. He hung his head, raking his fingers through his hair. "Bertie slipped me that condom as a sort of challenge. Taunting me to seduce you that first night we met. I don't believe he's ever accepted my decision to become a vicar. It's all a joke to him, really."

With a sigh, he turned to meet her gaze. "But you must understand, Marcella, I take my profession quite seriously. And at the risk of boring you with yet another speech, I can't possibly make love to you tonight and pretend that what happens tomorrow doesn't matter. It does matter, you see. The future matters quite a lot, actually."

Marcella hugged her knees to her chest and nodded numbly, trying to wrap her mind around what was happening. Or more accurately, not going to happen. "Wow. Yeah, I see."

She couldn't say she was surprised, just a little jolted by William's timing and awed at his strength. She told herself not to take this personally. They'd confronted this issue once before. But the thing was, she remembered William's words. He'd told her he didn't believe in making love outside of a committed, serious relationship. She couldn't help but wonder, didn't what they feel for each other qualify as serious?

Tears pricked at the back of her eyes. If this evening had gone as she'd hoped, they'd be cuddling beneath the sheets right now, wrapped in each other's arms. Maybe she'd be telling William how much she loved him. But they weren't, and he hadn't mentioned anything about love.

William stood and zipped up his fly.

"Since I've arrived, I've tried devilishly hard not to lose control. How could I've let things go so far?"

Marcella got up and padded to the closet for a robe. "Relax, you're human. It just happened."

"Well . . . that's not entirely true now, is it?"

Had she detected a hint of accusation in his tone? Marcella slung the robe over her shoulders as she turned to face him and pulled it tightly about her waist. "What do you mean?"

"I'd have thought you'd be a bit more supportive. Instead, you insisted we spend the evening at your flat, and you've been keen on making love since I walked through your door."

"Are you saying I seduced you?" Her defenses rose so fast, Marcella could barely think straight. "And I suppose you had only the purest of intentions when you stuck your hand in my panties." She folded her arms angrily. "Fine, it's my fault, then. The vicar and the tart."

His blank stare annoyed her further.

"The vicar and the tart?" he inquired.

"That is so unfair."

He leaned closer. "Sorry, did you say, the vicar and the tart?"

She glared until he started to grin, then as they continued to stare at one another, they burst into laughter.

"Forgive me, Marcella. Of course I'm every bit as responsible. I'm just a bit . . ." He drew a breath from the depths of his chest, "Well, frustrated, d'you know what I mean?"

"I know." Marcella shared his frustration. And if she felt frustrated, then she could only imagine the agony he was in. But if William could remain true to his principles under these conditions, Marcella believed he could do anything.

"I'm the one who's sorry," she confessed.

"No, I'm really sorry."

"I'm totally sorry. I served you a condom. Seduction doesn't get much more obvious than that. Look, why don't we just start over, okay? You go take that cold shower, and I'll brew a pot of coffee and serve up the cheesecake." She enticed him with a small smile. "Despite what I said earlier, chocolate's not such a bad consolation."

"I am rather peckish."

"Great. Bathroom's this way."

As she started for the door, he whisked his sweater off the floor and made to follow, only to pause at her opened closet door. "You've an unbelievably organized cupboard."

He was looking inside with such interest, for a moment Marcella thought the sex deprivation might have addled his brain.

"Yeah, me, organized. What a shocker."

"There's all these tidy little boxed shelves. Is this some sort of shoe filing system?"

Marcella suspected he was busting, but before she could arrive at a good comeback, he turned to her, saying, "Earlier in your office I noticed a shoe chucked carelessly in the bin. Seems a bit out of character for someone so obsessively meticulous."

"I-I am not . . . obsessive."

"Just curious. What sort of 'situation' would make you disabuse a perfectly fine pair of shoes?"

He was far too perceptive. Her conscience prickled as she

recalled the reason. And although she was squirming beneath her white terry robe, she replied casually, "Nothing important."

"Has something happened?"

She opened her mouth to respond with an emphatic "no" only to hesitate at his intense awareness of even her slightest expression. He'd know immediately if she didn't tell him the truth. Anything short of complete honesty would be an insult.

Resigning herself, Marcella explained, briefly, how she met the friend of a co-worker for lunch, unburdening the frightening experience that resulted and confessing that maybe the reason she agreed to the meeting at all was because she'd felt a little insecure about where things stood with William.

Not that she was making excuses.

"But it definitely wasn't a date," she assured him.

His expression turned stormy. "You met a stranger for lunch? Then stayed through dessert? I'm not a total git, you know. That bloody well is a date!" He looked as though she'd just socked him in the gut.

She hadn't meant to hurt him. She'd never have taken William for the jealous type. She had to make him understand, it was nothing. *Nothing.* "Believe me, you have absolutely no reason to feel threatened."

"Oh, but I am threatened. Absolutely! Totally threatened! Actually, the word I had in mind was 'jealous'. But 'threatened' sums up my feelings quite accurately." He pulled his sweater over his head and tugged it down over his torso.

"Look, let me be really clear, okay? Since meeting you, I haven't been interested in anyone else. It was just a kinda impromptu thing. And a decision I obviously regret." Marcella gave a small, nervous laugh. "If it's any comfort, I don't think Jack had any interest in me outside of my feet."

She had hoped for something a little more encouraging than a scowl.

"Jack. Right. Your feet? Sorry, not consoled in the knowledge you spent an entire afternoon in the company of a man whose intent it was to touch any part of your person with his tongue. And the sad part is, I have no right to feel jealous. A fact I'm perfectly aware of, as it obviously was to you when you decided to meet this bloke. We don't have any sort of commitment, or even a future for that matter. Not with me in England and you here in New York."

He looked so crestfallen, Marcella grew alarmed. She needed to reassure him. But she didn't know what to say. She had no answers herself.

"I believe we need to think about making some choices," he said.

"Choices?"

He nodded. "Sorry, but suddenly I've lost my appetite," he said, searching for his shoes. "Probably not such a good idea anyway, for me to stick round here tonight when you've such an important meeting in the morning."

He strode past her into the living room. Marcella followed him to the door, watching in shock as he opened it.

"We'll talk tomorrow," he said. Then he was gone.

What had just happened? Marcella wondered. What choice had William been referring to? His or hers?

There had to be a way to save this relationship. But she'd already examined her options and come up blank, so the thought of making a choice . . . well, it terrified her.

Chapter 16

Marcella hadn't heard from William since last night. Not that she'd expected a call first thing in the morning, but it would have given her confidence a nice boost as she went into her meeting. The moment it broke, she headed to her office to check her messages and phone his hotel—but instead she found William waiting outside the boardroom.

Hope flooded her heart as they walked towards each other, meeting in the middle of the hallway.

"This is a nice surprise," she greeted with a smile.

He'd worn his clerical collar in a French blue shirt with charcoal pants and was looking as handsome as ever. "I came with Aunt Lynne. Wanted to be first in line to offer my congratulations."

Marcella was impressed. Either his being here meant something really good or really bad. "William, Lynne was in attendance from the start of that three-hour meeting. You've been hanging around all this time?"

He gave a guilty shrug. "This is, after all, quite an important day for you."

Leaning forward, he pressed a kiss to her cheek, which seemed a little reserved after last evening. Marcella couldn't resist feeling a teensy disappointed. Although, realistically, they were standing in a hallway trafficked by her co-workers.

Lynne exited the boardroom, hesitating at the sight of them together. Her gaze moved from Marcella to her nephew, then back to Marcella, before she broke into a smile so uncharacteristically warm, for a moment Marcella didn't recognize her ex-boss.

Without a word, Lynne strode past them and continued down the corridor.

Marcella returned her focus to William. "I'm so glad you're here; you have no idea." For the first time all morning, she let herself get caught up in the excitement that had been bubbling inside her. "Actually, it's an even bigger day than you realize," she hinted.

Major changes had resulted from that meeting. It had taken some soul-searching and a reevaluation of priorities, but man! Talk about your promotion. William didn't know it yet, but he'd just jumped to the top of her agenda.

"I've been doing a lot of thinking," she said. "About us. And there's something I have to tell you."

"I'd like a word as well. But not here. Could we find a place more private? Oh, I don't mean your office. D'you think you could slip away for a bit? Go for a walk, perhaps? Before you say anything further, Marcella, there's something you need to know."

The seriousness of his expression sobered her, and immediately her mind envisioned the worst possible scenario. He was going to end their relationship.

Silly. Of course he wasn't. She refused to spaz. This was going to be a joyous day. It was.

"Sure, okay," she said. "I'll just let Lauren know I'm stepping out for awhile and then we can go."

They didn't speak as Marcella escorted William from the building. Did she sense a bit of nervous tension in the air? She couldn't be sure which one of them it was coming from.

Once outside, William strode to the curb and hailed a cab. "On second thought, a drive might be better, what d'you say?"

What could she say? Anything to get this show on the road. "A drive is fine."

William opened the door and Marcella swung her legs into the backseat, then scooted over. She watched as he whispered something to the driver before hopping in beside her.

Oh God, please give me a sign I haven't turned down the promotion for nothing, she prayed. "Thank you for your confidence in me," she'd told Beth Anne in the board meeting, "but I wonder if you might be willing to consider me for another position." Was she crazy? No, just in love. She'd taken a huge leap of faith, a leap which she hoped William would be happy about. It hadn't been easy to seize this opportunity and not be afraid. She refused to turn chicken now.

Then again, if worse turned to worse, she could always beg for her old job back and the chance to work under Jillian Navarro.

She'd rather throw herself from the cab.

The driver pulled from the curb, took a right on West 57th and headed down Fifth Avenue.

"So?" she ventured. "Where are we going?"

William turned from gazing out the window. "Somewhere away from the atmosphere of the magazine."

Evasive answer, Marcella thought. "I have an idea. How 'bout we find a Starbucks, grab a couple of lattes, and chat in some cozy corner?"

William frowned. "I've already consumed more coffee than I can tolerate, I'm afraid, waiting for you. But if you'd like something—"

"No, I'm good. What were you doing for three hours?" she asked conversationally, when suddenly she knew. "You were in the test kitchen, weren't you?" Her voice held a slight edge of accusation.

William's expression didn't so much as flinch from the truth.

"Exactly. M'Liss and Bree kindly offered to make me breakfast. A lovely but eclectic menu of eggs Benedict and banana chocolate chip pancakes."

"How generous of them." This talent he had for inspiring women to cook for him was beginning to get a little unnerving. "You know, they may be professionally trained chefs, but they can't cook authentic Italian the way I can."

He gawked, a little surprised, then burst into a grin. "Are we jealous?"

"That's what this is about? You're getting even with me for that terrible non-lunch-date I mistakenly got tricked into yesterday. Are you going to dump me for Bree? Those must've been some pancakes."

He started to chuckle. "That's not exactly what I had in mind, no. And I don't believe you see a'tall, Marcella. But you shall in a moment. Ah, we've arrived."

"Arrived where?" Even as Marcella spoke, she gazed out the window and saw that the cab had stopped before the Empire State Building.

"Would you mind?" William asked.

Now she was totally confused. "Huh?"

"Would you mind if we popped up to the observatory? To see the view. I've already purchased tickets." He slipped a pair out his pants pocket, explaining, "Online."

"Okay, this is getting too weird." On the bright side, Marcella's unease had disappeared. She still didn't know what William was up to, but it was shaping up to be something a little more fun than a breakup.

Of course, if it turned out she'd been overly optimistic and William did break her heart, she'd be conveniently located on top of the Empire State Building, so when it was all over she'd have a place to jump.

William had already jumped out of the cab and paid the

driver. He opened her door and took her hand to help her out. They entered the main lobby, passed though security, then rode the high-speed elevators to the eighty-sixth floor, where they stepped out on the observation deck to a breathtaking horizon that overlooked the glistening city of New York. Incredible as it looked, Marcella had a difficult time appreciating the view. The suspense was driving her crazy. What were they doing here?

They strolled for a bit before William pulled her aside. "Okay," he said with a swallow, "this is it. This is what I need to say. No . . . wait. Not here."

Taking her hand, he led her to another spot with a clearer view of the 59th Street Bridge. "Here, that's much more scenic, don't you think?"

"Beautiful," she said, but she wasn't looking at the skyline. The love shining from William's aquamarine eyes had totally mesmerized her.

"Sorry I got so upset last night, but I'm in love with you, Marcella, and I want you to marry me. In fact, I believe I've loved you from the first moment I saw you. You're the woman I want to spend my life with. I know life with a vicar is not nearly exciting enough to offer someone as truly spectacular as you, but it's all the life I have to offer. It's a lot to ask, surely. To give up your promotion and all this." He gestured to the city below. "Leave everything familiar behind and start a new life in England, but you're just the girl to make a smashing success of it. So, you have to say yes, you see, because it won't be much of a life for me without you. And we can't continue this separation. Well, I can't, at least. And that . . . that's it really. Oh-no, wait. One more thing."

Digging into his pants' pocket, he produced a small velvet box that had Marcella gasping even before he got it open. Inside . . . oh . . . *oh!* . . . inside was a vintage emerald ring set with a diamond baguette on either side.

"This once belonged to my grandmother, the Seventeenth Viscountess of Wiltshire. So, what d'you say?" he asked hopefully. "Will you come to England and be my wife?"

Marcella suspected he already knew her answer. The smile on her face hadn't stopped growing since he'd begun talking. She felt as though she were about to explode with joy. Here was an opportunity to marry the most incredible, wonderful, sexy man she'd ever met. Was she going to go for it? *Absolutely!*

"Yes!" she shouted, jumping into his arms. "I love you. Yes, of course, I'll marry you, William."

"You will? I mean, that's fantastic." He kissed her. "I couldn't be happier, but no regrets about giving up your job as a senior editor?"

She shook her head. "William, I love you so much that this morning in the board meeting I turned down that promotion. That's what I had to tell you. I've accepted a features editor position which is going to relocate me in England. Your aunt had already turned it down and I thought . . . well, like you said, it was time to make a choice. And I chose you, because the truth is, I only want to be with you."

Tears formed in his eyes. Marcella's hand trembled as he slipped the ring on her finger. Then he took her in his arms and they kissed, feeling on top of the world, which, in all practicality, they probably were. "I have one more thing for you," he said at length. He quietly slipped her a small package of . . . condoms.

Marcella could only gape.

"You're surprised?" he said with a laugh. "You should have seen the faces at the chemist's when I bought them. I'm, er, not suggesting anything, mind. I just thought, now that we're engaged, you might want to keep them on hand, you know . . . in case."

Marcella grinned. This just kept getting better and better. "In case what?"

He shrugged, leaving her to draw her own conclusion. "They're not in bright colors or anything. Hope you won't be disappointed."

"Oh, I'm sure I won't," she whispered, drawing closer to his lips.

He gave her a confident smile. "No, I don't believe you will be, actually."

ABOUT THE AUTHOR

Lisa Norato first discovered a love of writing when assigned to write and illustrate a children's book at the art college she was attending. Eventually, she abandoned the art career but returned to writing. Today she works as a legal assistant in the corporate department of a downtown Providence law firm. She enjoys the love and support of her close-knit Italian family and currently lives in Rhode Island with one very pampered, six-pound, designer Yorkie-poo.